DOORWAY INTO DARKNESS

GORDON STRONG

Cover photograph by Lucille Pine
Cover design by Gordon Strong and Dean F. Wilson

First Edition 2013

ISBN 978-1-909356-02-3

DIOSCURI PRESS

Published by Dioscuri Press
Dublin, Ireland

www.dioscuripress.com
enquiries@dioscuripress.com

Contents

"I've tried to control a chaotic universe and it's a losing battle."

— Harvey Pekar

"There is only one happiness in life, to love and be loved."

— Georges Sand

"Authority is always there to be laughed at. There is always room for one more custard pie."

— George Orwell

Preface

The origins of this saga came from a conversation at Stanton Drew in the Summer of 2012. The original setting and some of the characters remained, other elements got added. Figures from a distant, and not so distant, past lent something of themselves to the story. Magic plays a part, as it does in everything. Old wisdom, and the joy to be found in the company of ordinary folks, these things were important too.

Many thanks to Dean Wilson at Dioscuri Press for working so hard to get this out.

Gordon Strong
Portishead, England
April 2013

1

The water in the pool was always a particular shade of turquoise, one created at enormous expense. Clipped cypress hedges surrounded this Olympic lake and the endless lawns beyond were shaved closer than the thighs of a sumo wrestler. The property itself hinted that it extended further than the known world. It spoke too of privacy, one closely guarded by security men. All of these appeared to have been born with no neck.

The design of the house was so monumentally unpleasant it was difficult to imagine anyone admitting they owned it, let alone wanting to live there. At any time of day the sun beamed down on one of the countless terraces. In the middle of December, Phoebus was not always so obliging. Even with all his influence, Lord Douglas Folds could not determine the state of the weather.

Prockleby was an isolated bubble in the middle of the Yorkshire Moors. The estate consumed nearly as much in natural resources as a small town. In the main conservatory, the under-floor heating was permanently set at sauna-level, something his lordship constantly complained about. On the way to his office, he sharply addressed Lady Folds, in the same way that he talked to everyone.

"I can't understand why you have it so hot in here all the time."

"It reminds me of being in Belize, sweetie."

Lady Folds—skin like a python, lips as tight as a trampette—waited until her husband had removed himself before she carried on chattering into her mobile.

"These days ... with all this international trouble around ... you just *have* to be like that with these people. Don't you think so, darling? I mean ... why not? So ... well ... yes ... it sort of makes so much more sense that Dougie is *permanently* racist."

Lady Folds said this in the way someone else might say that their husband played golf, or bred prize carp.

"Yes ... it's all going to be *terribly* busy here at the weekend ... we've got the Sultan of Brenguna ... have you seen those pictures of him in *Hello* magazine? Absolutely dripping with gold ... I've never seen so much of it in my entire life. Some new people are coming too ... over from New York ... yeh ... flying in tonight. We're going to have the staff open up the big dining room. Dougie's got some mega-deal planned with all of them I expect. I stay well out of it, darling ... simply don't want to know. I've got enough to think about looking after this place ... we're having all the ground near the lake changed ... you know. Making a sort of landing place for little boats ... won't that be fun ..."

A discreet distance away, catering staff scurried in and out of the kitchens while in the shadows were the dark-suited men with eyes of flint. Other zombies—their way of walking reminiscent of the Nuremberg Rallies—constantly patrolled the perimeter of the grounds. Security was big in Lord Folds' life, as it always is in the lives of the rich and paranoid—two states often inseparable.

Like Schrödinger's Cat, his lordship's mind was always in two places at once, but mainly it stayed focused on his current scheme. Installed behind his huge steel desk, he regarded himself as Master of The Universe. Right now he was shouting into the phone—Folds never spoke quietly to anyone.

"I need this done now ... yesterday. You know what I'm like ... anything I want ... I always get it ... that's the way I am."

In response, faint mutterings could be heard.

"I don't care ... I want action ... I don't want excuses. Now just do it ... and call me back in ten minutes ... telling me it's all sorted."

Folds clicked off the phone and looked around him. The light from the window struggled vainly with the glare from the rows of halogen bulbs set into the ceiling. A vast array of filing cabinets against the wall looked accusingly at him. Since Folds had transferred every scrap of information he had accumulated onto digital alternatives, they knew their days were numbered. There were still papers that had to be preserved, and Folds was wondering how this could be achieved efficiently and impressively. He never liked to do anything unless it created an effect—a man of pomp in any circumstance. The phone rang again; Folds squinted at the display before answering its summons.

"Folds."

Plaintive squeaking.

"What d'you mean you can't get *five* rollers out to meet them? Have you any idea who these people are?"

Squeak, squeak.

"No! Of course that isn't good enough! What the hell are you talking about? I don't care if it *is* Christmas ... bloody Easter or Tom Tit's day ..."

Folds took his guests' visit seriously. Making deals involving huge sums of money has the effect of making people single-minded. Sometimes it blows their minds too. Folds ranted on, the metal of the desk clanging dully as he pounded it with his fist. A favourite trick of his to gain attention, he thumped away like a beaver's tail.

Like the furniture, the matching fabric of the seat covers and curtains—pastel, predominantly light tangerine—had been selected by a highly-paid firm of consultants. The amorphous shapes in the design bestowed a benign aura upon the staff-room at Eggleston Academy. How unlike the old-fashioned version it was—the kind of world celebrated in Giles cartoons! A cluttered cavern, filled with tobacco smoke and ill-assorted arm-chairs perhaps. But that was a long time ago and, in the ethos of modern education—alien and most definitely reprehensible.

Philip was perched on a vinyl-covered bench chewing on his tie, one decorated with a design involving red stars. His growing indignation at something he had just heard almost made him swallow it whole.

"That's so *Middle Class* ..."

Martin, sitting next to him, reflected calmly on his social status.

"Well ... I'm not Upper Class ... or Lower Class ... so really there's nothing else left is there ..."

Philip's cropped hair somehow had the effect of making his opinions even more forceful.

"The despised Bourgeois!"

"Probably ... but then ... so what? Anyone who has in any way influenced society in the last hundred years or so ... has been solidly middle-class. Politicians ... reformers ... entrepreneurs even ... artists ... writers. Pop stars are always middle class ... *lower middle-class* maybe ... but never *working class* ... though they might pretend otherwise ..."

Philip would almost certainly have argued at length against this thesis, if a shrill-sounding buzzer had not interrupted the debate. Eggleston Academy was about to begin its afternoon session and the mettle of the teaching staff would once more be severely tested. Philip and Martin left the sanctuary of the staffroom to make their way along endless carpeted corridors and into the bleak unknown. Waiting for them behind some door marked with an arcane code—XL7 or BZ5—lay, like a dormant volcano, the angst of adolescence only waiting for the opportunity to erupt.

Some hours later, as Martin crawled along the motorway back into the centre of the city, he reviewed the day. He had been sworn at several times and, outside the Sports Area, a chair had been thrown, possibly in his direction. While in the Craft Department, a waste-paper basket had been set on fire in an adjacent room. Martin was never entrusted with any actual instruction at Eggleston—the sacred imparting of knowledge—except in the most mundane manner. The date of the First World War, or the name of the ghost in Macbeth, might be the extent of what was required from him. The notion that any student might take advantage of Martin's scholarship, to hear an explanation of The Categorical Imperative, or an explanation of Wittgenstein's theory of language was unthinkable. The gap between his own education and those of his charges was wider than The Grand Canyon.

His course dictated that Martin spent part of the week 'observing' in a state school. He and Philip, both in their second year at Barstowe University, had opted for a module within their course that designated this 'hands-on' experience. After tomorrow, his placement would officially end, and it was unlikely that Martin would ever see Eggleston or its errant youth ever again. Avoiding being seriously injured by psychotic adolescents had been his primary concern. Martin reflected that those going about the business of education throughout the kingdom probably shared his approach.

Clinton, being close to the campus, was the student area of the city. Martin lived with four others in a Georgian pile in Bobbin Park. Presumably once an abode of the gentry, it had seen better days. The landlord had the view that any standard of accommodation should suffice for students. Like a whale washed up on the shore, an old van lay in the front yard, and the remains of a piano littered the whole of the back lawn. Unkempt shrubs and overgrown trees surrounded the property and—like the Triffids—threatened to take over the civilised world, or at least this corner of it.

Philip and Henry—who did English—occupied the top floor while Simon and Max—History of Art—had the rest of the rooms. A communal kitchen and a sitting room completed the domestic arrangements. Martin lived in relative splendour on his own, in the basement. That evening arrangements for Christmas were being discussed. It seemed that all except Martin were staying with the parents of their respective girlfriends.

"Trish's people are kinda cool about me being there ..."

"Yeh ... Lucy's Dad is a great guy ... takes me down the pub ..."

"They go to the Boxing Day Meet at Pokey Fiddleton ... get really lashed afterwards ..."

Martin did not contribute, it would have been impossible. In the matter of being in a relationship, naturally he would have preferred not to be single. Any enduring success in that area of his student life eluded him, the problem usually being to sustain any momentum. After initial progress, the prospective love always made it clear that she did not want things to continue. Fortunately for Martin's self-esteem, he took the accomplished view that nothing is fruitless in life, not even failure.

The conversation drifted into other territory and Martin and Philip decided to go to the pub. Passing the local supermarket, Christmas Carols honked out at them from speakers strategically attached to the wall outside. Martin realized that he had been excited by the prospect of the Yuletide Season when he was a kid—but no more. The inevitable prospect of spending the day with his parents depressed him. In his mind, filial affection was immutably linked with returning to his flat laden with Tupperware boxes filled with turkey and mince pies. Such things were on his mind when they were drinking in The Blue Badger.

"It just is so incredibly boring at my folks' place ..."

"Where do they live? Remind me ..."

"Brandyfoot ..."

Philip made a face.

"Where *is* that exactly?"

Martin had long ago resigned himself to knowing that his hometown was obscure to everyone except himself. If he had offered 'Hampstead' or even 'Swindon', a more enthusiastic response would have been forthcoming.

"About fifty miles away ... down the coast."

"Oh ... right. And at Christmas ... is it just you and your Mum and Dad?"

"Absolutely. Pretty full-on ..."

Philip tried hard to imagine such an intense little scene and gave up. His own home in Surrey would be stuffed with relatives and friends from Boxing Day until past the New Year.

"You don't know anybody down there anymore I suppose?"

"Never did really. I mean ... I went to boarding school in the middle of nowhere ... and then Clinton. So I never saw anybody in the town or got to have any real friends there. We used to stay with my uncle in

Canada a lot too ..."

Philip expressed marginal interest.

"Oh ... yeh? What was that like?"

"Well ... I can't remember that much about it. We stopped going there when I was around fourteen ..."

"Whereabouts was it?"

"Langley ... outside Vancouver ... right on the border with Washington State. Strange really ... being so close to America and never actually going there ..."

"Yeh?"

"Well ... Canadians are always trying to pretend America doesn't exist."

Philip adopted a censorious tone.

"A lot of people in the world would prefer that it didn't exist at all ..."

Martin raised an eyebrow, he was determined not to encourage Philip in slagging off the 'running dogs of capitalism', or whatever it was that Chairman Mao had put in his Little Red Book. They had another drink and made their way back to the house.

At the corner of Bobbin Park they were regaled by the sight of their neighbour Minnie Short. This extraordinary woman never failed to cause some reaction among those who encountered her. On this occasion she was wearing what looked like an apple turnover on her head. Renowned for her choice of eccentric headgear, there was always an uncanny resemblance to various puddings. Martin had definitely envisaged jam roly-poly and sherry trifle on occasions. It was rumoured that she wrote on the walls of her home, every room being covered in obsessive scrawling. Much of this was apparently libellous, according to Shane the local odd-job man. Insights from this quarter were generally not regarded as reliable, however, as the man was as notorious for his incompetence as much as his drunkenness.

As he and Philip turned in at their front gate Martin wondered—in rather an academic fashion—what sort of perception of the world Mrs. Short experienced. His own was mostly akin to an Impressionist landscape, with a few parts in predictable linear patterns—so it was a cocktail of reason and intuition. There were also more amorphous areas occupied by various emotions, these randomly changing from bold to timid. What sort of Christmas would Minnie enjoy? Visits from long-lost relatives anticipating a mention in her will? Meals on Wheels bearing the most depressing culinary invention ever conceived—an individual Christmas pudding? Hopefully there would be no bizarre incidents that would prompt enforced entry to her home by the Social Services.

The weeks after the University going down quickly passed, and Martin realised it was Christmas Eve. Alone in the house, he tried watching T.V. but, so moronic was the fare on offer, he felt the need to procure a bottle of Oz Plonk from the Off-License. Discovering a piece of stilton at the back of the fridge that was still edible and half-a-jar of pickled onions, he happily indulged himself at the kitchen table. When all had been consumed, he stumbled down the stairs that connected his quarters to the rest of the house, and fell into bed.

Martin woke on Christmas morning with a medium-sized hangover. He lay in bed listening to the bells of St. Ronald's calling the faithful to Family Communion until his mobile rang.

"Happy Christmas, darling."

"And to you, Mum."

"Hope you're having a good holiday break. That's what they say these days isn't it? So funny ... ah well ... and you'll still be coming over ... as usual?"

Martin detected a slight anxiety in her voice and reassured her.

"Yes ... of course ... I'll be there ..."

"We'll see you about twelve o'clock then ... don't suppose there'll be much traffic about today ..."

"No ... I wouldn't have thought so. Dad alright?"

"He's fine ... got his new slippers on so he's happy ... and he's made a nice fire up ..."

The thought of his father in his new slippers in front of the fire made Philip feel oddly dejected, but he was determined not to reveal his feelings.

"Oh ... that's alright then. I'll see you later, Mum."

"Yes, dear ... see you shortly."

Martin deliberately delayed leaving until the last possible moment, hoping someone might call and wish him the Season's Greetings, but no one did. The journey to Brandyfoot took an hour or so and, when he got there, his parents' home had not changed at all since he saw it last. There was really no reason why it should have. The rustic fencing, the winding path surrounded by snow-on-the mountain, the escalonia bushes and the big buddleia dwarfing everything in the garden, it was all there. The bungalow probably hadn't been painted for at least twenty years and the paint was flaking off from the woodwork. His father had taken early retirement so it wasn't as if he was pressed for time to set about these essential chores. Martin suspected that he spent most of the day in the garage tinkering with his model railway. This had been ostensibly bought for his offspring a decade ago, but Martin could never actually remember being given the opportunity to play with it.

"Hello, Mum. Happy Christmas."

"And you, Marty."

The appellation was never meant to be anything but affectionate, and Martin had got used to it over the years. In the sitting room Mr. Callow was in his armchair engrossed in a book, obviously another newly-acquired present. After meticulously marking his place, he put this on the small table next to him. Martin noticed the title—*Shunting Tales of the Somerset and Dorset.*

"Ah ... there you are, Martin."

"Happy Christmas, Dad."

Martin handed his father a gaudily-wrapped package. Another, slightly more sober-looking, went to his mother.

"Thank you, my boy. Very kind. I'm sure we've got something for you somewhere ..."

Martin's mother scurried off to find her son's gift. She returned with a large parcel and a Christmas stocking, a tangerine peeping coyly out of the top. Martin accepted both gratefully, though he slightly embarrassed about the stocking, considering this particular fetish should have been exorcised some years ago. The semi-nuclear family dutifully opened their presents and, not long after that, sat down to lunch. Martin saw his mother had set a bottle of what looked like half-decent claret on the table.

"Auntie Jocelyn sent this over for us. Wasn't that kind of her?"

Martin agreed that it was and helped himself to Brussels sprouts, the next instant recalling he didn't really like them. Turkey, sausages and the rest got heaped on his plate, the contents of which he consumed manfully. Conversation, not exactly sparkling from the beginning, quickly flagged, and it was not until the pudding stage that things perked up a little. His father, pausing in the delicate task of spreading some brandy butter on a mince pie, looked across at him.

"So ... everything alright with your course this term?"

"Yeh ... had to do some teaching ... go into schools ..."

"Oh? What was that like?"

"Um ... okay. Not sure I'd like to do that every day ... as a job I mean ..."

As soon as he had said this, Martin wished he hadn't. His father adopted a told-you-so tone.

"Got to go to work some day, son. Get out in the real world y'know."

Martin said nothing, finding himself wondering—as he frequently did—what exactly 'the real world' was. Was it all real or only parts of it? None of it even? Or did everybody have a different version of the Platonic ideal. He decided it would not be a good idea to introduce such concepts into the post-prandial small talk. The meal now over, Martin's father deftly slid the few feet required to reinstate himself in his armchair. His mother was already piling up dishes ready to clear the table. Martin went to help her.

"Now ... you take it easy, Martin. You and your Dad can have a nice little chat. I'll get on with the washing up ... don't you worry."

There didn't seem to be much to say to this, so Martin dutifully sat himself down on the sofa. Willing to embark on a scintillating exchange with his father, he knew full well his parent would much rather return to shunting in the sidings. Martin reflected that his father probably wasn't that much older than some of his tutors, yet he looked like an old man. The iron grey hair had something to do with it, but it was more the way he moved and spoke, with a gravitas that wasn't very convincing. He definitely *wanted* to be old, like some men did. Martin had noticed this trait occasionally and couldn't comprehend it at all.

"The Queen ... she'll be on in a minute ... we always watch Her Majesty. I miss it now they don't have Morecambe and Wise at Christmas ... don't take to much of what they put on telly though these days ... lot of bosh most of it."

Martin attempted to take part in this far-reaching critique.

"There's a flat screen in the sitting room in the house but nobody seems to ..."

His father, while fiddling with the volume on the remote, interrupted him.

"And you can't get the cricket any more ... unless you have that satellite thing ..."

The rumbustious sound of the National Anthem

and a line of Beefeaters marching up and down, intimated that patriotic proceedings were about to get under way. Martin glanced at his father—his eyes had speedily closed and he was now fast asleep. The Queen started on her speech—the usual auto cued stuff. Martin stole quietly out of the room. As he passed the door to the kitchen he whispered quietly to his mother.

"Dad's nodded off. I'm going to go for a walk."

Martin's Mother was earnestly drying a dinner plate.

"Oh ... alright then, dear. I shouldn't stay out too long though ... it gets dark quite early now. We'll have a nice cup of tea when you get back."

Martin set out into the approaching gloom, following the coastal path. As he walked between the laurel hedges at the edge of the golf course he reflected on his parents' almost inert lifestyle. Maybe his grandparents—neither of whom Martin had known—had passed on this innate yearning for stability. It was somehow reflected in the England of his father's childhood, one depicted in old black and white newsreels of the times—all Test Matches and bowler hats. Whether his father had actually *enjoyed* the Fifties, Martin had never thought to enquire. His parents never talked about 'the good old days' but that did not necessarily mean they were or weren't.

After mooching along the pebbles and gaining a glimpse of the sea, Martin retraced his steps in the gathering dark. Back in the bosom of his family, with an aura of coziness implicit in the tea and Christmas cake set out on doilies, Martin still felt isolated and alone. He began to feel almost guilty.

"What are all your friends doing this holiday, Martin?"

Martin snapped back into gear.

"Oh ... most of them are away ... London ... and places ..."

His father decided to contribute.

"I'm trying to think when was the last time your mother and I went up there ..."

"London, Bob? Oh ... a long time ago ... we went up for the day on a coach ..."

Martin wasn't listening. The day dragged itself into evening and later he retired early to his old bedroom. There he looked at himself in the mirror on the door of the wardrobe. His long straight hair hung down each side of his face and he thought he looked like a kid again. Back then, he had acquired a habit of hiding behind this blond curtain if he felt shy in company. Then, as now, it was the world he was hiding from. Martin was only too aware there was a big hole in his life, one that needed fixing. There was only one way that could be done—with love.

Rock is the body of the Earth and the stones within are her skeleton. From the very beginning, when Man took to putting one stone on top of another, he has built monuments. He recognized the permanence of stone and paid respect to it by constructing tombs and altars, even the Pyramids. At a time when Man felt the awesome power of nature, he paid homage to the Earth and the Heavens and built monuments in their honour. Thus stone circles and standing stones came to be, all over the world.

The stone circle at Rylock Wells had been a sacred place from its very inception thousands of years ago. The stones were more than twice the height of a man and weighed many tons. To explain how and why they had been dragged along the ground and eventually raised into the air was almost impossible.

Here, particularly in High Summer when the wind caressed the tips of the grass and the blue of the sky spoke only of paradise, was a world separate from any other. The clouds that lay above the hills—fluffy mounds and milky streaks- might play host to the vapour trails of a passing aircraft and hint at another era. But within the stone circle was a place unique, one where crows and hawks circled in unison.

In these honest fields and ancient ridges the feet of many had trodden, and the reassuring earth was blessed by god and goddess alike. Here they came, to gather, to celebrate and to conduct their rituals. To laugh and sing, light fires and above all to rejoice in being alive. Little had changed at Rylock Wells— or much, depending upon the imagination of the pilgrim. A few dwellings and an isolated farmhouse was all that punctuated the ring of trees. Ash, willow, oak and sycamore grew here, following the course of a once mighty river then ran along the edge of the circle.

And all the while these sentinels of stone assumed shapes that confounded all reason, one moment they were haystacks, horses, or mighty pillars. They could be held in the palm, thrown into the air or assume the vastness of an unassailable peak. One stood out from the rest, appearing to be pointing at the stars, as if announcing that the cosmos lay, not distant, but a mere thought away. Great power resided here, in this womb, temple, and portal into the next world.

2

By the middle of February the days began to feel they had some obligation to the coming Spring. Snow-drops were beginning to appear—clustered clumps of white and iridescent green, looking like nuns in starched wimples. More than enough evidence of the student population was evident. They were every-where—sprawling over the pavements and lounging on the grass in front of the library—like an army of occupation.

The Faculty of Arts and Humanities, known at Barstowe University as A&H, was located in a row of early Victorian houses. This took up one side of Beechdale road, while other departments that might have been regarded by some as more miscellaneous—Russian, Sociology, and Politics—were accommodated opposite. On the corner of Beechdale Road nearest to the Cathedral stood *The Willows*, once a hotel, now a conference centre. Its premises boasted a dining room for the university staff, and a canteen in the basement where students might gorge upon pizza and chips.

Compared to other more august seats of learning, Barstowe was a fledgling establishment. Founded in the late nineteenth century with the fruits of capitalism, its campus dominated the most select area of the city. The original buildings exuded an air of complacency and a raffish charm. With the expansion of higher education after WWII, it was found expedient to build new lecture rooms and halls of residence. A discordant note was struck when Victorian Gothic confronted Sixties chic. Traditionalists tended to prefer the aesthetics of Pater to Op-Art and said so—vehemently—at the time.

The clock in the Lecture Theatre proclaimed it was nearing ten o'clock; Ollie Pearson—a senior lecturer in the Philosophy Department—arranged his notes on the podium. The seats before him were steeply tiered, always reminding Martin of a Roman amphitheatre. Earlier, he had ambled in unhurriedly with the rest of them, many displaying a maximum of cool and a minimum of interest. Ollie walked up and down before slipping into tutor mode.

"Make sure you've all got a handout … if you could just pass them along … and please make sure you sign the register … and if someone could get it handed back to me at the end … thanks."

Martin noticed the trio of blondes near him—all flurried locks and pearls. Before the lecture started they had been yelling at each other at top volume, as the privileged classes are wont to do. Martin knew them—Shilly, Illy and Killy. Put together, the plums in their mouths would have made several pounds of jam. Draped over the seats in the row behind them were several tousled youths, obviously no strangers to privilege themselves. The clock ticked along to a few minutes past ten. Glancing at the front row he noticed the keener girls had red and green whatsits for highlighting and wads of post-it notes. Ollie, grasping the podium as if it were a surfboard, paddled out to catch the first thought wave of the day.

"Logic … along with truth … and the paradoxes inherent in the concept of truth … are what we are concerned with this morning. Logic can be defined as the mechanics of thought and analysis. It is the way we train the mind to think in a particular way. Logic is concerned with something 'as it is known.'"

While some of his colleagues had allowed middle-age spread to become a permanent fixture. Ollie had remained slim. A black shirt peeked out beneath the striped jacket; the latter tailored in a style once known as 'mod'. Black corduroys and designer-label boots completed the ensemble. His hair was longish about the ears, and only slightly greying. Ollie did not favour the 'pony-tail look' as sported by Terry Usher in the English Department. As well as being a blatant poseur, the man just looked plain ridiculous.

"Logic is not always logical. I won't go into that now either … but if I might suggest you look at how quantum has changed our view of truth. It will blow your mind … or it ought to."

This *bon mot* was greeted with a flurry of laughter combined with a sense of relief—his audience realising that the lecture was as good as over. They began to fidget with their bags.

"If you look at the handout you can see—in that first section—some numbered quotes attributed to those people I've been talking about. You should find those useful."

Tutor surveyed students.

"Thank you very much."

Ollie got a muttered response as he gathered up his notes and began to make for the door. Some students diligently packed the handout while Martin wondered what would have happened if Ollie had told them all to make a paper aeroplane out of it. He rather thought they would they have unquestioningly obeyed.

Martin would certainly have had to admit that of all his tutors Ollie had the most style -somewhere between early Byron and late Jim Morrison. Upon this stage—year after year, term after term—Ollie Pearson had given a practised performance. The rehearsed quip and the spontaneous aside were presented in equal measure. The caprice of his thinking never threatened to outshine the assigned thesis yet, if he felt like it, he manifested whatever was in his imagination. If his asides were lost on some, equally they delighted others.

Rylock Wells was one of those villages that were known intimately by those who lived there but rarely remarked upon, by those passing through it. Rows of stone cottages, a grand house or two, and a clutch of semi-hideous bungalows, built in the 1970s, made up the picture. The pub and a village hall—rarely used because the roof leaked—were the main features of the village. Naturally, the villagers knew about the stone circle but the site had never aroused much interest among the rural community. They considered such things were for outsiders to marvel at, not them. If asked, the male residents of the village would have said they had been a lot more excited by the arrival of Mandy the new barmaid.

Lunchtimes at the *Robe and Tackle* were hardly ever lively, and evenings could rarely be described as a riot of conviviality either. Country folks tend to raise their voices louder than urban folk, what with a lifetime of calling beasts, so the visitor might have believed more raucousness went on than it actually did. Any abandoned passions were mostly directed at Mandy, an asset to any publican's trade. She had raven hair with a touch of titian, eyelashes invariably laden with mascara, and her lips were the brightest coral pink. To many she resembled a Fifties pin-up—cool and dark like a choc-ice. Being country boys, and a good bit behind the times, teenage fantasies were still dominated by hot-rods and Buddy Holly. Mandy was their own Bettie Page, and just about as unobtainable. She would come in their dreams, and they might do too if they were lucky.

Admittedly, it was difficult not to keep staring at Mandy's breasts. She had a way of drawing attention to them too. Displaying a tattoo of a heart just where her cleavage began was one ploy. If she wore a t-shirt, her nipples stood out most prominently. All of Mandy was inviting, from her bare midriff to her well-rounded buttocks, every part invited a caress. Woe betide any who took that licence without express permission. Those who had foolishly done so found out that the serpent when it striketh, doth so with deadly venom.

Those who had enjoyed her charms, and there had been a chosen few, knew the play of her supple fingers and her darting tongue. Mandy gave them the feeling that she appreciated every move they made, no matter how clumsy. She was that paradox of woman, the temptress and the virgin, and Mandy had the power to change from one guise to another in the twinkling of an irresistible eye. Presently, this wondrous orb surveyed the lunchtime customers ranged about the bar, precisely to the number of three. Ernie was, as usual, the most vociferous of the trio.

"You 'ear that motor down our lane las' night?"

Ted shook his head.

"Don't reckon I did ... dead to the world I spec I woz. Four or five pints in yere do make sure o' that."

Clifford was more salient.

"I 'eard 'n ... an' I know what 'twas ... 'cos I looked out the winder."

"Ah?"

"Gurt big Rolls 'e were ... 'ad his 'eadlights on bright too ... bit narrow for'n up the lane ..."

"Wot woz 'e up to then?"

"I knows the bugger went up the stones ... parked up there too ... fer a hour ..."

Ted took an interest.

"That ain't right?"

"I knows 'e did ... shut the door of 'is motor good 'n 'ard ... woke I up ... an' then 'e must've went off round the stones. Then 'e come back later ... started off again ... an' gone."

Ernie reflected deeply while sipping his beer.

"Wos all that about then?"

" 'oo knows. Now then I'll tell 'ee summat else ..."

"Woss that?"

"When I took th' ole dog out s'mornin' ... I went an' found summat up by the gate to the field ..."

"Oh ... what were that then?"

His audience held in suspense, Clifford paused. Prolonged rummaging in a poacher's pocket produced a book, its covers smeared with mud.

"Yere 'tis ..."

The audience were interested but none over-whelmed with curiosity. Ernie asked the obvious question.

"Wos it about?"

Clifford shook his head.

"No ideal ... I did 'ave a look but it don't make no sense to I ... all long words and squiggles ..."

At this point Mandy started to take an interest. She leant over the bar, to the pleasure of all who beheld her cleavage in extreme close-up.

"Can I see?"

Mandy held the book and leafed through its pages.

"Wos think then, ar Mand?"

Mandy acted as if she had taken possession of this strange black-covered volume already.

"Lily ought to have it ... she'll know what it's all about ..."

Clifford shrugged.

"I suppose she might do ... 'er's into all that weird stuff I bin told."

That seemed to clinch it. Clifford laid the book on the bar, Mandy regarding it.

"Alright ... go on then ... I don't mind. T'ain't no use to I ... don't suppose nobody could sell'n anyroad ... all dirtied up like that ..."

Mandy put the book under the counter and conversation in the pub drifted off into rural matters. Tending to twist and turn like old paths through the woods, they inevitably involved the whole cast of the village. It did not take long before the matter of the book had all but been forgotten. Mandy did not forget it, however. When George the landlord returned from the local cash'n' carry later she was able to quit the premises. On her way home she met her friend Lily coming out of the Post Office.

"Hiya."

"Hello ..."

"I've just finished work ..."

"Oh ... come and have some tea."

"Oh ... yes ... yes ... lovely ..."

Mandy looked at Lily and, not for the first time, wondered what it was that made her seem so different. Her delicate, oval face was often smiling, but in a way all her own. She seemed to be constantly conjuring up some dream so she could be part of it. To everything she saw Lily gave life, from a moonbeam to a droplet of dew upon the grass. Other people might believe that they saw the same world as Lily, but they did not. That world was her production, and she was the director, the star and she designed the sets. Lily wore the same outfit for her every appearance too—black, silver and violet—making her a true Moon Queen. No one got to see the show unless Lily invited them. That was her way of dealing with other people. If she didn't want them to be part of her life she simply didn't acknowledge that they existed.

When Mandy visited the cottage she always thought she had somehow passed into another world one of fairy tale. She paused at the foot of the stairs to hang up her coat and wondered, as she often did, what Lily's bedroom would be like. More significant to Mandy was the question of whether she had ever invited any man there. She rather thought not, her friend may not have been a virgin, but she was the closest thing to it of the people Mandy knew.

"You go in ... I'll put the kettle on ..."

Mandy loving the sitting room because in no way was it designed to impress that was not Lily's way—she was entirely herself. No pagan tat, or framed posters of Hobbits were anywhere. There were a couple of cats of course, curled up on the sofa, lots of velvet draped over everything, and enough candles for a dozen birthday cakes. Mandy warmed her hands at the fire glowing red in the grate. Lily came out of the kitchen with a tray, floating into the room, as she always did.

"Oh ... thanks, Lily."

Mandy sipped her tea. She wasn't sure what was in it but it was like everything else that surrounded Lily, fragrant and gentle. They always seemed to sit in silence here and it didn't seem to matter to Mandy whether they talked or not.

"Have you seen Philomena?"

"No ... she hasn't been in the pub lately."

"Oh."

"She seems to be in Windleroot a lot of the time these days. Do you think she's got a fella there?"

Lily looked to right and left as if weighing up the options.

"I don't think anyone knows what she does ..."

"That's true ..."

Mandy suddenly remembered about the book and drew it from her bag. As she did so she stared in surprise. There was not a trace of it being soiled—it was pristine and glowing in the candlelight.

"I thought you might like this ..."

Lily smiled and took her gift.

"Thank you ... that's so kind of you Mandy ..."

She leant forward and kissed her friend.

"It seemed like your sort of thing ..."

Lily smiled once more.

"Yes ... it is."

She held the cover in her long sleek fingers for a moment then placed it carefully on a side table near her.

"I shall look at it ... later."

Mandy was aware that the air felt different in the room—much heavier. When she glanced through the window she noticed it had suddenly become dark. Mandy did not think it was late, but she felt somehow compelled to leave. She stood up and put her tea cup on the table next to a statuette of some Egyptian god—Anubis she thought.

"I really must go ... have a shower and then I need to have something to eat ..."

She realised she was talking too fast, babbling. Lily smiled, her eyes seeming to glisten in the half-dark in the room.

"That's okay."

She almost forgot her bag as she hurried for the door.

"I've got to back at work at seven ... there's a darts match tonight ..."

A fine drizzle was in the air as Mandy hurried home. Living with her parents had its disadvantages where her social life was concerned, but at least there would be a cooked tea waiting for her. The street lamp cast an unreal light as she went in at her gate, the night seemed blacker than usual. An image of Lily holding the book came into her mind. Even a long time after, when all the excitement was over, Mandy could never quite remember what prompted her to ask Clifford if she could have the book. She wondered later if somehow she wasn't responsible for the all the strange things that happened.

For as long as anyone in Clinton could remember Anton Ludowski had lived in Clarence Terrace, the street adjoining Bobbin Park. Martin had greeted the dapper little Pole one day and they had started talking. Anton had announced proudly that he had shot many Russians during the Hungarian Uprising, and he was obviously a man to be reckoned with, mainly because he was never at loss for an anecdote. Late one afternoon, at the end of a depressing day of constant rain, Martin—who knew where his quarry resided—was prompted to set out in search of Mr. Ludowski.

When Anton answered the door, he squinted at Martin from behind the thick glasses that he wore. The lenses refracted the light from the street lamp into diamond shapes.

"Hello, Anton. It's Martin ... I ... hope I'm not disturbing you."

As always, the response was a surprise. Anton was never predictable.

"I am eighty-nine years old today ... God has been very kind to me."

Martin was genuinely amazed, even with his silver-white hair, Anton looked younger.

"Many happy returns of the day ..."

"Thank you ... thank you. Won't you come in? Perhaps we shall celebrate my birthday a little ..."

Martin was unable to resist the bright smile of welcome and he followed Anton along a passage and into the kitchen. A cupboard decorated with flowers in a folksy style stood in one corner. The room was dominated by a table made from thick timbers of pale wood. Delicacies in dishes were set out neatly on the linen cloth. Had Anton been expecting company?

"Were you planning on having a party?"

The old man's eyes twinkled.

"Yes ... always ... for whoever comes."

Anton busied himself preparing coffee while Martin took a chair by the window. His host's style of conversation was marked by his embarking, without any warning, on some reminiscence.

"I learned the marching songs of my peoples when I was a youth in Poland ... We drank much Tokay and sang them ... very loud ... all my friends did the same. I am proud to be Polish ... my country ... that was once called Silesia ... was always tolerant ... very *liberal*. We did not harm the Jews hundreds of years ago like others did. Those who followed other religions ... we did not mind. We were great warriors too ... defeating the Teutonic Knights ... we were the only nation ever to do so."

Martin thanked Anton for the coffee and also the

glass of vodka that accompanied it.

"*Na zdrowie!*"

Martin did not attempt to echo this.

"Cheers!"

Anton sipped his vodka and carried on.

"I was already in the Polish Air Force when Germany invaded my country. My aircraft was a PZL from the State Aviation Works ... I flew as far as I could towards Romania and then ... when I ran out of fuel I crash landed and walked to the nearest railway station. I hid on a train. So, you know what I did then? I took another train through Hungary and then Austria. I knew it would be dangerous to travel through France and so at the border I climbed underneath the train ... there I was ... all through France. Can you imagine that? I nearly froze to death."

Martin tried to imagine it, not without some difficulty.

"That's incredible ..."

"It is true. Some of my friends went to Greece ... to Gibraltar and that way to England. I thought I could do it differently ... it was all the same in the end. We all met at Duckworth airfield. That was where the R.A.F ... they started The Polish Squadrons. We were all quite mad ..."

Martin was feeling a little insane himself; he put it down to the 99% spirit.

"Really?"

"We would fly upside down in the sky ... do all sorts of tricks. We were as warriors of old ... we had no fear of death. That belief has stayed with me. Now ... we will go into the other room."

A miniature version of some European interior greeted Martin. A heavy chandelier hung from the ceiling, its crystal light reflected in a pair of ornate mirrors upon the walls. A low table with carved legs, and lined with elegant chairs was set out with heavy silver upon it. Framed etchings of old Cracow took up one wall and, on a bureau were photographs in dark leather frames of fierce looking men in uniform. A picture of a woman with a Rita Hayworth hairstyle stood in pride of place on another polished surface.

"My wife Margaret ... everyone called her Peggy ... I did not. To me she was a queen ... a goddess. In 1944 I married her ... a good English woman who I admired and loved until the day she died. She knew that I regarded her that way and thus she became so ... that is the nature of being ... we become the world about us. I made sure she had everything she wished for, I was honoured to do that."

Martin was completely absorbed in this account of another's life, one so different from his own.

"When the war was over I had to decide what to do. I knew I wanted to remain here in England and study ... philosophy. My English was not very good. I learned your language by studying literature. First I read Josef Conrad, because I had already read *Heart of Darkness* in Polish, then I read D.H. Lawrence ... Hemmingway and Sherlock Holmes. After that I studied hard ... the works of all the great men who have ever lived ... those who attempted to explain the nature of the universe ... and everything in it. Why we see things as we do ... and why we are here at all."

Anton had the habit of directing his gaze at a

point some distance away, as if he was conversing with invisible beings who he knew intimately.

"Do you know what prevents us from becoming as one with the gods?"

"Um ... no ... I don't ..."

"It is *time* ... as simple as that. It appears to be moving slowly and inevitably towards us along a track ... like a slow train. We stand on the station platform waiting for various moments to arrive. It is as if we are rooted to the material from which the platform is constructed ... and we cannot in any way hasten or slow the progress of our lives. All men believe that they are at the behest of this force ... but they do not realise it is one that does not exist."

Martin attempted to contribute, albeit most briefly.

"I'm sure that's true ..."

"None of us need be limited by this thing called time ... *past* ... *present* ... or *future* ... they do not exist. Neither does space ... and we may wander in as many dimensions as we like. If we do not regard existence in such a serious manner then all will disappear and we may make progress. We may become a mountain ... or a river if we so wish. We may enter the soul of a wolf ... or an eagle if we want ... by ceasing to be just an observer we become the spirit of that world and everything in it. Come ... we will eat."

They returned to the kitchen and ate spicy saus-age, pickled herring and after that, a cake made with poppy seeds. All the time, Anton continued to explain the nature of reality as he saw it. His audience was by this time befuddled with spirits and could only gape in wonderment. At some point Martin wondered what he was doing there, half-drunk in the company of an extraordinary man from Poland, one who talked of those who had lived many hundreds of years before as if they were still in this world. As if by some sort of clairvoyance, Ludowski answered the unspoken question.

"No one knows what it is that makes up this world ... our ancestors knew ... and somewhere hidden deep in the atoms that make up this shell that is our bodies is the same message ..."

Martin tried to focus, first on the words he was saying and then on Anton himself. His features were beginning to spin slowly, not so rapidly as to cause too much alarm, but enough for Martin to place his glass carefully on the floor. He realised that Anton was staring at him intently.

"I know that you will go to a strange place ... a circle of stones at somewhere near here called Royston Wells and find your destiny there ... you may even find true love ... as I did once in my life."

Martin merely stared, he was now beyond speech.

"One must be a little mad perhaps to embrace the unknown. The nature of the night is no different from the experiences of the day. When we open the door into other worlds we gain the infinite."

Martin was suddenly aware of feeling tired. Listening to Anton for any length of time would have fatigued an Olympic runner. He stood up, somewhat shakily, and with an attempt at a wave, indicated that he intended to leave. Anton led him outside. On the doorstep he still continued to talk.

"Shall I tell you what is the greatest gift that we possess? It is laughter, my friend. Mirth frees us from the bounds of the material and thus we are not limited by the nature of any event ... or indeed its outcome. Then we exist in a new universe ... one that has laws that are different to any in the known and visible world."

By this stage of the game Martin could only mumble his thanks for what had proved to be an overwhelming hospitality. After that he did not remember a lot more, except being somewhat relieved not to see Minnie peeking out from behind her net curtains as he stumbled along the pavement. At the third attempt he managed to unlock the front door of his flat and fall inside. As he tumbled, fully clothed, onto his bed and into unconsciousness he heard Anton's laughter once more.

3

To describe Royston Score as shifty would have been like saying Caruso sang now and then. Lord Folds, however, found him useful. If any dirty business was required, Score could be sent to do it, and rarely did he ever fail. It was perhaps unfortunate that he was so unattractive. He owned an oily moustache, and a nose that looked like it had been sculpted out of putty. Lady Folds particularly objected to his appearance. She had chanced upon him only once, considering that was enough of a disturbing experience for her to protest to her husband.

"I am fully aware, Douglas that you are often forced to employ the worst kind of riff-raff to get done whatever it is that you wish to do. I do not enquire into your business arrangements ... because I do not wish to know what they are ... they do not interest me in the slightest. It is simply the case that a particular *person* ... who I had the misfortune to encounter by the herbaceous borders ... offended me. He actually made me feel ill ... like something out of those terrible fairy tales our Transylvanian nanny used to read us in the nursery. That was until my mother found out the reason why we were all having such dreadful nightmares ... after that she sent her packing."

Thereafter, Folds had to insist that Score make his way to the office by some other, circuitous route, one that guaranteed he would not be observed by her Ladyship. Score was due to make an appearance that very morning, and Lord Folds was taking particular pains to ensure that nothing upset his spouse. The weekend guests had tried her *savoir faire* to the utmost. The Wall Street element—with names like Jakovich and Kedrova—had been most impertinent. To make matters worse, the Arab contingent were aloof and expected constant deference, something Lady Folds was not prepared to bestow upon anyone. The hostility between the two parties then made for a ludicrous situation, and Lady Folds' work was cut out to persuade them even to talk to each other.

The series of business meetings over the two days was a different matter. Here, Score came into his own. Although he had found observing the negotiations extremely tedious, he knew his own role was often more important than his employer. Folds too had little interest in the minutiae of commerce. Meetings with accountants bored him, and the progress of his stocks and shares he did not meticulously check every morning as some did. His only interest in wealth was that it gave him power over others.

Score also found it extraordinary that those who were providing the finance for Folds' schemes seemed to have a minimum of interest in what they might actually be. As long as their investment resulted in guaranteed profits what Folds wanted to do with their money was almost irrelevant. Score knew too that in the past Folds had always contracted a Rottweiler—of either sex—to do his bidding, but this method had its disadvantages. They tended to snap and snarl at everyone regardless of their status, their behavior tending to be counter-productive.

The success of the whole enterprise relied on how quickly Score could persuade others to agree to Folds' proposals. To his amazement both the Americans and the Saudis easily fell in with everything that was suggested. If any individual even mildly demurred, Score would gently but firmly indicate that their objections had absolutely no foundation. Unbelievably, they would agree to the exact opposite of what they had insisted upon only moments before. Even if Score gave way on some point, he did it in such a way that the other party always doubted he had gained a victory, and felt guilty if he thought he had. The only glitch in the proceedings was that by Saturday evening his guests were showing signs of restlessness. As that day's meeting drew to a close, Folds took Score discreetly aside.

"I want you to tell 'em there's no hookers laid on here ... or porn ... or cocaine or any of that sort of lark. They won't find that in the villages round about either ... and the bright lights of the city are a long way off."

Score, who had suffered a long day, uncharacteristically protested.

"Why has it got to be me who has to tell them?"

Folds had looked at his most superior

"Simple ... I've decided you're the man for the job."

Thus it was Score's unenviable task to relay this news to the guests. They did not take to it too well, and there might have been open protest if Score had not applied the usual unassailable logic, combined with yet more helpings of the old oil. His duty done, he spent an uncomfortable night sleeping on a camp bed that might have been designed by the Inquisition, in the staff quarters. He had departed for Selly Oak and home on Sunday morning.

Now it was Monday and, still tired, he was facing Folds across the desk in his office.

"Well ... the house is empty of Johnny Foreigner I'm glad to say ... our American cousins have cleared off too. I wouldn't want to be playing host to that lot every weekend. Still ... what we wanted to get settled we did ..."

Although he nodded, Score's expression was neutral.

"Right."

Folds moved his chair a fraction closer.

"There's a lot of money involved in all this business that I'm setting up ... shed loads."

"Yes."

"You got any idea of what sort of people they are ... these yanks and ayrabs ..."

Score ignored the racial slur.

"I think so ... yes."

Folds felt he had to leave his hired hand in no doubt as to what he was implying.

"Let's put it this way ... if you or anyone else were to be chatty about any of their affairs to anyone else ... they'd have you snuffed out ... straightaway."

Folds made a clicking sound with his fingers, one that denoted finality.

"I see what you mean ..."

Folds stared, darkly.

"You do don't you? And I won't need to tell you ... these guys have blokes on their books who knock people off. When they decide they're ... surplus to requirements."

"Okay."

Folds moved his chair back, changing his expression as he did so.

"Just thought you ought to know. Now ..."

Folds dragged a file from a locked drawer, at the same time bringing to life the flat screen on his desk. Score moved his chair so he could see the display more clearly. Graphics, in a bewildering array of colours began to appear. Folds shuffled papers around on his desk, squinting at them from behind his glasses. There was a knock at the office door. One of the staff—a young blonde—appeared with coffee on a tray. She paused for a moment, enough for Score to leer. Folds, shielding his papers, merely looked up and snarled.

"Just put it down over there ... we're very busy."

"Yes, sir."

The girl silently closed the door behind her. Folds then delivered a remark in such a way that Score wondered if he was actually hearing the words correctly.

"I want to control ... not only the mind of every individual in this country, but their soul as well. And this is how I'm going to do it ..."

As he continued, describing how he would bring this about Score had the alarming realisation that his employer was bordering on insanity.

The suit Mr. Tonks was wearing had, like its owner, seen better days. Once, he had been renowned at Barstowe University as one of the great minds of the

West. His students thought him eccentric but loveable, his lectures were inspired, his tutorials anticipated with delight. Mr. Tonks guided his Postgraduate students into realms of knowledge that lay far and beyond the call of duty. The head of Humanities at Barstowe considered him an invaluable asset, a state of affairs that raised his standing with the then Vice-Chancellor to extraordinary heights.

"Brilliant man your Tonks. Do you know his name was mentioned when I was at a conference in Havana last month ... ?"

"He is somewhat of an international authority in his field ..."

"Indeed. Even Berkeley frequently requests his opinion I'm told ..."

"Ah ... yes ... and when the Americans begin to take notice ..."

"Quite. You're really on the map then."

In those days Mr. Tonks was regarded as a genius, every utterance of his the greatest wisdom. Whenever he said something, it was as if a coloured ball had been thrown into the room and all were then transfixed by its glistening trajectory. Some who think deeply are at heart institutional animals and they thrive only within a system. Mr. Tonks was such a one, without the hallowed walls of Academia about him he would have not felt complete. The rigour of the academic life more than suited him, it defined his very being.

His income enabled Mr. Tonks to live in a manner that suited him. His apartment was modest but it could accommodate his library, and enable him to set aside one room as a study. He required little else, for he was not a man who needed company or entertainment; he found all those things within his discipline. All went well for several decades, changes occurred around him but Mr. Tonks did not change, he liked being himself—he was content. The tragedy came when he retired, for he discovered, to his chagrin that he could no longer afford the rooms that he had grown to love. The area he had always lived in had become so up-market, so chic, that he could not possibly compete with the merchant-bankers and other young thrusters who owned property there.

He took on private tuition to increase his income but found only disappointment. Clint and Topple Tuition—and particularly the manager Sid Fryer were not to his taste. Thus, when his academic career was no more he was obliged to move to an indifferent part of the city and live in a block of flats for which he had little affection.

Mr. Tonks accepted his lot, and once a week allowed himself time away from his hermitage.

"Top Man Taxis!"

"Oh ... hello ... Archie Tonks here ..."

" 'ullo, sir ... nice to 'ear from you, Mr. Tonks ..."

"I was wondering if ... this Thursday ... you might ..."

The voice politely took over.

"... pick you up from Peason Drive ... Conkerville ... take you to *The Robe and Tackle* in Rylock Wells ... pick you up tennish ... your usual run ..."

Mr. Tonks laughed.

"If you would be so good."

"In the book, sir."

Mr. Tonks was a man of regular habits. In

the allotted time at *The Robe and Tackle* he would consume two half-pints of Guinness and a packet of bacon-flavoured crisps. He took a book, more likely three, and the notes relevant to his current research—Mr. Tonks prided himself on continuing to learn. And there would sit Mr. Tonks, always at the same table—the only one in the place that was circular.

"The Round table ... or *The Table Round* as Welsh pedants prefer to title it ... has an association with the Circular Tomb of Jerusalem. The Knights Templar ... as I'm sure you may have heard of ..."

The majority of the clientele at The Robe may have regarded him as a harmless oddity, but the more discerning considered Mr. Tonks an asset to the establishment. Shy to approach him at first, he quickly came to be looked upon as some great sage from afar, one dispensing wisdom to those with ears to hear. And Mr. Tonks never patronised them, he listened to what the cowman had to say as carefully as he would have some pundit from Princeton. Word went around that the newcomer was 'as sound as a pound'—and that is high praise indeed from country folks. Clifford was once moved to quiz their resident professor upon a subject that puzzled him.

"Some o' these ackeedemical types ... ain't they a bit out of touch, Mr. Tonks?"

Mr. Tonks felt moved to take a sip of Guinness before responding.

"I heartily agree ... you're absolutely right. Few seem to bother with what might call ordinary discourse with their fellow man. Minds as closed as a redundant coal mine ..."

Clifford paused, shaking his head.

"Bloke can think too much I reckon ..."

"Certainly. There have been great thinkers who have lost their wits ..."

"There you are then ... blowed their brains out ... sorta."

"You may very well be right ... their theories possessed them to the extent that nothing else existed ... a dangerous situation in any walk of life."

There came one Thursday when Mr. Knowle, the boss of Top Man Taxis, had informed Mr. Tonks he would be obliged if he could leave an hour earlier for his usual trip to Rylock Wells. Mr. Tonks readily agreed, he would take the opportunity to reacquaint himself with the stone circle, something he had been meaning to do for some time.

"Absolutely no trouble at all, Mr. Knowle. If your chap cares to come earlier that's fine with me ..."

"Fanks, Mr. Tonks. Sorry to mess you about ... but these fings sometimes is out of our 'ands ... like."

In the taxi Mr. Tonks pondered on the day being the Spring Equinox. He had a great respect for the old ways—the rhythms of the land, the cycle of nature. These were the things that mattered, and he sided with Blake's view that all creation was wondrous, from great to small. The great poets ventured into the unknown, exploring the uncharted territory of the imagination. As musicians attempt the impossible, discovering new ways of hearing, the true poet boldly risks all to find new horizons that will enchant us.

When Mr. Tonks entered the field that held the stones, the Sun was about to set, casting an amber glow over the scene. The mighty pillars were haloed with light, their faces turned towards him seemingly in greeting. He duly acknowledged their presence with a bow and began to walk slowly towards the circle. An avenue ran from West to East and Mr. Tonks processed slowly along this until he entered therein. He walked in a deosil direction about the stones, formally greeting each one in turn. Then he paused to give thanks to the spirits whose presence he felt so strongly there. The light from the West was still bright enough to give the impression he was entering some Solar Temple. Mr. Tonks halted in the very centre of the circle, closed his eyes and stood absolutely still and in silence.

At first he was aware of the stones observing him intently, as they had watched thousands before, then Mr. Tonks shifted his consciousness gently but surely into the void. Both aware and unconscious, he was in the highest state of meditation. The version of himself that was not part of the material plane moved in and around the stones, travelling in their world, becoming familiar with their essence and their very being. Mr. Tonks knew they held life as much as anything else upon the Earth. They understood what had once been and what might be, and he was astonished at what he learned. First the ancients came to him, the very ones who had caused these monuments to be placed here, and they told him much of the power and significance of the stones. Mr. Tonks listened gratefully and understood, passing elsewhere then, into another time.

Here, he was unaware of being an individual— simply a reflection of the energies around him.

Although he moved back and forth through time and space he was aware that he kept returning to a place in the circle of stones. He was aware of a pulsating rhythm that echoed through the Earth and into the deeps, and at the same time into the skies beyond. It would have been the natural beat of life had it not intensified then almost ceased.

Mr. Tonks realized that the stones were awaiting some event and wary of its inevitable coming. This warning of danger broke into the transcendent world and with a jolt returned him to the self that stood in the field. Such was the transition that Mr. Tonks was nearly flung to the ground, and only with an effort stopped himself from falling. For a time he waited, aware only that the sun had disappeared and the dusk was slowly approaching. All very strange indeed! Slowly he became aware of the shapes of the stones and he regarded them almost with protective eye. They responded as if asking him to ensure they were safe from any who intended to harm them.

With measured tread Mr. Tonks left the field almost not aware of his surroundings. He walked into the lane that led to the main street of the village and suddenly recognised the bulk of St. Wadworth's church. He glanced at his watch, another aspect of his returning consciousness albeit an artificial one. What did hours mean to the stones of Rylock Wells? But Mr. Tonks reasoned that he had time in hand before he retired to the Robe so he turned towards the gate that led into the churchyard. He would step from the pagan world into The Kingdom of Christ—with certain trepidation. When he encountered the figure of the vicar in the church porch he knew his caution was warranted.

"Hello ..."

"*Good Evening.*"

Stiff, unfriendly. Mr. Tonks regarded the un-smiling countenance of this man of the cloth with curiosity. The cuff links on his shirt peeked out from the sleeves of his jacket. His brown leather shoes were polished adequately, although the dark pink socks he sported were distinctly surprising.

"I've just been to the stone circle ... most interest-ing."

The Rev. Dunlop-Matthews was dismissive.

"Ah ... yes."

"Now I thought I might investigate your church ..."

"*Investigate?*"

Mr. Tonks fixed his gaze upon the umbrella stand in the corner of the vestibule.

"Middle to late ... twelfth century?"

The vicar hesitated, not sure if he was being mocked.

"Er ... 1159."

Obviously feeling it was incumbent of him to perform a guided tour, the vicar led the way into the well-proportioned nave, one crowned with trussed rafters. Neither overwhelming in its magnificence, nor uncomfortably cramped, Mr. Tonks experienced that agreeable feeling that invariably came to him in centuries-old places. Lines of simple seating for the common folk were interspersed with box pews for the gentry. The gallery above the south door sagged from age but still owned a quiet dignity, even after half a millennium. Still quite visible on the wall next to the pulpit were large painted figures, unusually a jester and an angel. Mr. Tonks examined these with a wistful expression.

"Ah ... the traces of your Catholic foundation ..."

Mr. Tonks evoked a vision of Mass, a ritual conducted by gloriously costumed dignitaries, amid clouds of pungent incense. In this imposing space, decorated with statuary and colourful pennants—a grandiose spectacle it must have been. Rev. Dunlop-Matthews sensing this Popish imagery looked profoundly pained.

"We are all Anglican ... here ... a small congregation but devout ..."

Mr. Tonks was even.

"Ah yes ... that extraordinary faith those such as you adhere to ... one determined by an obese tyrant ... Henry VIII. The Reformation ... merely an excuse for the rape and looting of some of the most beautiful abbeys in the whole of Europe. The libraries, the books and documents all destroyed. A tragedy ... would you not agree, padre?"

The cleric huffed and puffed, he was not used to hearing the Church of England—his employers—regarded with such open scorn. He could offer no worthwhile defence, his own knowledge of doctrinal matters so full of holes as to resemble a Swiss cheese.

"I could not say ..."

"But you would agree that the popular notion of worship ... the Mass ... had about it a magic and mystery ... even superstition ... one that had all but disappeared by the time of James I. Kept alive by Shakespeare perhaps ... undoubtedly a Catholic himself ..."

The cleric went a shade of lobster pink.

"Your attitude is positively ... um ... um ... not in the least *Christian*."

Mr. Tonks pondered.

"What was it Nietzsche said ... 'There was only ever one Christian and he died on the cross.'

Pink became deep chartreuse.

"That might be considered outright blasphemy ..."

"My God ... you actually mean that don't you?"

At the mention of God the cleric's face assumed an expression of distaste.

"Really ... this is too much ..."

Mr. Tonks was unabashed.

"I consider myself to be a metaphysician ... and no philosopher has ever been afraid of the accusations of The Church ... even Galileo himself did not ever fully retract his convictions concerning the nature of the universe."

The Reverend gentleman recovered a little of his loftiness.

"Perhaps your own philosophy could benefit from a little *faith* ..."

Mr. Tonks eyed the prelate, slowly.

"Your faith has no more significance than the tweeds and flannel trousers of your congregation ... 'The Tory party at prayer.'"

Matthews' temperature began to rise once more.

"I really fail to see the point you are making ..."

"My point is that you ... and those like you ... miss the point entirely ..."

The vicar was fast approaching a volcanic state.

"And *how* do we do that?"

"The actual nature of your consciousness seems to me to be implausible ... you do not *see* ..."

"*What don't I see?*"

"Anything and everything ... and while I agree with Locke that the passions may determine reasoning ... your display of anger is as trivial as the power of the lightning is mighty."

The Rev. Dunlop-Matthews started for the South Door. In the churchyard, the evening was slowly creeping about the walls. He espied two figures, one small and bearded, crouching in the lych gate. The vicar peered into the gloom seeming eager to identify them.

"Ah ... Edwin Kew from the Chapel ... but who is that with him?"

A rather down-at-heel figure in a distinctly stained and grubby robe shuffled towards them.

"Edwin?"

The Methodist minister had a lively Midlands accent.

"Hello, Vicar! This is Stibs Gulley over from America ... Boise, Idaho to be precise ... he's an ordained minister at the Church of The Triple Trinity over there."

Rev. Dunlop-Matthews regarded him in an even more unfriendly fashion than he had Mr. Tonks. Before he could speak, the scruffy priest began to drawl loudly.

"Hey ... Lemme tell yuh I belong to a few other ... uh ... highly regarded where I come from ... spiritual organisations too. You won't have heard of the Sons of Silver Sundown I don't suppose ..."

Dunlop-Matthews shook his head vehemently.

"No ... no ... never ..."

"Yer aristocratic Lord Folds is very interested in my researches I been staying in a Priory ... Raviepartier near his place ... Prockleby ... where he's got a swanky spread. Y'know it?"

No reply seemed to be forthcoming from anyone. Mr. Tonks had been regarding the newcomers with interest. He considered the robed figure to be a slightly sinister article, and in his mind Mr. Tonks associated him with the anxious pleas from the stones. He left this trio of hierophants to discuss the prospects of unity among faiths, and went on his way to the pub. As he walked along Mr. Tonks could hear their voices, raised in dissension.

In Beechdale Road, a pale sun loitering in the morning sky was attempting to herald Spring. Martin sprang up the few steps that led to the entrance of the Department of Philosophy. After he had punched a few numbers into the security lock, the door swung back with a pneumatic wheeze and he was permitted entry. Crossing the foyer, he mounted the flight of stairs that led to his tutor's room.

Ollie Pearson had arrived in the building an hour earlier. When he opened the door of his room the furnishings greeted him in the same way they had done for nearly forty years—laconically. Over time, books had gradually gained the upper hand over everything else. The couch, where files and essays got dumped, was still under the window, but there was never any room for anyone to actually sit on it. Thus a chair was religiously kept clear of any miscellaneous stuff and assigned to students and any unexpected visitors.

From the window, a tiny courtyard could be spied. Part of the original garden—the rest usurped by Modern Languages for a car park—there a lone laburnum grew. By the end of April, handfuls of yellow spray would be cast up to the skies, a splash of colour against the grimy backs of the houses opposite. Before sitting at his desk, Ollie spent some moments watching some doves making purposeful forays into the undergrowth and being rewarded with material for their nests.

Ollie took up an essay from the pile in front of him. Reading a few sentences confirmed to him, as if it was needed, that only a minority of students were capable of writing 'good English'—even in the loosest sense. Reading some of this stuff was like being served a badly-cooked dinner and knowing you had to finish it. Ollie's mood lightened a little when he took up Martin's essay 'Monitoring Modern Metaphysics' once more. Ollie had from the beginning appreciated this student's presence in tutorials. He grasped ideas quickly and made pertinent remarks, and if ever politics were discussed he didn't offer the usual banalities. A knock at the door announced his arrival.

"Come in ... Hi, Martin."

His visitor looked sheepish, in the way that

students occasionally do. Martin knew the purpose of their meeting was to discuss his essay, one composed with a more than painful hangover, later revised when he was sober.

"Hello."

"Have a seat."

"Thanks."

Martin looked around having only ventured into his tutor's room on one previous occasion. He didn't think the framed portrait of Nietzsche was there because Ollie wanted to impress anybody. Nor the unframed photo of Brigitte Bardot, looking at her most toothsome. Martin was amused to see that the top of one bookcase was taken up with puzzles, toys, a small globe, and a plastic Buddha.

"I was just looking at your essay again ... most interesting, Martin ..."

Martin visibly showed his relief.

"Oh ... good. Glad you liked it. I hoped you wouldn't find the alliteration a bit ..."

"OTT? Do people still say that?"

Martin laughed, quietly.

"Well ... I don't."

Ollie smiled.

"No ... I thought it was very good ... not only because it was a comprehensive and well-written account of that aspect of philosophy ... but for other reasons too."

"Yeh?"

"I was intrigued by these personal researches you've done ..."

"Ah ..."

"This Hungarian guy ..."

"Polish ..."

"Yes ... sorry ... Polish. He sounds like quite a character ... and the conclusions he comes too ... as a result of his own personal experience ..."

"That's right. I totally believed what he told me ..."

Ollie was quick to agree.

"Of course ... no reason why you shouldn't. The researcher has to faithfully reproduce and collate the material he's presented with."

"Mmm."

Ollie went back to academic mode, putting on an invisible mortar-board.

"As I see it ... this offers a totally original account of our experience of the world ... one different to what is generally assumed. Now I know philosophy attempts to do away with assumptions ... in the cause of critical thinking ..."

Martin listened.

"... the closest I can get to assessing these accounts of yours ... in any way that is *related to the course* ... is by applying Wittgenstein's dictum that the world is a totality of facts ... not things. By arranging these in a different way we come to form a different world than the one we thought we had established. Do you ... um ... follow that?"

"I think so. Kind of choosing how we see things ... and if we do that from a different perspective ... then they change."

"Exactly."

Ollie pressed on.

"The other thing that rather obviously springs

to mind is Kant's idea of the noumenon ... or the noumenonal world. This is the idea of a particular world ... the unknowable ... that we can only ever approximately define. *The Ding an sich* is how he expresses it ... sometimes it sounds more convincing in German ..."

"Maybe that's why there's a lot of German philosophers ... they all sound so authoritative."

Ollie didn't allow himself to be diverted.

"Anyway ... in English ... *per se* is the best way we can put it."

Ollie realised Martin was looking at him in a way he couldn't quite interpret.

"It's all pretty amazing though ... for someone to actually experience these things rather than just ..."

"Writing about them? Indeed it is ... I mean ..."

Ollie suddenly ran out of things to say, unusual for him. Martin, however, carried on for him.

"Most of Anton's paranormal ... if we can say that ... experiences in this country anyway ... are in this particular place ... Rylock Wells ... where there's a stone circle."

Ollie shook his head.

"I know ... I saw all that ... I've never heard of it. I don't really go in for that sort of thing ... but I'm prepared to see its relevance in your argument."

"I *have* heard of it ... but only vaguely. I'm thinking of going there though ... particularly after something Anton said ..."

"Oh? What's that?"

But Martin chose to move on to something else.

"Anton talked to me once about some pretty

amazing things that happened to him in Czechoslo-
vakia ... before World War Two. Prague mostly ...
witch cults ... the golem ... vampires ... all sorts ..."

Ollie was gently probing.

"It's this account of the rituals inside the ... uh ...
stone circle that is the most fascinating though ..."

"Yeh ... right ... the *portal* thing ..."

Ollie tapped the essay lying on his desk.

"I thought you explained that very well ...
examining the whole aspect of imagined and concrete
reality ..."

"Thanks ... I did get into Leibniz and his 'possible
worlds' a bit ... but it was more the people who came
later ..."

"Yes ... I saw your primary sources. William
James is a lot more accredited now ... and the idea of
phenomenology ..."

Martin looked slightly apologetic.

"The multiverse ... then quantum ... or rather
quantum entanglement ..."

"Buckyballs?"

"Well ... yes ... they were mentioned ..."

Ollie beamed, now in thoroughly good humour.

"Sorry, Martin ... I just had to say it. The Philosophy
of Physics ... Scientific Realism isn't really my field ..."

Martin looked slightly abashed.

"Oh ... right ... I'll remember that ..."

"No worries. You're doing fine."

Ollie was strangely elated by the conversation
and found himself in a buoyant mood when he left
the Department later to walk back to Clayville where
he lived. Unable to afford a house in Clinton, Ollie

had acquired a rather undistinguished bungalow in Hornbeam Crescent there. His home almost from the moment he had come to Barstowe, Ollie had done nothing in the way of improvements, apart from having the outside painted. The front garden was a sea of gravel, the back a parched patch in Summer, and a quagmire in Winter. Carefully opening the front door, he stepped over the mail that lay on the mat. His mobile began to play Beethoven's Fifth—insistently.

"Ollie … it's Mick."

"Hello, mate. How's tricks?"

"Fine, fine. You?"

"Oh … getting used to realising that another term has actually begun … that sort of thing … you know what I mean …"

"Indeed I do. I swear it gets more tedious every year. I'll put money on my tutorial group being duller than ever … and my colleagues in the English Department even worse …"

"Oh … hard luck."

The prelims over with, came the real McCoy.

"We ought to get together for a …"

"… drink or two. Yes, quite right. Let me just glance at the old diary … When were you thinking of?"

"Sometime next week? I think I'm pretty free then …"

"Wednesday?"

"Sounds good. Around sevenish?"

"Okay, see you in Hardy's."

This was the wine bar where began any evening of jollity for these comrades-in-arms. Later they would adjourn to Roussos, a Greek restaurant Ollie and Mick had been subsidizing for a decade or two. The place totally suited a couple of unattached academics whose main purpose was to get moderately legless. Of the pair, the state of perpetual bachelorhood was more ingrained in Mick than Ollie. The former was rumoured to live somewhat unrepentantly in a degree of squalor. Most of Ollie's colleagues were either married, or in some long-standing relationship. He had once been engaged, a state that became so prolonged his fiancée eventually returned the ring informing her betrothed it had gone rusty.

4

Although security men had been a fixture for as long as Prockleby had been her home, Lady Folds had never felt comfortable around them. She particularly disliked the one who wore a rope of bling about his neck. Lady Folds was convinced his body was covered in tattoos, as she had noticed one or two peeking out from under his cuffs. Lord Folds was indifferent to their presence, engaged as he was most of the time in his office.

Spreading a map of England on the desk before him, at intervals he carefully circled various towns and cities with a red felt-tip pen. At the same time he made notes on a pad at his elbow. Everything he did had the same motive—control of everyone and everything around him. Right at this moment he desired the soul of England.

Folds had concluded that if he could command enough influence in the way the country was run, he would gain his objective. Politics was not the answer; he was intent on enslaving the very mind of the English. He considered the way to achieve that was through education, specifically the universities. Entering higher education was still the intellectual goal of over half the population and, if knowledge could be regulated and delineated then the country would be his. Lord Folds, sensing this still might not be enough to win his campaign, was determined to own the very spirit of the country as well. To this end he knew he must venture into dark and unfamiliar places, and to this end he was about to embrace all things occult.

When Folds was initially looking to raise finance for his schemes he had turned to old money, but to no avail. Giblette—the Earl of Plywood, had turned him down as had Poissonelle and Rougaire, his ridiculously named brothers. Folds soon realised that the families who were the descendants of William the Conqueror's thugs—had loot and land enough not to wish to acquire any more. The only kind of money that was available to him was from the sources he had already approached—Wall Street and offshore banking. The electronic universe of digital transactions, and that of the laundered variety, was nowadays almost indistinguishable.

Folds had already set other balls rolling and wheels turning, contacting Hancock Butcher—the well-known firm of Management Consultants. The choice was between them and Ketchburn-Virelli, and Folds had taken an irrational dislike to the latter's name. As soon as he contacted Hancock Butcher and heard their top operative Julian Flora's voice, Folds deduced he was more slippery than a tub of mackerel. This did not, however, prevent Folds from summoning him to Prockleby. For the appointment, Flora flew from London in his private plane. He landed at the commercial airport nearest to Prockleby and was met there by car. When he met him, the shiny suit, modish shoes and aluminium attaché case only confirmed Folds' low opinion of his visitor. Once ensconced in Fold's office, Flora started in with the high-octane guff, as was only to be expected.

"Basically ... in return for your investment you'll

be receiving the most expert advice in the country ... our expertise runs through the whole field of organisation."

Folds merely grunted.

"I should hope so too ... what you're bloody charging ..."

Flora had a way of smiling that just avoided being impertinent.

"I see this as being a 'future-based' approach ... aligning people within an organization to a common vision of the future. Performance correlates to the motif of the world that is presented. Employing future-based language is essential to any strategy."

Folds took to snorting.

"If you think that kind of tosh impresses me ... it doesn't. You keep your buzzwords ... and the rest of it ... for the idiots you rip off ... not me."

If anything Flora's smile appeared to glow even brighter.

"Your project, Lord Folds ... interests us greatly. Hancock Butcher would be more than pleased to come aboard ..."

"D'you know anything about the way higher education works?"

Flora didn't miss a beat.

"I think our strategy would be the same as in any area ... be it entertainment the media or *higher education* ... in the end it's all product ... and the way that is presented."

Folds shrugged.

"Organization ... that's all I want from you. The thing almost sells itself. Okay ... you can have a glossy prospectus that says Uni will be nothing but partying for three years ... that sort of bumf ..."

Flora nodded almost imperceptibly.

"Yeh ..."

"What you ought to know straightaway is that I intend to run every university in England ... simple as that. Oxbridge will be the hardest nut to crack ... but they're totally isolated anyway. We'll put the squeeze on them eventually ... they'll join in ... they'll have to."

Flora took to adjusting his lapels.

"Hancock Butcher will make sure you achieve your ambition, Lord Folds."

Folds tapped on his desk.

"Right. So how are you going to go about it then?"

Flora leaned forward eagerly.

"The way I see it we need a team of project managers ... one at each stage of the restructuring ... to coordinate any corporate strategy ..."

Folds was on the case straightaway.

"No ... we don't! Just one overall administrator in every university is all we need. The whole place ... and everybody in it ... answerable to them. The way I'm going to work it is all the staff will be told about the way things are going to be run ... and they'll do what they're told."

"We might want to insert a consultative body at the initial stages ..."

"Why bother? If anyone doesn't like it they can push off."

The mask slipped into place.

"That's an alternative approach ..."

"They won't be able to work anywhere else will

they? So they've got no choice ..."

"Of course ... there's bound to be wastage ..."

Folds dismissed any consideration of humanity with a wave.

"So what else have you got in mind?"

"The American model has high profile leadership ... specific specialization areas ... student affairs ... academic affairs ... administration."

Folds became impatient.

"You really don't understand where I'm coming from do you? Listen ... if we've got ... say a hundred universities ... that means we've got a total of hundred reports coming in every so often ... somebody's got to read those. I don't want the minutes of twenty committees coming in as well. Keep it simple ... then I know what's going on ... what needs sorting out. This is business ... and that's how I run things ... not like some sort of Oxfam gig. And that's why I said I wanted just one boss ... me. I don't want to be attending sodding meetings all the time either."

Flora was determined not to be fazed.

"I think that's good strategy ..."

"You do? Fine ... that's good ... now we're getting somewhere. So what else?"

"Finance."

"Right. What about it?"

"Student loans ..."

"Scrap 'em."

Flora's response came slowly.

"Okay ..."

"They pay up front or they don't go ... simple as that. This is a business arrangement ... dosh for a degree. Make the universities self-sufficient, and not run by the government. Since they kicked Thatcher out nothing's worked. They paid out billions with these stupid loans and getting anything back is a complete joke. Income and expenditure ... what's left over equals profit ... eventually. We won't make any for the first three years I know that ..."

Flora had been busy punching keys on his i-pad. He looked up.

"What's the ramp-up time on this project?"

Folds gave him a look, not of the friendly variety.

"What balls are you talking now? Just go away and bring me some numbers. I want you back here in a week."

Flora clicked off his iPad and stood up.

"I assure you, Lord Folds ... we'll have a complete game plan by then ..."

"Right ... and after that we go and see what they've got to say for themselves at Barstowe University ... over in the West Country ... that's the first one on my list. You can put in a bit of spadework there too ... get someone on the inside ..."

Flora stood up and extended his hand, Folds absently took it.

"We'll be straight onto task tomorrow ..."

"Good idea ... and don't send me any of your bloody bills yet. Alright?"

Flora contented himself with the all-purpose grin.

"Good to meet you ..."

Folds kept Flora in sight as he made for the parking area and the smartish enough motor waiting for him. Score, who had been sitting mutely in the outer office, joined his lordship.

"We'll say how they shape up ..."

"Yes, my lord ..."

Folds eyed him.

"Now what I want you to do is this ..."

Score waited.

"... you'll need to contact certain people ... London ... Cambridge ... one of them is down near Barstowe. They're the bunch I want to get together for the *other* part of all this ... I'll tell you about that later. Here's the list ..."

Despite himself, Score could not help but look quizzical.

"Cattermogg Hicks? Bonzo Bailey?"

Folds made a clicking sound with his tongue.

"They'll be a bit off the wall ... I can tell you that. When you get in touch with them tell them I need their expertise ... their insights for a research project ..."

"Is that all I'm supposed to tell them?"

"For the moment ... yes."

Score continued to stare at the list.

"This last one ... *Florin Farish* ... his name's been underlined ..."

"I know ... he's a *crim* ... tea leaf ... different league from the rest ..."

Score was bland.

"What do I say to *him*?"

Folds showed his impatience.

"Same thing as you do with the others ... just say you've got a job for him. I want all these people on standby until exactly the right moment ... that's why

I'm paying them a retainer."

Score shrugged; there wasn't much else he could do. He didn't ask any more questions, particularly as Folds was now staring out of the window preoccupied with his thoughts. His employer was actually considering what role Score should play in the current scheme. Given that his most accomplished skill was lying—an art he might have invented himself—Folds used him sparingly, like a deadly but efficacious draught.

The First of May marked the triumphal entry of Summer, and also the occasion when Ollie would sample the delights of Clinton nightlife. Strolling past the restaurants and bars lining the main street, he arrived at Hardy's Wine Bar. Benson had already been quaffing substantially. The giveaway was him greeting Ollie a touch too effusively.

"Hello, Ollie, old chap. How are you? What'll you have? I was just going to get another one in ... I was only saying to Steve here that ..."

Ollie glanced along the bar.

"Just a half of lager ... regular stuff ... none of that imported rocket fuel."

Mick's hand dived into his jacket pocket.

"Coming up ... I'll get these."

While the redoubtable Steve went about his business, Ollie surveyed the interior of the establishment—with little enthusiasm. Dark hues predominated, modish images in pine frames being set at intervals along the walls. The effect was startlingly mundane. He was, however, relieved to see no other members of the university staff in evidence. The false bonhomie evident in chance meetings with colleagues always nauseated him.

"Cheers."

"Indeed ... indeed ... cheers."

Ollie pondered momentarily.

"So what's been happening with your lot in English lately? Anything exciting?"

Mick took a few hefty swallows from a frothing stein.

"Not that I can think of ... I mean things happen but nothing you could call ... riveting ... no ripe gossip ... that sort of thing ..."

"No?"

"Fred Waters is retiring at the end of this year ... I expect you knew that anyway. Maggie Brougham our resplendent Head of Department continues in her own singular manner ..."

"No real changes then?"

"None. Derek Mint and Bob Bride carry on being their usually shitty selves ... but that's to be expected."

Ollie was all too aware of Mick's feelings towards this duo—doyens of post-modernism, and poseurs *in excelsis*. They were of an academic ilk that found no favour with Ollie either. He drained his lager.

"Okay ... let's go and sample the delights of *Roussos* ... Celestial Centre of Cypriot Cuisine."

The eatery in question was in Botham's Hook, an alley next to the Post Office. When Mick and Ollie came in Ulysses the owner was listening intently to the Arsenal game on the radio.

"Luffly to see you. Luffly."

At the customers' request, the soccer was replaced with a tape of balalaikas going at full bore. Ulysses smiled ecstatically, swaying a little in homage to his culture, one now many miles, and many years, distant.

"You sit here ... usual table ... yes? Luffly ... luffly."

Ollie and Mick always insisted on the same spot, facing the mural of the Parthenon. It had been painted in the Sixties and, like the original artefact, showed certain signs of wear. Ulysses hovered for a moment with a pair of redundant menus encased in brown plastic. It was part of the ritual to produce these, a pointless gesture as they always ordered the same meal—the one they had ordered on every visit in the last twenty odd years.

"*Kleftiko ... sheftalia ... taramasalta ... dolmades* ... thenk you ... thenk you. No proplem."

A carafe of the house paint-stripper arrived promptly and making that reassuring sound as it went glugging into their glasses. Ollie slid out of his leather jacket and hung it over a chair at the next table. They could always afford to spread themselves out a bit here, the likelihood of any other diners showing up being markedly slim. Before long, a basketful of *pitta* and various plates of stuff slid into view, signifying starter's orders.

"Dolmades ... tara ... thenk you ... thenk you."

Ollie had already detected that Mick had some-thing, on his mind. The earlier revelations concerning the business of the English Department were mere froth. Ollie was also interested in learning more about the direction the university's ruling elite might take the academic empire in the immediate future. He knew he had to obtain this information before Mick became too incoherent. Ollie estimated that the point when this would occur was about half a carafe away.

"Have you heard anything about the way Senate wants to run things next year?"

Mick was as the proverbial rabbit caught in the headlights.

"Well ... I did hear about a few ..."

"Changes?"

"You could bloody well say that ... yes."

Ollie noted the tone.

"More dramatic than usual?"

Mick got in the groove.

"Basically ... they can't balance the books. With all the new building that's been going on ... the new library ... the union ... the science research block ... plus all the updates of facilities ... that crap new email system for instance ..."

"Mmm ..."

"They're in a massive deficit ... and digging themselves in deeper all the time ... hoping the good fairy is just around the corner."

Ollie grew more interested.

"Really? Is it as bad as all that? I had no idea ..."

"No ... well ... you wouldn't would you? They're hardly going to go round blabbing about how they're totally in the shit."

"But ... it's hard to keep something as serious as that completely quiet ... surely?"

"Oh ... they have their ways and means ..."

Ollie paused.

"Of course … you're on the *steering committee* …"

"S.M.O.G."

"What?"

Mick allowed himself a brief smile.

"Or *smug* as I call it … Senior Management Operations Group … we meet once a month. Supposed to monitor every proposal that goes through Senate and Council and make sure the way it's dealt with is all kosher … then we report to the University Senior Management Committee. I'm not sure you can make an acronym out of that one."

"So what do *they* do?"

"It's a total farce … if they don't want us to know about something they're doing they just don't tell us. No one can monitor what they don't know about … can they?"

Ollie was genuinely alarmed.

"Is that the way it's all done these days? Totally hush-hush? I thought Council had some policy about being 'publicly accountable' … and making known their Code of Practice. They set that up some years ago I remember. Round about the same time Blair waffled on that everything was 'open and accessible' in government …"

"Well … yeh … and that was a lot of bollocks too as we know. You can say anything can't you? Doesn't mean you're actually going to do it."

This observation seemed to prompt Mick into applying himself once more to the contents of the carafe.

"So … is there any actual prospect of the University actually being *bailed out*?"

Mick sighed, whether from approaching intoxication or world-weariness was hard to tell.

"Well … no … there wasn't … until last month when one or two on the committee got wind that it had all changed. Now this is interesting … Norton Bradley …"

"He's a member of this exclusive cartel?"

"Yeh … but he's straight … and I'm not just saying that because he's one of the few people in my Department I actually respect …"

Ollie hastened to keep Mick on track.

"No … no … I appreciate that …"

"He told me … and I don't actually think he told anyone else … that there was going to be money about … pots of it. Of course, no one has any idea who was putting it up … only that it was enough … and more … to sort things out. Even to the extent of putting everything on an even keel for the next five years."

"Well … that's good then …"

Mick eyed him, in somewhat sinister fashion.

"No … it's not."

"How d'you mean?"

"What we're looking at, Ollie … is a complete restructuring of how Barstowe University is going to be run from now on … all of it … every department. Mine … yours … even right down to that potty little annexe where they do the M.A. in Creative Writing."

"But that was bound to happen … they've been talking about changing the Faculties round … putting everything into 'schools' or whatever for ages …"

Mick was dismissive.

"Don't kid yourself, Ollie … this is going to change everything … for me … for you and every other bugger … apart from certain people in the university who want it to happen … because it's to their advantage."

Ulysses chose that moment to slide plates of steaming stuff onto the table. Conversation took a back seat for the present. As he ate Ollie could not help feeling distinctly uncomfortable at Mick's words. Had control of his academic destiny suddenly evaporated? His deliberations stopped abruptly when he realized Mick was tapping the empty carafe with his fork. Ulysses, who had slipped away to get an update on Arsenal's progress, reappeared at the summons.

"Another wine? Hof course … luffly."

Another pitcher of plonk was set down, zithers shimmered, dryads and nymphs sported in Elysian fields. Chat drifted off into other byways, all the time Mick determinedly making a dent in the second carafe. When Ulysses was clearing away the debris he went outside into the street to smoke. On returning, Ollie noticed he was coughing more than usual, and was definitely looking like a man at the end of his tether. Ollie just hoped Mick didn't start adopting the patrician habits he had observed among some of his colleagues—sporting lunettes, or ties with obscure insignia. After staring glassily at the wall for some time, Mick lurched across the table.

"Some geezer from outside is going to take over everything in the Uni. The VC … his deputy … the Registrar … *and* all those pro-VC nobs are going to let him do it too."

"That can't happen."

"You watch … wait and see."

Ollie stared in disbelief, unable to tell if Mick was now simply catatonic. When they came to leave, Ulysses continued with his usual chorus.

"Luffly to see you … luffly … luffly … luffly …"

Ollie felt duty bound to make sure Mick gained his own front door without any mishap. They set off towards Spencer Heights which was vaguely in the direction of Clayhill. With Mick duly dispatched at his flat, Ollie started on his way home, still turning over in his mind what had been said over the *dolmades* and the rest.

Martin had heard tell that Windleroot was the Mecca of the New Age. The town lay inland—in Withyshire, an hour's drive from the city. He drove across the moors wondering what he might find in this mysterious landscape. His journey terminated in Lowe Street, the main thoroughfare of the town. Martin was astonished by this New Age Disneyland— row upon row of luridly painted shop fronts, each one festooned with a name more obscure than the last. *Paganorama, Krazy Krystles, Unicorns United.* Lolling on benches along the pavement were figures in soiled fatigues begging for alms.

Martin hurried past displays of broomsticks, velvet capes and illuminated skulls in search of some establishment that might resemble a bookshop. At last he came upon *The Babbling Plinth* where he spent some time staring at the bizarrely titled volumes in the window—*The Twenty-six layers of Millennial Karma, The Mystical Circle of the Pentagram within The Pyramid*. Quite half of the space was taken up with the mystical novels of Mirabelle Canasta, whoever she was. The words of Anton came into his head, giving him the will to enter this esoteric emporium.

One must be a little mad to embrace the unknown

The owner of the shop, a woman so corpulent that she resembled a barrage balloon, smiled at him vaguely as he came in. There were no other customers in the place and Martin felt distinctly conspicuous.

"Er ... I was wondering if you had any books about the stone circles at Rylock Wells ..."

The Lindenbergh look-a-like assumed an air of superiority.

"Not really ... no ... most of us Windlefarians think the energies are totally all wrong ... really negative ... so nobody goes there at all ... can't help I'm afraid ..."

She waddled out from behind the counter and Martin had the distinct impression he had been dismissed. A little further up the street was *The Squeaking Peanut*. The proprietor, a wraith with a wispy beard, was even more unhelpful. For the second time in a matter of minutes Martin found himself standing in the street wondering what to do next. On the other side of the street he noticed *The Ghastly Mirage*. A notice in the window announced that the business had recently been taken over by Wally Moonstone and his partner Smudge. Within, was a lively scene as punters tried on plastic elf ears and witches' hats made of recycled cardboard. Tolkienesque trappings twinkled alluringly in glass cases. Martin repeated his request to a figure in a tea cosy hat, who he presumed was Mr. Moonstone himself.

"Right ... let's see ... *Rylock Wells* ... *Rylock Wells* ... We've got *Tibetan Tantric Transformations* ... Prof. Sturmey Bourneville ... that's not you want obviously. Here we are ... *The Mystery of Rylock Wells* ... sounds like an Agatha Christie novel doesn't it? Ha ha ..."

Moonstone squinted at the screen.

"Published 1999 ... Scotch Froth ... ten ninety-nine ... author Standley Strange ... oh dear ... out of print ... I'm afraid ..."

So great was the crowd now gathered about the counter that Moonstone, in stepping back, upset a quantity of powdered lungwort into a tub of tripe oil. Smudge, his partner, was not pleased with this improvised mixture and said so—vehemently.

"Watch what you're doin' Wally ... that gear ain't cheap y'know ..."

"Sorry, love ..."

In the crush Martin found himself next to a sculptor who told him he carved flowers out of old railway sleepers. He stank of dank hassocks, the result of living in a converted monastery in Meddle, a village nearby. Stibbs Gulley, en route from Rylock Wells, announced he was an Archpriest of what sounded to Martin like 'The Church of The Sacred Flowerpot'. Anxious to leave behind what passed for life in Windleroot he made for the door, walking along Lowe Street to where his car was parked. As he took out his keys, a girl with violently coloured red hair approached him.

"Hi ..."

Martin paused. The girl looked at him intensely.

"Are you going to the circle?"

With a start, Martin realised he probably was. If he could not find anything written about Rylock Wells then it seemed obvious he ought to go there and find out about the place for himself.

"Yes ... I think I am ..."

"Can I come with you?"

Martin was not used to being approached by girls in strange towns soliciting him.

"Yes ... I suppose so ..."

"It's only that ... I live in the village ..."

"Oh ... I see ..."

By now they were in the car together.

"I'm Philomena ..."

"Martin ..."

She clapped her hands together, apparently in spontaneous joy.

"Isn't this great? I heard you talking about the stones in that shop and I thought ... I know that guy's going to just where I want to go ..."

"Very handy ..."

Martin found being in Philomena's company a novel experience. She had a habit of launching into some tuneless lament, and he wondered if she had been taking drugs, but he did not like to enquire. The moors all around had assumed an otherworldly beauty, but when Martin remarked on this Philomena only smiled in a quixotic fashion. As they came into Rylock Wells, the church bells were ringing for some reason.

"You can drop me off at the pub if you like ..."

"Alright."

"Unless you fancy coming in for a drink?"

Martin paused.

"Why not?"

When they got inside, the sound of folk music of the kind played in pubs these days emanated from a corner. Pints of Old Todge were being consumed at a steady rate and a gale of laughter engulfed Philomena as she bounced up to the bar. Martin hung back, looking round rather shyly until his attention was taken by an ethereal figure in black poised upon a stool. Her eyes would not meet his. Philomena was talking to everyone around about her and gaily ordering drinks. She introduced Martin to Mandy the barmaid and the vision in black.

"This is my friend Lily."

Martin experienced a rush of emotion entirely unfamiliar to him. A man may offer a woman his heart or his fortune, but he can never determine how she will respond. In this instance not at all and Martin felt more bereft than he had ever done in his entire life. He had yet to experience the forces that are not seen in this world but are constantly in play. They are personified in the ways of woman and they are secret—always must it be so. Martin was also unaware, as many before him, that true love is built upon rock, never shifting sands. Much confused, he decided not to visit the stones and instead turned his attention to the entertainment on offer.

H.P. Umber, the night's star turn, was not a prepossessing character. Looking like an even more wizened version of Willie Nelson than the original, his act did not whip the audience into a frenzy—rather the opposite. His introspective ballads were so melancholy as to induce suicidal tendencies in those who heard them. At the end of the evening he received his fee from George the landlord, and politely refused the portion of melon and peanut curry offered him by the landlady. After putting his guitar in the back of the van, Umber decided a nocturnal jaunt to the stone circle would be in order and wandered into the field. Seated on a convenient megalith, he opened a tin of pilchards and uncorked a flagon of Kinnocks cider to accompany this feast.

By midnight an absolute blackness surrounded all. As Umber fingered a piece of oily fish, the Moon, gliding out from behind a cloud, lit the scene. Umber could see the outline of the stones clearly, their presence seeming more extraordinary than he had ever known before. The more he gazed the more he ate and drank, finally convincing himself that the stones were becoming animated. The pair that formed an arch way to the West had moved closer together he was sure of that, and several of the outlying stones were slowly moving to join them. The pilchards all but forgotten, Umber stared open-mouthed as these mighty pillars seemed to bend towards each and confer in low whispers. Umber noticed that from the base of one particular stone a blue light glowed, one that more than hinted at unearthly things.

As he watched, this stone seemed to rise until there was a space between it and the earth below. From this came a golden beam that perfectly harmonised with the blue above. In its centre was an intense silver point and, the more Umber looked at it the more intense it became, so that eventually he was forced to look away. When his opened his eyes once more, the lights had disappeared, the Moon had drifted behind the clouds and all had returned to something near normal. H.P. Umber addressed the night, almost with a sense of recrimination.

"What was that all about then?"

5

On most days Ollie lunched at *The Willows*, its ambiance unchanging—set between *Ye Olde Tea Shoppe* and a motel in Kansas. On his way to the canteen he slid past the suits that occupied the bar. Picking up a tray, Ollie joined the queue behind Jack Fitch, a colleague in his department. The latter was engaged in examining the shallow tubs on the counter.

"Hello, Jack."

Fitch replied in his usual laconic way.

"Hi … .fancy seeing you …"

Served, and spying an empty table in a corner, they moved in that direction. Ollie set down his Chicken Provencal, Fitch—the Mediterranean Pasta.

"Somebody was telling me, Ollie … can't remember who … that you were actually a student here in the bad old days …"

"Mmm … I did my M. Phil here … Seymour Widgeon was my tutor."

"Widgeon! No! Not really? You mean that incredible old chap in tweeds who you sometimes see wandering about by the Library?"

"The very same … he was getting on a bit when I knew him too …"

"Well … I'm blowed. So when was this?"

"1972."

"What was that like?"

"1972 … or doing my degree?"

Fitch, pausing with a forkful of pasta in midflight, eyed him.

"Now, Ollie … don't give me a rundown on the

greatest albums of that year. I've heard you doing that sort of thing before at parties … the celebrated walking encyclopedia of rock'n'roll … ."

Ollie smiled, somewhat depreciatingly.

"Okay I'll refrain from telling you about Hawkwind's 'Silver Machine' getting up to number three in the Charts …"

"Yes … I'd rather you missed that out … if you don't mind …"

Ollie grinned once more.

"Okay … I promise. Well … I got a Double First at Cambridge if I say so myself … and I was bit full of it. Widgeon sorted me out good and proper. There was no getting past old Seymour. You certainly couldn't blag your way through any tutorial with him. He knew exactly how much reading you'd done … or rather *not* done. Not like now … when we don't expect students to even *look* at a book unless they're forced to do so."

Fitch presented a gloomy profile.

"I know. If they can't find what they want on Wikipedia … as far as they're concerned it doesn't exist."

"Not all of them. I've got a few very bright post-grads."

"But *they're* here because they want to be … not like little Sophie who thinks she's *entitled* to go to Barstowe … because she's got a bloody pony in the paddock …"

"True."

Ollie found his thoughts wandering back to the 'The Thatcher Years'. Then, a great many academics were convinced that the Iron Lady had done for every university in the land. Widgeon was not one of them. He could see a harsher dawn approaching—one which duly came in the 1990s—around the time he retired. Everything in Higher Education began to take on a harder edge—the modish phrase 'customer satisfaction' was everywhere. Management teams were brought in, 'productivity' assessed. What had before seemed impossible to quantify, and thus never attempted, was made accountable. Society began to regard 'qualifications' as a given rather than a reward. It did not take long before it was decided that a degree should be included in society's wares for sale. The new thinking went like this: if not enough candidates were gaining high marks, then the standard had to be lowered. Cynicism had won the day.

" 'Eh oop … you two!"

Ollie's reverie was interrupted by the familiar Huddersfield twang, an accent its owner had been trying to jettison for a decade or two, albeit unsuccessfully.

"Hello, Lucy. How's things?"

Dr. Tucker, who had something of the Earth-Mother about her, sat down jauntily and eyed the company.

"Alright. So … .what's goin' on then?"

"About what exactly?"

"C'mon, Jack … you know as well I do. There's something goin' on we don't know about … basically because nobody wants to tell us."

"You think so?"

"I'm sure of it."

Lucy shifted in her chair, acres of print dress

moving in unison with her.

"It's all to do with Dick. I mean … we all know he's a funny old boogger at the best of times … but have you noticed something else about him lately?"

"Like what?"

"He's worried about something … frightened almost …"

Ollie could feel himself getting tense, determined not to reveal what Mick had told him. Fitch merely shook his head.

"Well there's *always* rumours going round of what might or might not be going to happen in the Department …"

Lucy looked arch.

"This isn't just about the Department … this is the whole bloody Uni. I think Dick knows about it … but not as much as he'd like to. So … he's not sure where he stands. Not really fair on the rest of us though is it?"

Fitch leaned back in his chair.

"That *would* explain why he's so jumpy in Departmental meetings … Dick certainly likes to be in control all the time …"

Lucy turned towards Ollie.

"What about you, Sunshine … have you heard anything?"

Ollie deliberately assumed a casual tone.

"Nothing *definite* … no."

The June *day* was warm, and the chatter from the tables outside could be clearly heard. All seemed timeless, inviolable.

"My guess is that Dick will call a meeting before

long … if he thinks that people are wondering what's going on …"

Lucy looked at Fitch then her watch.

"Ooh … 'eck … nearly half-past. I'm off … said I'd meet Emily and Pamela for coffee. I'll see you all later."

Ollie beamed, as best he could.

"Okay. Keep us informed."

"I will, love … and you do the same. Promise me."

The Summer, after her initial glories, had become exceedingly coy. The first day of July announced itself with a tempestuous storm. It began in the early hours of the morning, and woke Lord Folds. Unable to get back to sleep, he rose and went downstairs. At dawn, all suddenly abated and he was able to walk out onto the terrace, steaming in the early morning sun. Making his way to his office, Folds began to organize his notes ready for the arrival of Flora in a few hours time. At seven he rang through to the kitchens to order coffee, and an hour later he fell asleep in his chair. Woken by the crunch of tyres on the gravel, Folds opened his eyes. With some difficulty, he kept them that way. Flora was his usual self—a persona which combined Uriah Heep and R2D2 in equal measure.

"These are the figures … I think you'll find they cover everything …"

Folds examined the file handed to him.

"Right … every student pays twenty grand each year for three years … for that they get everything …

accommodation … all the university facilities … the lot. That makes it all simple."

"The numbers are based on Barstowe's current intake …"

"Okay … and we have a maximum of forty departments each with two hundred students that gives us an income of sixteen million … enough to pay the staff and have a reasonable profit."

Flora was cautious.

"Of course … that's not taking into consideration maintaining the buildings … ancillary staff …"

Folds was terse.

"I know that … the income's just a drop in the ocean compared to the actual upkeep of the place. I've thought about all that … it's the Government's legal responsibility … comes under Health and Safety. You can make anything comply with that these days. They can foot the bill … or the local councils can. The Government is responsible for the upkeep of the buildings too … they've got to be … they're all Grade I listed. Anywhere else … all the other modern crap … gets hired out … or used for storage. That can all bloody fall down as far as I'm concerned."

Flora looked relieved.

"We did look at the turn around …"

"When we actually take over you mean? It can't be this academic year … have to be the year after."

"All the changes will be implemented and in place by then …"

"Right … and I've been thinking about a name for all this. We'll keep the name Barstowe University … but the organization … *my organization* … will be known as *Pride of Prockleby—A Degree of Promise.*"

While Flora responded by beaming mechanically, Folds also allowed himself a grin of triumph.

During August, Barstowe bid farewell to its student population and welcomed the hordes of tourists that made the West Country their Summer destination. Rather than loaf around at his parents' house, Martin remained in his flat, determined to spend his second year there. The days drifted along without incident until one Saturday morning when a small crowd gathered in the street outside. Their gaze was fixed on a figure clinging to the chimney stack. Ollie knew it had to be Winnie.

He learned that she had climbed onto the roof wearing nothing but an apron. Grasping a pink feather duster tightly in one hand, she was singing 'How Much is that Doggie in the window' over and over again, in a tuneless soprano. Among the neighbours, comments were tinged with a censorious air.

"She'll go too far one day … that Winnie will …"

"What? Fall off the roof when she's climbing around up there you mean?"

"No … I don't … I mean she'll get put in the old loony place … binned up with the rest of 'em."

Martin was only mildly diverted by all this. He was determined to discover the secrets of the stone circle at Rylock Wells. Grabbing a light coat, Martin set off in the direction of the moorlands of Winslet. As he left the city he noticed the skies had an obstinate look about them, and it was raining heavily when he reached the outskirts of the city. After the downpour, the trees shone with an iridescent green. Set against the smoldering grey, they appeared to vibrate. He found his way to the stones, and felt as if he was returning home. Martin had never felt such a sensation before; it was as if he recognized every single detail in the landscape.

Surrounded by trees and a river, on the horizon knolls and mounds, were the fingers of stone— pointing at the heavens. They suggested all manner of things that Martin could not as yet understand. He wandered in and around and among these stone people, until he felt he knew them a little better. After a little time, they acknowledged his presence and welcomed him into their midst. Martin was strangely moved, as if he had been reunited with his ancestors from the ancient world. In the immediate present he espied a man—tweedy, corduroyed, and topped with an old felt hat. Immediately, this strange figure hailed him.

"I say ... sorry to bother you ... but I wonder if you would be so good as to tell me whether *I'm seeing things.*"

Martin followed the direction in which a finger was pointing.

"There ... there ... can you see it? Coming out from the middle ... lines of silver ... lots of them!"

At first Martin could see nothing, then gradually the vision took shape and he could see clearly what was described.

"Yes ... like wires ... vibrating ..."

"Exactly ... exactly ... oh ... I'm so glad you can see them too ... that does give me a certain sense of relief."

"Oh ..."

The new acquaintance held out his hand.

"Do forgive me ... Tonks ... Archibald Tonks ..."

"Martin Callow."

"Delighted to meet you, Martin ... a fellow pilgrim upon the celestial way that leads to Rylock Wells. Not all highways are so congenial ... don't you agree?"

The cows grazing nearby regarded the pair with a singular lack of interest, while Martin regarded Mr. Tonks, smiling so joyously. He wondered if the eccentric figure might perform an impromptu jig.

"Do you know a lot about ..."

"This place? A little ... but mostly of a speculative nature. Who were the folks who came here to construct these fantastic megaliths ... these monuments to sky and Earth together? After their labours ... did they laugh? Did they regard their work with satisfaction and dance in celebration? I like to think so ... and I think they were of a noble sort ... who believed in great things. I would dearly love to have met them."

Mr. Tonks continued, as if delivering a lecture to an invisible audience.

"I am certain a whole network of underground streams is to be found here. The very name ... Rylock Wells ... tells of the nature of the land round about. It is as if this place is a microcosm of a greater pattern that exists ... one encompassing the whole of England ... I don't know."

He paused and there was a sound like rusty bolts being drawn back—Mr. Tonks laughing.

"Bless me … the idea of anyone actually knowing anything *for certain* … what a thought … eh?"

Martin had been considering what had been said.

"But … tell me the point of a network like that …"

"What indeed would be the purpose of a connection between springs … lakes … and rivers? But then water is so extraordinary … it flows … often undetected … even invisibly … it possesses a mysterious energy. We might imagine that the whole globe is criss-crossed with these patterns of life. Perhaps they cause subtle changes within ourselves … and our predecessors knew this. Were they in tune with these influences? Perhaps it is yet another part of our consciousness that has been lost."

Martin considered.

"So you think the Earth was telling these people something … and because they were who they were … ready to listen?"

"Exactly … and also a sort of 'early warning system' …"

"Warning about what?"

Mr. Tonks paused.

"When our ancestors saw shooting stars … or the Moon's phases … that would have been extraordinarily profound to them … and the sight of a comet would have been awe-inspiring. They may have experienced monumental changes in weather conditions too. And … of course … a stone circle would serve as an astronomical observation post … as well as a cosmic conductor … activating and transferring energy. It would have encouraged solar energy to gather within … and attract lunar energy when needed … hence the water."

"So all this energy gets used to …"

"… to generate force … perhaps even enabling them to raise other great blocks into position."

Martin stared at the stones around him, near and far.

"So … you could say all this built itself?"

"Exactly … and for another reason too …"

"Which is?"

"Constructing a megalithic monument like this would provide a portal … a doorway … into another dimension."

Martin was not au fait with esoteric matters. A few movies, a video game or two, this was the closest he got to the Otherworld.

"But … um … why would anyone want that?"

Mr. Tonks was matter-of-fact.

"The business of the shaman … witchdoctor if you like … is to communicate with the world of spirits and the ancestors. He journeys to the Otherworld and returns with the wisdom he has been given … this he passes on to his people … answers their questions."

Martin took all this in, or tried to.

"And this is where it all happened? In this circle …?"

Mr. Tonks went up to the nearest stone and stroked it gently.

"Quartz … we respond to it … and its crystals … often unconsciously. It has the power to manifest the invisible you know …"

Martin stared at Mr. Tonks and saw in him something he was not aware of before. A key had been turned, and things he had never imagined could exist were being revealed to him. Ideas flooded into his mind, and he tried to seize one or two of them before they disappeared.

"Inspiration … the artist creates …"

"Exactly. The artist instinctively switches off any conscious thought, knowing that visions will appear. That's where the idea of the muse or 'divine inspiration' comes from. People always imagine artists being in some kind of trance."

"Keats writes about *negative capability* …"

Mr. Tonks nodded enthusiastically.

"When children play they are deadly serious about what they are doing … the game … totally involved in some other-worldly experience. The great artists never lose that power and use it … almost to amuse themselves. Some became rich or celebrated but that is almost irrelevant."

Martin and Mr. Tonks continued to regard these silent sentinels.

"And where are you studying? At Barstowe?"

"Yes … doing Philosophy …"

"I was in the History Department myself some years ago … I expect things have changed a little since my day …"

"I think they have …"

He and Mr. Tonks shook hands.

"Remember there is no such thing as a coincidence, Martin. You were drawn here … your destiny is closely bound up with Rylock Wells."

"Yes … someone else said that to me not long ago. I feel it too … I'm not quite sure how or why …"

Mr. Tonks eyed him, kindly.

"Mystery surrounds us constantly."

Martin made his way to the gate that led into the field, his head heavy with ideas. The next task would be to make some sense of them all.

6

Dinner at Prockleby was never a happy affair. In deference to protocol—*pas devant les domestiques*—Lord and Lady Folds did not openly argue. The atmosphere, however, was always palpably tense. Folds always insisted on having the entire complement of staff in attendance, a habit which irritated her ladyship. 'Standing by' might have been a better description of their duties as, apart from the butler and the under-butler, the rest stood in a line against the oak panelling, like a row of skittles. Whenever Lady Folds remonstrated about this she always received the same rejoinder.

"I pay them ... I want to be able to see them ... I don't care whether they *do anything* or not."

Folds was also inclined to regularly complain about what was served.

"Salad? Salad! Why has it always got to be bloody rabbit food every night?"

Lady Folds took an intake of breath.

"If you want something particular on the table you can always tell the kitchen people in the mornings ..."

"That's not the point is it? What I want to know is why they think it's perfectly alright to bring this in at all. Why am I expected to eat this?"

Lady Folds was having none of it.

"It's the Summer ... the weather's warm ... people eat salad."

Folds was petulant.

"Well ... *I* don't. I want them to bring me something else ..."

Lady Folds was icily patient.

"What is it you would like prepared for you?"

"Peas ... broad beans ..."

Lady Folds regarded her husband with some severity.

"Too late in the season for both of those, Douglas."

Folds fumed.

"Alright I won't have any vegetables at all. I'll probably get scurvy or something."

Lady Folds waved the servants away. She fixed her husband with a look—one he knew only too well.

"If you are going to be so unreasonable at dinner all the time you must take your meals in the library."

"I'm being *perfectly* reasonable ... I just don't want ..."

Lady Folds had heard quite enough.

"I think they're probably aware in the next county of what you want ... and don't want. Now either you change your tune, or I shall take *my* meals upstairs. *You choose, Douglas.*"

Such a tone meant Folds was beaten and he knew it. As he toyed with his *steak au poivres* he was aware these squabbles were becoming more and more frequent. He and his wife had ceased to share a bed a long time ago, and the only time they ever spoke to each other was at dinner. Folds put down his cutlery and ignoring his wife's most disapproving gaze took out his mobile, and began texting. He had decided he wanted Score to come to Prockleby in the morning.

When he left Birmingham some time before dawn the next day, Score was only vaguely aware of the maze of grey and blue gantries stretching above him on the motorway. Spaghetti junction reminded him of the maze of deceit that enabled much of the world to function. By constantly denying the truth, people had created an alternative world, one they forced others to acknowledge. Score had been helping to shape this artificial universe all his life, and felt he was one of its pioneers.

At Prockleby House he found Lord Folds perched behind his desk looking malignant.

"What d'you know about *the occult?*"

Score looked sideways.

"What do you mean, my lord?"

"Ritual magic ... that sort of thing ..."

"Well I ..."

Folds tutted impatiently.

"I thought so ... nothing at all."

"No ... I suppose not, my lord."

Folds waved him into a chair.

"Right. Now sit down and listen ... you might learn something."

Score adopted as meek a pose as he could manage at such short notice.

"First of all ... it's nothing to do with bloody Harry Potter or that sort of nonsense."

"No ..."

"I've been studying it ... I intend to use this power in any way I can ..."

Score was genuinely baffled.

"For what?"

"To make sure this University thing works ... that's what."

Score shook his head.

"I'm sorry, my lord. I don't follow you at all ..."

Folds sneered openly.

"No? Well never mind ... probably better you don't know too much about that side of things anyway. The only bit that concerns you is getting these people together I asked you to ..."

Score was relieved to return to the mundane.

"All done, my lord. There was only one of them I couldn't reach ..."

"Who was that?"

"Boggy Ogwit."

Folds shrugged.

"Doesn't matter too much about him ... as long as we've got some of the heavy mob ... Angus Rookley ..."

"Definitely got him ..."

"He's *The Great Beetroot* himself ... 10.10.10 ..."

"I think he told me he was bringing ... er ... a trio of *Vermillion Women* ..."

Folds nodded vigorously.

"Good. Yes ... I know all about them ..."

Score deliberately stuck to business.

"They've sent you a lot of documents, my lord ... I put those out for you ..."

"Yes ... yes ... most helpful."

"They were all asking me where they should meet you for the ... er ... *ritual* ... I think they said. I informed them I'd confirm a date with you."

Folds adopted a knowledgeable air.

"Time and place is very important ... the forces get charged up on certain days at these old sites. I've chosen Rylock Wells for our *event* ..."

"Really, my lord? Where's that?

"Down in the West Country ... all yokels ... straw in their hair ... that sort of thing."

Score wrinkled his nose, as if at that moment detecting something rural and pungent.

"I see."

Folds suddenly sat upright.

"I've got to go down there again ... very soon too ... last time I went there I lost something ... essential for our *business*."

"My lord?"

"A book ... a very valuable one ... a sort of instruction manual in all this sort of thing I was telling you about."

Score took a breath, summoning up as much courage as he could, not a quality he often displayed.

"Can I just ask, my lord? Is it actually *safe* to be getting involved with all this ... witchcraft or whatever it is? And these people ... some of them sound very odd indeed ..."

Folds smiled, patronisingly.

"I know what I'm doing ... I know a lot about that Rylock Wells place ... and how its power can be controlled. You wouldn't believe what I've found out ..."

Folds' eyes had assumed an unholy light.

"If you don't mind me saying so, my lord ... I think this is all very dangerous to be involved with. I ... I ... don't like the sound of it. Fooling with things nobody really understands ..."

"*Dangerous!* Have you ever known me be afraid of anything, Score?"

"No, my lord ... but ..."

Folds raised his voice, just enough for it to be noticed.

"Be quiet! I'll do this my way. Now ... arrange all this for the First of November ... *Samhain* ..."

"As you say, my lord."

Folds began muttering to himself.

"I'm sure I know where I lost that book Florin got for me I'll go down there in the next couple of days and make sure I get it back ... I don't want any of those wurzels to find it."

Score piped up immediately.

"Is that Florin *Farish*, my lord?"

"Yes. What about him?"

"He gave me another contact number ... his new girlfriend's mobile ... Mandy ... she's the barmaid in the local pub."

"Is she now? Some peasant trollop no doubt."

Score made no comment, Folds began thinking aloud.

"Flora will be showing up here again by the end of the month ... that bloke's as smooth as a baby's whatnot ... but I want to see what him and his Metropolitan Mafia plan to do next."

"As you say, my lord."

"Flora's got this Zandra Croop woman in tow now. He's already fixed it so she has some executive position at Barstowe ... one with enough clout to have an influence right where we want it. She's started things moving nicely ..."

Folds' deliberations gradually began to fade.

"Lot going on ... lot of balls in the air ... let's hope it doesn't turn into a complete lot of balls, eh?"

Score's attention wandered towards a parchment that lay on the desk. The initials O.R.S.R. seemed to stare out at him, below was inscribed *Order of the Royal and Sacred Radish*. All this talk of 'magic' and 'the unknown' made him distinctly uneasy, and he continued to fix his eyes on the parchment. To his horror the strange symbols seemed to writhe with a sinister life of their own.

Autumn brought the new term and Ollie was more on edge than in the previous academic year. The university was rife with rumour and counter-rumour and in the second week of term Ollie decided to have things out with Dick Trencham. When the time came and Ollie slid into a chair opposite his Head of Department, the latter looked distinctly pale as if not relishing the encounter.

"What's … what's … on your mind then, Ollie?"

Dick sounded as if this was the last thing he wanted to know about. Ollie went straight for the jugular.

"Look, Dick … I know what's going on. Don't kid yourself I don't."

A haunted look stole over his superior.

"What d'you mean? Nothing's going on … nothing at all."

Ollie sighed wearily.

"Yes it is … and you jolly well know it is. For a start … this Zandra Croop who we all get half-a-dozen emails a day from …"

"Yes ... Zandra ..."

Dick repeated the name as if it were some kind of mantra.

"Who the hell is she?"

"What do you mean? Zandra's quite entitled to send mails out to everyone ... it's ... er ... part of her brief ..."

Ollie was direct.

"She's a bloody fixer."

Dick drew in his breath.

"What ... what are you saying, Ollie?"

Ollie was tight-lipped.

"She's a stooge for these gangsters who are going to take over the Uni. at the end of this academic year."

Dick's voice suddenly assumed an unpleasant whine.

"I really don't know what you're talking about, Ollie ... and as for Zandra ... I think 'stooge' is putting it a bit strong. 'Exterior Academic Advisor' is Zandra's official title ..."

Ollie grunted.

"Call her what you like, Dick."

Trencham adopted a lofty tone.

"Like all of us ... she's only doing her job, Ollie."

"That's what they said at the Nuremberg Trials."

Dick showed a more than pensive profile.

"I think she's doing a great deal that's very positive for Barstowe ... and she will carry on doing that I hope ..."

Ollie said nothing.

"... and I would support her ... *and* I don't know what you mean about anyone *taking over* ..."

"What are you going to say when this new lot tells you you're out on your ear then, Dick?"

For a moment the mask slipped.

"That won't happen! It can't."

"Won't it? Okay … so they might spare you … *for a little bit* … give you a cushy little executive number for a year or so … but not the rest of us I don't think. Myself … Lucy … even Fearnley … we'll all be for the chop soon. They can't really do anything else can they?"

Dick started to remonstrate.

"Ollie … where *do* you get these ridiculous ideas from? Nothing like that's going to happen I can *assure* you of that. And I hope you haven't been bandying this sort of nonsense about in the Department and getting everyone all worked up. That wouldn't be very responsible on your part would it?"

Ollie stared at Trencham, making him feel uncomfortable.

"Dick … do you know why I'm so certain as to what's going on? I've seen the figures … how much is earmarked for staffing out of the budget for the year."

Dick looked petrified.

"What figures? They're not … not …"

"Available? They've been *leaked*, Dick … that and everything else. I'm not the only one who *knows* … several people in other departments do as well … it's no secret any more … what these bastards are going to do …"

Ollie could see beads of sweat starting to form on Dick's brow.

"You mustn't call them that …"

"Really? I think that's a fair description of the bunch of corporate tosspots who resemble the Gestapo on some real juicy mission ..."

Dick was almost gasping for breath.

"Everything's above board ... full consultation ... all down the line ..."

Ollie ignored this.

"Dick ... let me ask you something. Whatever happened to things like—*integrity* ... the actual worth of what we in the Department were doing? What we used to believe in ... qualities you yourself were proud to uphold. All that's gone out the window pretty quickly hasn't it? As soon as the mighty dollar starts to figure above everything else ... that's what happens."

Dick thrashed around, trying to save himself from drowning.

"Ollie ... there always has to be changes."

As soon as he said it Dick knew how feeble that sounded.

"Is that all you've got to say? And what sort of changes are they going to be, Dick? Changes for the better? I don't think so. Zandra and her sort don't see things quite like that do they? Or *Lord Folds* ..."

If Ollie had thrown a bucket of offal onto his desk, the reaction would not have been more dramatic. Dick visibly jumped.

"What? What! *Lord Folds!* He's only a figurehead ... a ... a ... sponsor if you like ... he won't have any say in what happens ... any changes. If there are any that is ... *and I'm not saying there will be.*"

"But, Dick ... I know he intends to totally alter

the way Barstowe is run."

Dick made a see-saw motion with his head.

"Nothing's anywhere near finalized. There's got to be evaluations, assessments ... a study group ... reports."

Ollie was nodding.

"Okay ... but we know what the outcome of all that's going to be don't we?"

"Do we?"

"Opening the gates and letting in the Mongol Hordes! We'll have an executive structure ... a bunch of managers ... they'll do away with departments. Every member of the academic staff will be answerable to some kind of *politburo*. All the decisions will be made by a faceless bureaucracy ... simple as that. We'll be like those new places they call *colleges* ... the ones the government have just opened ... Brougham and Marchdale ... it'll be just the same here."

Dick was all set to deny this too, but one look at Ollie told him he would have been wasting his time.

"I think you're being ridiculously pessimistic, Ollie. Anyway ... be fair ... those two you've mentioned ... they're now in the top fifteen of unis."

"And who do you think puts out these league tables? The *government*, Dick."

Dick resorted to a spot of humphing.

"It's the way things are going, Ollie. You can't stop progress."

A sudden feeling of exasperation gripped Ollie. He stared hard at his Head of Department.

"I know it is, Dick. And the only places that have stood up to this kind of Stalinist tactic is Oxbridge and one or two others. But then they're *proper* universities aren't they? The only ones that have ever meant anything really. Why? Because they've stayed autonomous ... and been run ... believe it or not ... by *academics*. Barstowe could have given a good account of itself once. Not any more, Dick ... the Senate have made sure of that ... by caving into this *crap*."

Dick shuffled about uncomfortably.

"Now ... don't get all bitter and twisted, Ollie ... that's my advice ... it's just not worth it. Life's too short."

Ollie looked arch.

"Depends how you regard *time* doesn't it, Dick. But ... I'm not going to start a discussion about *quantum* just right now. We can do that when we're both on the dole ... there'll be plenty of *time to kill* then I'm sure. Good to have a little chat with you ... sort things out a bit. Cheers."

Dick stared after Ollie's retreating figure and, not for the first time in recent months, wondered what was going on in the world.

George—the landlord of *The Robe*—didn't care too much for music. He probably associated it with girls from Barstowe, the sort who got pie-eyed in his pub on a Saturday night and disported themselves. Sounds were filling the air in *The Robe* this lunchtime and unusually, prompting comment. The D.J. on Windleroot Radio was offering a little background to the song that had just been played.

"*After The Jam and Cream in the swinging psychedelic Sixties ... came The Scones ... no ... not the Rolling Scones ... but The Phoney Buns ... and that was their big Nineties hit ... Womble of Thanet ...*"

Big Dave gave his verdict.

" 'ere that were a load of old cobblers then ..."

Little Rog, standing next to him, looked up from his pint.

"Woss that?"

"They on the rayjow ..."

Rog apparently shared the landlord's indifference to melody.

"Didn't notice ... weren't listening ..."

Big Dave turned to address Ernie, Clifford and Old Ted who were playing cribbage at a table in the corner.

"I'd rather 'ear old Bill Emmett goin' up through the farm with his tractor and trailer than that bleedin' row ..."

At this, Dennis the Thatcher spluttered into his Old Todge. The debate on the merits of The Phoney Buns ended when the door opened, with more than a touch of officiousness. The figure of Lord Folds was revealed, glaring at all around him. After a brief enquiring glance at the newcomer, the locals simply returned to what they had been doing. Folds bustled up to the bar. George appeared from the cellar where he had been changing a barrel. The landlord wiped his hand on a convenient cloth.

"Morning, sir. What can I get you?"

"Small scotch."

"Coming up."

Folds continued to eye everything and everyone around him with blatant loathing. To him they were without exception thieves and sneaks, and all as guilty as hell. He had not yet worked out his plan of campaign, but he was determined to bring these peasants to heel. George set his drink in front of him.

"There we are. Two pound—fifty."

Folds slid a twenty-pound note across the bar. He accepted the change without comment and continued to stare about fixedly. When Mandy appeared from the other bar, she caught Folds' eye.

"Are you Mandy?"

She was so surprised she did not deny it.

"Yes ..."

"Do you know anything about a book of mine that I lost here ..."

Under Folds gaze Mandy began to hesitate.

"I don't know ... what sort of book ..."

Folds knew he had hit the target with his first shot.

"One that was picked up near the stones ..."

Mandy was not a little frightened.

"Um ... I don't know ..."

"I rather think you do ..."

Mandy rallied.

"Anyway ... who *are* you? How d'you know my name anyway?"

Folds adopted a judicial air.

"It doesn't really matter does it. You know where my property is ... so that means you stole it ... or you know who did ..."

No other sound was heard in the bar except Folds'

hostile tones. In a flash of spirit, Mandy suddenly rounded on her accuser.

"I don't know who you are ... coming in here and saying things like that to me. You push off!"

Folds, not used to such straight talking by those he considered to be his social inferiors, comprehensively lost his temper.

"You thieving ... lying ... little whore!"

Big Dave, who up until now had his back to the proceedings, turned round.

"'Ere! Who do you think you are? Talking to our Mand like that?"

"*I am Lord Folds.*"

Big Dave squared his shoulders.

"Oh ... are you now? Well ... I tell 'ee what ... I don't care if you'm King Arfur and all his Round Tables put togevver. You mind yer manners when you talks to a lady ... in yere or anywheres else."

Folds faced his adversary, words spewing out of his mouth in a violent torrent.

"You brainless oaf ... you're all the same in this filthy place ... criminal scum ..."

Folds got no further, both Big Dave and Little Rog, with Dennis the Thatcher in support, began to move in Folds' direction—more than a little menacingly. Folds was many things, but he was no fool, and knew he was outnumbered and outgunned. He strode out of the pub, slamming the door behind him. George looked up.

"What was that all about?"

Mandy, letting go of her emotions, began to cry. Big Dave stood in the middle of the floor seething with righteous anger. Mandy grabbed a handful of tissues from behind the bar and disappeared. Clifford went to the window and looked out.

"Yere ... I thought so. Tha's the same motor ..."

"How's mean?"

Clifford briefly retold his story. Big Dave still fumed the more.

"Don't make no difference ... about his bleedin' book. I still ain't 'avin' 'ee talk to our Mand like that."

He quaffed his pint and began to move towards the door. Little Rog called after him.

"Wos gonna do Dave?"

The other paused, a hand on the doorpost.

"I'm off to get me tractor ... an' I might 'ave the slurry tanker on behind ... we'll see."

All in the pub exchanged significant glances. Folds, meanwhile, had set off towards the stones, partly to see if there was any sign of his missing book, but mainly to calm his racing heart. He would have been better advised to remain in sight of his Rolls. When he returned twenty minutes later the pristine vehicle he had left outside the pub resembled a gigantic mud pie, one the colour of dead moss.

Folds might well let loose vile imprecations, but his curses achieved little. If anything they encouraged the faces in the window of *The Robe* to be more animated. The locals took to hooting loud with laughter and slapping each other on the back in their mirth. If ever they believed a pompous townie had got his just desserts it was now—an occasion in the annals of village life when justice was done. The sight of Lord Folds trying to squeeze into the driver's seat without rendering himself in the same state as his motor car was one they would never forget. Mandy squealed with delight, tears of joy now running down her cheeks.

"You ruffians! Numbskulls! Country Bumpkins! I'll sue you ..."

Hoarse with shouting abuse at his tormentors, Folds peered through the windscreen as he edged the green monster along the narrow road that led out of Rylock Wells. He was aware that most garages boasted a car wash but, as the miles slowly unwound before him, Folds discovered they were not much in evidence in this part of the country.

7

Lord Folds spoke to his lawyers, but they advised caution. His lordship eventually abandoned his intention of taking proceedings for criminal damage against a person or persons unknown in Rylock Wells. Bringing the Barstowe campaign to fruition was also occupying him more and more. Flora had arrived that morning with a stooge in tow, both of them eager to report on progress.

"Lord Folds, can I introduce my colleague Hugh Smigg."

Folds regarded the duo; he would not have trusted either of them to tell him the right time. The question was whether their proposals would impress the Vice Chancellor and the University Management Committee of the Senate. Folds was certain he had the measure of the Vice Chancellor and the Registrar—pigs snuffling around a trough.

"So … what have you come up with?"

Smigg, who had been staring into his laptop, looked up momentarily.

"I don't anticipate any problems with accepting our package, Lord Folds … particularly as it offers such advantageous terms to the administration of Barstowe."

Folds raised a speculative eyebrow.

"I wouldn't be so sure … there's always problems with getting people to do what you want … even if you're paying them off …"

Smigg volunteered the ghost of a nod.

"I agree … the first step is to establish a forum …"

Smigg had a pronounced Welsh accent. The effect of this was to turn the buzzwords that rolled from his tongue into pseudo-bardic cadences.

"We have to set out an overall mission statement … aims and objectives set out clearly. Scrutinise and evaluate organisations … operational plans … managed and drafted by the individuals and teams who will be implementing them … establishing rolling programmes of activities … and continually evaluating their success and impact …"

Folds stared into a corner of the room as Smigg's volley of jargon reached a crescendo.

"We never forget SMART … objectives must be … Specific … Measurable … Achievable … Realistic … Timed."

At last Folds raised a hand in abject protest.

"Yeah … yeah … I get all that. It wasn't going too badly … before you started on all that crap …"

Smigg lapsed into silence Flora immediately took up the reins.

"Is there some specific aspect you feel we ought to concentrate on, Lord Folds?"

"Definitely. Dealing with old brigade … that's where any trouble will come from … some of them are bound to kick up good and proper. I wouldn't be surprised if they weren't already …"

Flora was equal to this.

"The approach is to show empathy … maintain connectivity … and above all avoid confrontation …"

"So how do you do that?"

Smigg was smug.

"We've already installed one of our top operatives

116

Zandra Roope at Barstowe as you know … she's introducing our initial procedures as of this moment …"

Folds was tight lipped.

"Nobody kicking up a fuss about her being there? How did you make sure that didn't happen?"

Flora pitched in.

"Mainly by maintaining information security. To put it simply … don't tell anything to anyone who you don't want to know what's going on … remove paper based processes as soon as possible. The old brigade … as you call them … they rely on that approach still. They're not likely to access any of our secure data systems …"

Folds nodded, slowly.

"I'll take your word for it …"

Smigg was now busily collating spread sheets on his iPad. Flora pitched the question he really wanted to ask.

"The investment aspect, Lord Folds … I just wanted to clarify with you about the external funders …"

Folds was wary.

"You did? Why's that?"

"For the purposes of quality P.R. any corporate investment has to be seen to be financed appropriately."

"Really? I thought *Goggle* and *Spaceboot* funded some of the top universities these days …"

Flora smiled, only slightly.

"That's certainly what happens in the States … yes … where legislation in this instance is … shall we say … less tight. There are exceptions here of course

... and really it all depends upon the way things are presented ..."

"Exactly. That's what I'm paying you for ... to make sure everything sounds kosher to these Uni. wallahs."

"We still have ... for our own peace of mind ... to guarantee sufficient working capital ... assets against liabilities ..."

Folds cut him short.

"You don't have to bother about of that side of things ... that's all taken care of ..."

Smigg clicked a box on his screen.

"Thank you for your confirmation, Lord Folds."

"The big carrot for Barstowe is that they'll automatically get a return on the investment they have to put in. I'm guaranteeing ten or more times their original investment within five years ... *and* their percentage contribution is minimal compared to what I'm putting up front."

Moments passed, punctuated only by the rhythmic click of electronic devices—messages launching into the aether.

"Do you have anything further you need to clarify with us, Lord Folds?"

Folds was abrupt.

"I'm still not entirely convinced you guys can pull this off ... not that you don't talk a good game."

Smigg's confidence showed not the slightest dent.

"I had a brief conversation with Jools about the way to approach this ... there's an element of quite clever psychology in this. Not only getting people to support the policies you implement but also to make sure they themselves believe they're doing the right thing ... not just paying lip-service to what's going on."

"How do you do that then?"

"By creating an environment in which they're comfortable ... namely ... one they've totally created for themselves. It can't be done overnight of course ... and they have to trust us completely ..."

Folds looked amazed.

"Does anyone trust anyone these days?"

"Interesting you should say that ..."

"Oh?"

"The government in America has recently done a lot of research about what makes a period in history seem to be a time of unity. The Thirties or the Sixties ... for instance ... the Sixties being the better example. Then ... there was such a very strong bond among youth it almost amounted to a universal consciousness. That kind of thing hasn't been experienced since ..."

Folds was vague about anything that could be described as social, cultural or psychological.

"Maybe not ..."

Smigg continued.

"Then came the Seventies and everything became fragmented. You could say that extremist groups ... terrorist organizations began to thrive because of the loss of that unity."

Folds was gruff, in his usual manner.

"So how is all this relevant to what we're doing?"

Smigg allowed himself a tight little grin.

"These researches show that with the right input it's possible to achieve total agreement on policy in any organization. That's Zandra's role ... the impact of which will increase as she gains a pivotal position as part of the university administration ..."

"So I hear."

"... and she's done the same sort of undercover work in some mega corporations very successfully across the pond. These university people will be small change to her."

Folds shrugged.

"We'll see. Universities really do have some ridiculous customs ... like *the academic year* starting in *October*. What's the sense in that? If I have my way that'll be scrapped."

Flora tried to sound as neutral as possible

"Would that work?"

"I don't see why you shouldn't start the year in January ... makes a lot more sense to me."

"But don't students have to wait until August to get their school exam results?"

Folds regarded Flora coldly.

"That'll be irrelevant. After a year or two we'll introduce a system that won't depend on exam results at all. Entry to *my* Universities will only be open to those who can afford it ... and as we shall have the monopoly on Higher Education ... we'll steadily keep bumping up the fees too ..."

Flora and Smigg exchanged a brief, almost undetectable glance.

"Our long term strategy?"

"You could say that. Anyway let's concentrate on what we're doing right now ... everything has to be in place by next Summer ... ready for the beginning of October when *my* new students come in. So ... if your Zandra has softened them up enough ... then the next stage for you is a presentation to the whole university ... that's what I want done next."

"Introducing strategy ... overall policy ..."

"Right ... get all your power-point stuff working full bore and blind 'em with science ..."

Smigg shut his laptop with a snap.

"All in hand, Lord Folds ... data logged and uploaded ... just a matter of delivering it at the agreed time."

He stood up, rather like an old-fashioned mechanical toy, Flora did the same. They faced Folds, a neater version of Tweedledum and Tweedledee. Folds leant over his desk.

"There is one more thing ... or should I say person ... that needs attending to. You might get your Zandra working on this little problem ..."

Smigg flashed the ubiquitous iPad.

"Yes? I'll make a note of it ..."

"Bloke called Fearnley Wilmot ... has a bit of clout on some administrative committees ... he's dead set against all this ... and people appear to listen to his point of view."

Smigg looked alert.

"Anyone else?"

"Not for the moment. There's a little squirt called Trencham ... Head of Philosophy or something ... I've got him right where I want him ... he might be able to spike this bloke's guns too."

"Right ... I'll be in video conference with Zandra later I'll mention it ... get something done about this character."

Flora nodded briskly.

"We'll be in touch ... very soon."

Folds perfunctorily shook the hand offered by Smigg. It was clammy, and he tried not to wince.

It was more than a month since Martin had encountered Mr. Tonks at the stone circle. They had agreed to meet at *The Robe* and continue with their discussion and even the painful possibility of encountering Lily did not put him off. When Martin arrived that evening, Mr. Tonks was already holding court, Ernie and Clifford being in attendance. Old Ted was quietly musing in the corner. Somewhat to Martin's relief, Lily was not in evidence. Mr. Tonks rose to greet him.

"Martin, my dear boy ... how marvellous to see you."

"Can I buy you a drink?"

"I shall regretfully decline your offer as I have already embarked on my second half of Guinness. My doctor insists I ration myself to only a modicum of alcohol ... you see."

"Fair enough."

Mr. Tonks looked along the bar.

"Old Todge is the local brew ..."

"Oh ... I ..."

Seeing his hesitation, Ernie stepped in.

"Yere ... there be two wot be the best ... Wickdipper and Todge ..."

Mandy eyed him, Martin spoke up manfully.

"Pint of Todge then ... please."

Ernie nudged him in a matey fashion.

"Go on, young'n ... get some of that down 'ee ... that'll make thee pecker whistle ..."

Mr. Tonks raised an eyebrow, minimally.

"What better recommendation, Martin ..."

Mandy handed Martin his change, at the same time addressing Mr. Tonks in a low tone.

"I suppose you heard about that *man* coming in here ..."

Mr. Tonks inclined a sympathetic ear.

"Tell me all, Mandy ..."

"He was called Mouldy ... no Folds ... *Lord* Folds ... he certainly didn't act like a toff ..."

Certain synapses began to vibrate inside the brain of Mr. Tonks as Mandy told her tale. He listened to the end of her tale, then casually mentioned one episode.

"This book ..."

"The one he thought I pinched?"

"Yes ... where is ..."

Mandy dropped her voice even further.

"My friend Lily's got it."

"Oh ..."

"I didn't tell old what's-his-face though ... no way."

"Quite."

Mr. Tonks appeared to deliberate.

"Can you give Lily a message from me?"

"Yeh ... sure ... I can see her tomorrow ... in the morning ... I don't start here till later."

Mr. Tonks looked serious.

"If I'm right in thinking what book it is ... it's dangerous for it to be in her possession ... for several reasons ... none of which I can explain right now."

Mandy took this in.

"So what should she do? Burn it ... chuck it away?"

"No ... actually ... I think she should give it to me for safe keeping. I mean your friend can have it back later if she wants."

Mandy pulled a few frothing pints for Clifford and his cronies.

"I wanted her to have it ... and I just knew I had to get it out of sight somewhere. Just as well I did as it turned out."

Mr. Tonks hastened to reassure her.

"You did the right thing, Mandy. Fear not ..."

Mr. Tonks drew Martin to his table, talking as he did so, almost as if he were thinking aloud.

"When power is used for selfish ends ... polarity is reversed. The forces within the Earth cannot themselves determine for what purpose they are employed ..."

Martin chose to be flippant.

"Going to the Dark Side you mean?"

Mr. Tonks did not respond.

"Jung would have called it 'the shadow' ... that part of ourselves we often wish to conceal ... or even deny we have. The hidden elements of our nature are just as significant as those qualities we are keen to display. Unfortunately ... destiny sometimes gives the tyrant the opportunity to let his delusions run riot ... the self casts an even darker shadow. Eventually, the wicked hurl themselves into the pit. But it is the destruction wreaked by them along the way that makes for the tragedy."

Mr. Tonks then fell silent, as if ruminating upon

the intrinsic evil in mankind. A figure at the bar was deep in conversation with Mandy, who was recounting Folds' visit to him.

"How did he know my name? Who told him ... that's what I want to know ..."

Her companion, Farish Florin, was quick to lie. Mandy, blinded by a growing passion for him, did not detect it.

"Wasn't me ... never heard of the bloke ..."

Mandy was anxious to share the news she had of Philomena.

"She says she's going to *do* a magic ritual at the stones at Samhain ... that's the First of November."

Florin was deliberately casual, disguising his interest.

"Oh ... yeh ..."

"I told her she's mad to do that ... you never know what might happen ..."

"Yeh ... right. And she's definitely going?"

Mandy nodded her head vigorously.

"Getting all kitted out in her black clobber an' everything ... she will look amazing though with her red hair and all that ..."

Mr. Tonks carefully observed Florin take out his mobile as soon as Mandy went to attend to the needs of her customers. Score, who received his text, assured Florin he would pass on the information concerning Philomena to Folds. Score also suggested to Florin that he obtain another book to replace its lost predecessor, and to this request Florin agreed.

Martin was being observant also, and noticed that an envelope was lying on the floor underneath their table. He picked it up and put it in his pocket meaning to hand it in at the bar but forgot. In less than sixty seconds, many a fate had been decided.

Score was aware that Lord Folds regarded the forthcoming Samhain ritual as a trial run for some greater endeavour. He had been informed that having the occult fraternity in attendance would oil the magical wheels for the future.

"*Samhain*, my lord."

Score pronounced the word in a way that would have made any self-respecting Druid wince in pain.

"Now who have we got for the final line up?"

Score read out a list of half-a-dozen names, as he came to that of Boggy Ogwit Folds interrupted.

"So ... he's back ... eh? Fair enough ... he'll be perfect for *the front line*."

Score looked mildly puzzled.

"How do you mean, my lord?"

Folds adopted his lofty air.

"The purpose of the ritual is to open the Gates of the Otherworld ..."

Score looked even more puzzled.

"... another dimension if you like ... one that exists alongside this one."

"Ah."

"Needless to say ... much is *unpredictable* in these realms."

Score echoed the italics.

"*Unpredictable*, my Lord?

Folds assumed an expression half-way between smug and sinister.

"According to Cattermogg Hicks ... who's running the show ... the first sphere beyond the portal is *Twyfin*—the Land of Darkness ... and the denizens of that world are not the sort you would want to meet. Demons ... iron teeth ... razor claws and all the rest ... so Cattermogg tells me."

Score's eyes whirled around like bingo balls.

"But you aren't planning to go there?"

Folds was curt.

"Certainly not ..."

Score swallowed hard, thoroughly perturbed. His employer was looking at him in a way he didn't like much either—with a sort of leering amusement. The same look was almost permanently present when he mingled with the miscellaneous occultists at Rylock Wells. Folds had thought it wise to bring two of the security staff from Prockleby in case any of the locals took too much interest in proceedings. They positioned themselves at the entrance to the field, unaware that Martin knew of another way to the circle.

He had taken up a position an hour or so before the arrival of Folds and his party. Somewhat apprehensively, he viewed the scene from behind a large oak. The Moon was in her most fulsome splendour, the clouds a milky luminescence, partly streaked with black. The wind rattled the leaves and the shadows danced. Martin watched as a group of extraordinary figures made their way towards the stones.

Carrying staffs and lanterns, and in an array of garish costumes these amateur sorcerers began to parade widdershins about the circle. With their ponderous puppet-like steps Martin thought they looked more ridiculous than eldritch. Finally they stopped before one particular stone and began chanting in a tuneless monotone. This went on for some minutes and the effect was strangely unnerving, as if some force was being coaxed out of Mother Earth. Martin was suddenly aware of another figure approaching across the grass.

Philomena Planet Weaver! Sightless eyes directed towards the stones, the girl appeared to be in a trance. Her arrival in the midst of the unholy group caused them to begin cavorting animatedly. Their leader led Philomena towards the stone that, moments before, had been the focus of their chanting. To Martin's amazement, this began to glow with an iridescent blue light and appeared to abandon its solid state. Slowly, but with the utmost deliberation Philomena approached what was now a doorway lit from within. A yard wide, it could easily accommodate any figure travelling into the unknown realms. Still pulsating with a vortex of energy, the light became even brighter until it glowed with ferocious intensity. The next moment Philomena disappeared completely. She had been swallowed up, and was now presumably in the bowels of the Earth!

Martin stared transfixed at the glowing arch which soon began to fade as the outline of the stone was restored. For the first time in his life Martin was aware of some other force determining the nature of the world. Another universe existed, one invisible and incomprehensible, beyond ordinary reality. Sudden panic making his heart thump uncontrollably, he fled into the darkness.

8

Unaware that any of his students had been witness to sorcery, Ollie had been content with the more innocuous delights of Guy Fawkes Night. At one time he had got as excited about rockets and roman candles as any other boy but, with advancing youth, his enthusiasm had waned. While a student, he had nearly fallen into the bonfire after drinking too much cider. In Hornbeam Crescent, preparing for the following day's tutorial, Ollie was dimly aware of showers of sparks in the sky, and muffled explosions in the distance.

The next morning, as the clock crept towards noon, Ollie felt like Gary Cooper at the railroad depot. Apart from Martin, he was hard-pressed to recall any particular individual, even after studying his list of students several times.

> Martin Callow
> Suzi Dobbs
> Jenny Fairbush
> Scott Finley-Ross
> Eleanor Hobart-Horrocks
> Toby Quinn
> Katherine Tigwell
> Lin Yee Tong
> Luke Walters

After a slow start, the seminar got into gear. Frege and Wittgenstein were summarily dealt with, despite Ollie's dread of philosophical principles that came accompanied by elaborate mathematical formulae. Next it looked as if Nietzsche was to be given the same perfunctory treatment.

"He concludes that existence is awful and absurd …"

Toby mimed putting a revolver to his head causing some merriment and Eleanor Hobart-Horrocks to mildly chastise him.

"Oh … you are *so* silly …"

Her tone reminded Ollie of the shires, unmistakably redolent of honking commands in the hunting field. He suspected that if Eleanor actually did take exception to anyone, she would go in with both barrels blazing. Those haughty features told of an ancestral line who had trounced murderous trespassers and insane servants.

Sharply at one, the group disbanded. Ollie noticed Martin, who was obviously keen to engage in a chat, and looking uncharacteristically a little pale. Ollie hailed him cheerily.

"If this was the 1960s I would have probably offered you a glass of sherry … I'm sure any tutor who did that now would be hauled up in front of some disciplinary committee."

Martin smiled.

"Definitely. Acting inappropriately … health and safety …"

Ollie laughed.

"So, Martin … how are you finding the course this year? You seemed to enjoy yourself in tutorials last year … that was a fine first essay …"

"Well … I actually happen to like doing Philosophy."

Ollie tried not to sound patronising.

"I'm glad to hear it."

Martin looked frankly in his direction.

"I do know people here who couldn't care less about what degree they're doing ..."

Ollie was genuinely astonished.

"Really?"

"Yeh. They might have been clever enough to get here ... but that wasn't really why they came to Barstowe."

Ollie smiled.

"Not to further their knowledge ... as you might say ..."

Martin shook his head.

"Probably half the students in Philosophy wanted to do History of Art ... English ..."

Ollie sighed.

"Yes ... I did hear that ..."

"Does that worry you?"

Ollie looked towards the window where the November greyness looked impenetrable.

"Yes ... it does. I've never really thought of it like that. I know sometimes students hand in poor work ... so I assume they're less than exhilarated by the subject but ..."

"Barstowe's very *fashionable* ... gets checked on all the blogs about cool unis and all that blah ... Facebook ... Twitter ... y'know ..."

"Yes ... I'm sort of aware of that too. I don't do a lot of *clubbing* myself ..."

Master and pupil regarded one another, both

feeling the desire to share some insight, but neither sure what that might actually be. Martin had experienced the fabric of reality being dramatically enhanced, while Ollie was uncomfortable with the nature of the world he knew. Would describing the goings on in the dark at Rylock Wells mean much to Ollie, any more than detailing the machinations of University Council meetings to his student?

Their combined awareness may have amounted to great wisdom, but at this moment neither knew the way to manifest it. In the classical era to discover universal truths was the goal, knowledge being simply a tool used to acquire wisdom. Now, enlightenment was not part of the *zeitgeist* as it was not quantifiable. Thus abstractions inevitably took the place of confidences. Ollie found himself thinking aloud.

"I was reading an article about Global Domination the other day ... one that would have been dismissed as just the worst kind of conspiracy theory a few years ago. It actually seems pretty plausible now ... governments being in the pay of corporations and banking that sort of thing ..."

"I'm sure that's true."

"And doesn't that make you ... personally I mean ... feel a bit helpless? To know that you're a young person with everything in front of you ... and you're faced with this behemoth controlling you ..."

Martin grimaced, not a little.

"No ... not really ... I believe change can happen anytime ... and for the better."

"That's what they believed in the Sixties ... though I was a little bit young for all that ... so I missed the real involvement."

"I think that generation had the right idea."

"Nothing did seem to change though ... my student years were in the Seventies ... and that was pretty bleak ..."

"Mmm. Nowadays ... for us ... it's just that much harder to be an individual ... the pressure to conform is pretty much there all the time ... almost in everything. You can buy your identity on e-Bay if you want."

Ollie moved towards the door.

"So we're all trapped. And to you are my colleagues ... and myself ... just lackeys of the fascist state?"

Martin followed him out.

"I don't see you ... particularly ... as anything like that."

"Good ... I don't see most of my colleagues as like that either ... in fact I think we're the ones who are being controlled by the forces of repression ..."

Martin looked at him strangely and his tutor suddenly realised perhaps he had revealed a lot more than he had intended. Ollie was aware that it would not do to make such provocative and unguarded remarks to any student, not even a discerning example. Martin took out an envelope from his bag and handed it to Ollie.

"What's this ... not your resignation I hope ..."

Martin looked serious.

"No ... it's something I found ... but I think you ought to have it. I just have the feeling it might be important ..."

Ollie was puzzled, but apparently not enough to want to open the envelope immediately. It stayed in his briefcase for some time before he transferred it to his desk, then he later promptly forgot about it. The endless corridors of the Department swallowed him up, eventually releasing him into Beechdale Road.

Along the pavement, Autumn gusts whirled the leaves into heaps of golden sovereigns. Ollie, aware he had to attend a Faculty Committee meeting in less than half an hour, went off in search of lunch. Since its recent refurbishment, the Social Sciences Library had the ambiance of an airport lounge, and was the hang-out of many an idler. Entering the cafeteria section on the ground floor meant encountering tables full of crimson-faced farmers' sons braying away at their equally flushed partners. He dutifully made a purchase, but when he bit into his baguette the cress garnish tickled Ollie's nose, and the egg mayonnaise flew in great gobbets down his chin.

Swallowing the last of his lunch and, remembering he needed a particular book, he hurried up the library stairs. As he wandered up and down the stacks he was aware of I-pods crackling and mobiles jangling, in total defiance of library rules. Students flitted about like feral pigeons, or clustered in clumps on the stairs, a maelstrom of humanity, programmed by the universe to do he knew not what.

During the faculty meeting, which was tedious and achieved very little, Ollie pondered yet again on the real decisions that were being made about Barstowe. They were inevitably made in secret and, for all he knew, at this very moment. He now trusted no one in the university hierarchy. They were no better than the grasping financiers and corrupt politicians that seemed to run the entire world these days. And whose world was it? Certainly not his. The meeting over, Ollie came out into Hume Square. As he passed the Woodbine Building the university clock chimed three. Suzi and Jenny from his tutorial group gave him a coy wave. They skipped up the steps arm in arm, emerald leggings making them look like a pair of mischievous elves. Already the charcoal skies were moving inexorably towards dusk. The rear lights of the cars in Macarthur Street shone with all the brilliance of rubies.

Earlier in the day a mist had gathered on the moors, entirely surrounding Prockleby, so that the stable buildings resembled a castle in some fairy tale. Folds was on the phone in his office, liaising with Trencham. He had just been informed that any presentation at Barstowe would have to wait until early in the next year. This news did not bother Folds overmuch, as he already had plans in place to exert his influence on the hierarchy. His current obsession was how he could eliminate any opposition in the ranks at the university. Zandra had already identified another loose cannon, and Flora had been informed.

"I have a feeling there are going to be one or two people who are going to get in our way ... they've got to be dealt with."

Trencham, not used to such baldly expressed sentiments, did his best to concur with this.

"Of course ... I'm sure you're right ..."

Folds was calmness itself.

"I want you to see to one particular person ... someone who knows a bit more than he should about my negotiations with that Senate lot ..."

"Er ... who's that?"

"What's his name? *Benson* ... that's it."

"Mick Benson? He's in English Department ..."

"I don't care if he teaches bloody Chinese ... this is the second time I've found out he's been nosing in my affairs ... and I want him out ..."

Trencham spluttered in protest.

"But I can't just tell the uni to sack people ... I don't have the authority to do that ..."

Folds was icy.

"Then you'll have to find someone who does and speak to them about it ..."

"That's a tall order ..."

"I don't care ... I'm not having my plans messed up by some interfering little nobody. I've invested a lot of time ... not to say a lot of money in all this ... and if you want your share of the sweeties then you've got to do your bit. Savvy?"

Trencham could feel sweat forming on the inside of his collar.

"Alright. Alright ... I'll see what I can do."

Folds was deliberate in his reply.

"I expect the people who work for me to *do* things ... not *see* about doing them."

"I will ... I will ... I promise."

"Good. Let me know when it's all sorted."

Trencham was left holding a phone that made a buzzing noise. He stared at the red handset for some moments as if it were a deadly serpent—one about to strike. Lord Folds made such impossible demands, and he was under pressure from everywhere these days, it was all too much!

No sooner had Folds dismissed the Head of the Philosophy Department than two more senior members of Barstowe University announced their arrival. Fred Bingley-Brass, the Vice-Chancellor, and Willie Slate, the Registrar pulled into the car park. Their Fiat Uno was dwarfed by the line of Lord Folds' own vehicles—a Land Rover, Bentley, Ferrari and a Rolls Royce Phantom.

Few bob knocking about here then ... eh, Willie?"

"Aye, lad ... you're right there ... someone got right jammy."

Bingley-Brass surveyed the landscape, or what could be seen of it through the mist. They followed a sign that proclaimed Office: Reception.

"Oop here then ... long by this snicket ..."

Slate followed along the path, all the while gazing about him.

"Aye. I were brought up not that far from here y'know. This were big house when I were a nipper. Been knocked down and boogered about though ... looks like ..."

The latter's accent had once been described, with some justification, as Geoffrey Boycott on speed.

"You've not met his Lordship then ..."

Slate dropped his voice.

"Nay ... I've not ... only heard he can be a mite mardy ..."

"Oh ... aye."

Presented with the unsmiling features of Lord Folds, the impression seemed wholly confirmed. Bingley-Brass recovered enough of his natural bounce to extend a hand, one which Folds accepted languidly. Introductions over, they entered the office, Folds commandeering his desk. His visitors, sitting side by side on a beige coloured sofa, betrayed a surreal resemblance to Morecambe and Wise. Folds began casually.

"I'm aware Barstowe University needs funding ... I can do that to almost any amount you require ..."

The two exchanged glances, they both felt like little lads being promised a new train set. Bingley-Brass offered his practiced blandishments.

"Well ... the government is most unhelpful in these circumstances ... and so Senate has been forced to look for outside funding ..."

"Yes ..."

The Vice-Chancellor hurried on.

"That's almost inevitable these days for any university ..."

Folds looked away.

"Of course ... you lost a lot of money recently ..."

Slate looked uncomfortable, but only briefly.

"There were a few investments that were unfortunately timed ... yes. But that's all behind us now ..."

Folds fixed him with a searching look.

"You're still up to your ears in debt though aren't you? I know you are ... I've got the figures here ..."

Bingley-Brass sucked in a breath.

"I didn't know *that information* was pooblically

available …"

"It isn't … I just make sure I'm informed about things … so I know what I'm dealing with … all the time."

Bingley-Brass remained chirpy.

"Great idea … must pay big dividends."

Folds examined other papers arranged strategically on his desk.

"I'll make sure you have all the funding you could possibly need …"

Slate smiled glassily.

"That's good news."

"… up to five billion if need be."

"Oh … nice …"

Folds' audience were beginning to sound like a pantomime chorus.

"Overseas backers … impeccable pedigree …"

Bingley-Brass, momentarily overwhelmed by such largesse, recovered enough to make what he considered a pertinent remark.

"This would completely revolutionize the present financial structure …"

"Exactly. Out with the old … in with the new. In more ways than one …"

Bingley-Brass heard the ominous note.

"Erm … how d'you mean exactly, Lord Folds?"

"Well … if I'm paying the piper then I want to call the bloody tune don't I?"

Slate sounded funereal.

"In what way?"

"Obvious isn't it? With the help of a few people I've signed up … Barstowe University will in the future be run in the way I want it to be."

Bingley-Brass tried his best.

"There might be some objections to that …"

Slate thought his colleague's voice sounded faint, as if coming from a long way away.

"I can't see why there should be … everything will be a lot easier for everybody. No one needs to worry about a thing."

"Aye … I know what you mean … but …"

Folds looked at him as if he were dealing with the village idiot.

"Fees come in … outgoings … upkeep … wages … catering … all taken care of by subsidiary companies who'll be contracted to do that."

Slate tried to assert himself, without much hope.

"There's bound to be people who won't want the changes …"

Folds was matter-of-fact.

"Your choice then isn't it? If you want the dosh you'll have to sort out a way to make everyone agree to the new arrangements. Which I've been working on … by the way. I'll give you a file before you go."

Bingley-Brass stood up, in the hope of being counted.

"I still don't think it will be as straightforward as all that. There will have to be a consultative committee … sub committees probably … it could take some time to sort out all that … ratify their findings … y'know."

Folds shook his head decisively.

"I don't work like that. I'm not really interested in anyone who doesn't agree with what I say. What

I would advise you to do is this … if you get any troublemakers you tell 'em … if they don't like it they can work somewhere else. If anybody will have them …"

Slate detected the latent threat, it was barely concealed. He wondered if Bingley-Brass realized the implications if they accepted Folds' offer lock, stock and barrel. But then, how could he know Barstowe was only the first step in Folds' master plan? Slate spoke up.

"With all due respect, Lord Folds … I'm not sure if you are fully aware of the way in which Barstowe University is run at present."

Folds simply ignored him. Bingley-Brass, sensing the growing tension, quickly stepped in.

"There won't be any problem wi' pro-VCs, Willie … that lot couldn't organize a set of fat bobbies most on 'em."

Slate seeing where the land lay, decided to stay silent. Folds shuffled his papers into a pile. The meeting was obviously over. Bingley-Brass was breezy.

"Well … thank you for your time, Lord Folds … I'm sure everybody knows where they stand now. I'll present findings to Council at next meeting …"

"When's that?"

"Er … don't rightly know off 'and like."

"No?"

Slate saved the day.

"It's a week this Tuesday …"

Bingley-Brass slapped his thigh in slapstick mode.

"Aye … course it is … what am I thinking about … I don't know …"

Folds was steely as he led the way towards reception.

"I won't expect there to be any problems then …"

"No … no …"

Before they realized it, the two visitors found themselves ushered outside. Bingley-Brass began to stamp his feet.

"Hellfire! I'm fair frozzed … what say we get t'nearest poob an' 'ave a bit o' loonch … like."

"Grand idea. Might even be a bit of a celebration …"

"Aye … mebbee. That bloke … he'll give oos brass alright … but he'll be bloody runnin' things. Don't know what others will make 'o' that …"

"They'll 'ave to loomp it won't they. If we don't take what his lordship's offerin' we'll be boogered."

Slate started the car, Bingley-Brass peering out through the windscreen.

"Might be a good idea drivin' a bit further on … out this fog … and go to 'otel. If Uni's getting' all this brass … least they can do is put a decent bit o' scran oor way."

The Fiat negotiated its way through the electric gates at the end of the drive and into the open road. On the journey through the outskirts of Huddersfield, both men were thinking hard. Nothing was said until they pulled up outside the grandest hostelry they could find.

"Funny bloke that Folds …"

"Aye … he is that, Willie."

"Summat not right somewhere …"

"Mebbee … not oor problem though is it?"

"Know what y'mean, lad. ..."

Still in his office, the subject of their deliberations spoke to Score who during the meeting had remained obediently in reception.

"Did you see those two?"

Score was guarded, as always.

"Not really ..."

"Bloody clowns. I'm not surprised Barstowe University is in trouble if the place is being run by people like that. Still ... they're as bent as Uri Geller's spoons so they should be no trouble ..."

"No, my lord."

Folds was his usual officious self.

"Some more people I want you to get I touch with ... first some chum of Cattermogg Hicks ... he'll be useful for The Winter Solstice."

"My Lord?"

"December the twenty-first. 'The Darkest of Nights' it's called it ... .I'll bet it'll be the bloody coldest too. Next year it'll be the Summer Solstice ... middle of June. That'll be the real thing ... around the same time as we take over Barstowe ..."

Although the room was warm, the temperature had dropped abruptly. Folds had finally embraced the persona of the despot, always just one step away from paranoia and madness. Score could feel his lips moving, and heard discarnate sounds.

"Right, my lord ... of course ..."

"This bloke ... Stibbs Gulley ... Yank ... he's staying near here in some monastery ... no ... Priory of Raviepartier ... that's it ... on a retreat."

"Yes, my lord ... I'll get in contact with him."

"I've got an idea he's much better suited to what I want to do … more experienced. Cattermogg got far too excited when some stupid girl appeared out of the blue at the Samhain thing. She bloody *disappeared* … that wasn't supposed to happen. I've no idea who she was … or what happened to her. Cattermogg told me that the Earth sprits often take sacrifices … so I suppose it all helps the cause."

Folds' casual attitude made Score shiver momentarily. Would anyone miss him if he was to be ritually murdered?

Mr. Tonks settled himself in his armchair to read *The Garden of Squagbo*. One of those overpriced limited editions with 'hand-tooled lettering', it was a mixture of dissertations on the occult, some mis-informed magical history and a few spells. To the uninitiated it would have seemed so obscure as to be laughable, yet Mr. Tonks still detected a malevolent air emanating from its pages. As he read on his expression became more grave, and he realised why Lord Folds would have been so distressed that it had left his keeping. Despite its amateur status it was still a book of sorcery—a key to using phenomena. Such power in the hands of the dabbler or the egotist could so easily be misdirected.

Now he had gleaned certain insights about Lord Folds, Mr. Tonks concluded that the abuse of power was second nature to him. He had also investigated Stibs Gulley, the adopted son of a plumber from

Wisconsin, with the equally unbelievable name of Perko Wiley. The latter had in later life been a leading light in the Deophisical Lodge in Boise, Idaho. Since his youth, Gulley had fallen foul of the law on several occasions for quite serious offences. His mug shot bore an uncanny resemblance to Charles Manson.

Mr. Tonks read more of the *The Garden of Squagbo*, at intervals searching out obscure volumes from his own bookshelves. Gradually he was piecing together a landscape that accurately reflected Lord Folds' own vision. As the sketch became a more finished work, his lordship's intentions were revealed—and only too clearly. Such a scheme, if brought to fruition, would result in the greatest evil and tyranny the kingdom might ever endure. Mr. Tonks could feel his pulse quicken, his breathing become labored. Gradually he calmed himself, though aware that the days ahead would be spent conjuring a counter plan to all this base ignominy.

His own researches into metaphysics had led him to one conclusion—that magic had only one purpose: encouraging the light, and doing good. If the practice of magic was undertaken with any other motive it was not true magic. Mr. Tonks strongly suspected that Gulley and his ilk glibly embraced 'the left hand path'—with all its treachery and false glamour. It was little consolation knowing that those who attempted to use power for their own ends inevitably came to a sticky end. Mr. Tonks was certain that the stone circle at Rylock Wells featured large in Lord Folds' infamous plans, and he pondered long on what they might be.

9

Many an academic nurtures a fleeting affection for the month of December. The University goes down some time in the middle of the month, and pleasing thoughts of the approaching Yuletide abound. Inevitably a time of reflection, Ollie recalled his introduction to Barstowe University in the 1970s. He had been shown into the Senior Common Room—a kind of gentleman's club, with comfortable looking armchairs and thick carpets. A place of quips and laughter—senior men holding forth in front of the gas fire—it was fogeyish, but welcoming and unselfconscious. In the next decade the space was commandeered as a lecture room. With the removal of the common-room any degree of conviviality in the Department departed. The new millennium brought other changes, most of them demonstrating the worst of the institutional ethos. A weary resignation then set in, a state soon to be tinged with a hoary cynicism among students and staff alike. Ollie was in melancholy mood when he encountered Dick Trencham in Beechdale Road. The latter was grinning like the proverbial feline.

"Ollie … just the chap I'd hoped I'd see …"

Ollie was taken aback by the warmth of his greeting, recalling he and Trencham had not parted on particularly good terms on the last occasion they met.

"Hello, Dick. Something up?"

Trencham clasped him by the arm, in a way Ollie considered rather too familiar.

"I thought we might have a quick drink together

this evening … something I really do want to run past you …"

"Oh?"

"Yeh … desperately need your input … how about this evening? Around six?"

Ollie found himself agreeing to this arrangement without any protest and Trencham, obviously pleased, went on his way grinning even more. Returning to his room, Ollie watched the amber sun glimmering behind the trees—at this time of year mere skeletons. A sky streaked with blue and grey replaced the disappearing sun. Ollie sat in silence, not even bothering to get up and turn on the light. Glancing at his watch sometime later, Ollie realized it was time to go and meet his Head of Department in The Willows.

It was perhaps inevitable that Trencham would choose this venue for their *tete-a-tete*. Although alcohol was served, the coffee house atmosphere always remained, setting a permanently genteel tone. Trencham ostentatiously laid his wallet on the bar; possibly believing this was *de rigueur* when ordering pints of ale.

"Now then … what'll you have, Ollie?"

Without much enthusiasm Ollie requested a half of lager, Trencham ordering a pint of *Old Sheepshagger* or something equally ridiculous. He paid for the drinks with a flourish, handing over a twenty pound note so crisp and new that the barman was at risk of being injured on its razor edge. Ollie moved towards a table in a discreet corner, but Trencham apparently preferred one nearer the bar. They sat down, talk being uneventful at first.

"Term going alright? Your new groups settling in?"

"Can't complain … as always … some more involved than others … a few bright sparks …"

Trencham was immediately garrulous ...

"Always the way isn't it? Some of them are just here for the beer."

The irony of the remark was not lost on Ollie as, in less than half a minute; Trencham had almost emptied his glass. He was obviously building himself up to come out with something and Ollie felt he should offer a prompt.

"So … ?"

Trencham was succinct.

"You're a mate of Benson in English aren't you?"

"Yes … see him for a drink now and then …"

"What do you think of him?"

Trencham uttered this in such marked way that Ollie was immediately put on his guard.

"Mick and I came to Barstowe round about the same time …"

"Would you trust him?"

Before Ollie could answer, Trencham was up at the bar ordering another pint. Returning, he sat down heavily, beer dribbling down the side of his glass. Belatedly, Ollie answered his question.

"As much as anybody … yes … why?"

"I've heard he's been making trouble … in committee … telling them a lot of things he has no business to say …"

Ollie was deliberately non-committal waiting to see where all this was leading.

"First I've heard about it."

"Oh … come on, Ollie … you know what he's like … has a skinful and shouts his mouth off …"

"Mick does like a drink … but I've never known him be indiscreet."

Trencham looked triumphant.

"I've got *proof* he has been … *very* indiscreet. A third party has informed me … in some depth … of his … *attitude.*"

Ollie was almost inclined to laugh but decided not to. He also noticed that Trencham's second pint was fast disappearing. No matter which way the conversation went, he decided to introduce some sort of decorum into proceedings. He rose, more steadily than Trencham.

"Having another?"

The question was almost superfluous; Trencham drained his glass and passed it over, gapingly empty. Ollie did not order anything for himself, just returned with another brimming flagon for his head of department. When handed to him it was immediately grasped tightly with both hands, whether this was because the drinker's motor faculties were on hold, or it demonstrated an unadulterated lust for alcohol was hard to tell.

"You know Lord Lupin …"

"Not personally … no."

Trencham looked at Ollie uncomprehendingly; he was past the stage when subtleties were rewarded with joy by the synapses.

"He's just released this report about government spending on higher education. If his recommendations

are taken up … it's the end of the road for Barstowe …
I'm telling you."

Ollie was inclined to disagree.

"Lupin's only interested in keeping standards as
high as possible … I support him there. I'm not sure
his proposals are that draconian either …"

Trencham raised his voice.

"They bloody well are … it's criminal how any
minister could even suggest what he's doing."

Ollie eyed him.

"So your point is …"

Trencham was holding onto to the edge of the
table as if to steady himself.

"I'll tell you what the point is … *Lord Folds*. I
know you don't think much of him … none of you
lot do …"

Ollie was amazed that sides in any debate had
now been delineated. He was prompted to sarcasm.

"You think *his* scheme is going to save us all …"

Trencham turned an interesting shade of vermillion.

"I know it will. It makes so much sense … don't
you see that …"

"Not sure I do actually, Dick. But setting all that
about Lord Lupin aside for a moment … what's Mick
got to do with all this?"

Trencham's expression darkened, now the colour
of cherry brandy.

"He's been going about rubbishing Folds …
buttonholing people in Senate … even wrote letters to
the Vice-Chancellor … damned little idiot. He ought
to mind his own business … stick to T.S … .bloody …

Eliot ... or whoever it is he writes books about."

Ollie was stunned, but not into silence.

"So this heinous crime that Mick's committed amounts to what? Expressing his opinion? Informing people about things they may not be aware of? Even telling the truth perhaps?"

Trencham took a more than good pull on his pint, before attempting to answer.

"*He's not telling the truth!* It's all a pack of lies he's touting around the place ..."

Ollie was measured in his reply.

"Is it? I'm not so sure that quite a few of my colleagues wouldn't agree with Mick. I have a strong suspicion those who are so firmly behind Lord Folds ... such as yourself ... are doing so because it's to their personal advantage. Tell me ... what do you stand to make out of it if Folds takes over, Dick?"

Trencham started to wave his arms about like a windmill in a hurricane. One or two people at nearby tables stared.

"Now you're talking just like him ... none of you understand politics ... let me tell you ..."

Ollie interrupted, swiftly.

"All this has nothing whatsoever to do with politics ... that's not the issue. It's trying to stop the ethos of the university being undermined by people like Lord Folds ... and Barstowe being destroyed ... irrevocably."

Trencham was now hysterical, his words almost a screech.

"We're going to get rid of that bloody Benson ... and anyone else who won't see sense ... I've got Senate on my side with this one … you wait."

Ollie almost whispered his reply.

"This stinks, Dick. I didn't really quite realize how much it did until this moment … now I know."

In the features of his half-drunk Head of Department, Ollie could read guilt, petty defiance, and ultimately despair. He slurred his words when he replied.

"Not my fault … got to get rid of the rotten apples …"

Ollie almost shouted back at him.

"Dick! Dick! What are you doing? Mick might get pissed occasionally but basically he's a good bloke! Sound … a man with integrity! Can you say the same about yourself these days? I used to consider you were like that … decent … reliable … I'm damned if I think of you that way now."

Now extremely angry, Ollie abandoned what remained of his lager and strode out of The Willows. He left behind the slouched figure of Dick Trencham grasping his pint as if for support and staring unseeing in front of him. As Ollie climbed Spencer Hill on his way home thick grey clouds pressed down on the roof tops, and he nuzzled into his scarf for warmth. By the time he reached Hornbeam Crescent he had calmed down enough to think about what he was going to do for the rest of the evening. Coming to a swift decision, he turned into Lionel Road and picked up a Prawn Biryani from the Raj Toot.

As soon as he gained his front door, Ollie went into the kitchen and spooned the contents of the aluminum containers onto a plate. He went into the sitting room, switched on the T.V., sat down, and began to eat. The News did not evoke much response in him. What followed was a documentary about volcanoes and he fell asleep during a digitally enhanced lava flow. When he woke up he realised that the programme had ended, succeeded by a feature on earthquakes. Ollie got up and applied the remote, after that he went upstairs to bed. The onset of sleep found him wondering if the Earth was ever still.

Mr. Tonks, in loose jacket and equally shapeless corduroys, passed between the ornate Edwardian gates of Beck Park. Probably the only part of Conkerville where it was possible to engage in anything resembling contemplation, the orderly flower beds and tree lined walks achieved the desired effect. The chill air did not encourage dawdling, and Mr. Tonks hurried past the bandstand and the squat clock tower, intent on his perambulations. His inner self was focused upon puzzling out the intentions of Lord Folds. The nature of the book, his sudden appearance in Rylock Wells, and the subsequent disappearance of Philomena—a source of much head-shaking and anguish in the Robe—could not be considered coincidence.

A brief email from Martin was for Mr. Tonks another matter of concern. In it he had hinted at certain goings-on in the stone circle at Samhain, but had not mentioned any details, as if this was all too painful to recall. That Martin wished to distance himself off from any more dealings with the occult was quite apparent. Mr. Tonks consoled himself with the knowledge that an adverse reaction to things transcendental often happens to the most promising of neophytes. Not that Martin had in any way pledged himself to the esoteric path, but that, Mr. Tonks was sure, would inevitably follow.

Folds was seeking to employ magic for some nefarious purpose, and Mr. Tonks suspected that he wished to control the minds of others, in the tradition of the tyrants of Ancient Rome, or the propagandists of the Third Reich. His reflections were interrupted by a whole flurry of peals ringing out from the church tower of St. Mowat's. This reached a crescendo, as if all the gods were acclaiming their new champion. The Heavens had chosen Archibald Tonks to grasp the sword of justice and return divine harmony to the world. In that same instant was revealed the truth to him—Lord Folds was seeking to hold captive the soul of England! And where better to begin dominating her mind than the intellectual hub of the universities? Mr. Tonks gave thanks to those deities that had bestowed such an insight upon him, and returned home to celebrate with tea and crumpets.

Mr. Tonks had correctly concluded that Martin had been troubled by his experiences at Rylock Wells. As a result, he had thrown himself into academic work with fervour. The world of logic and reason seemed suddenly greatly attractive, free as it was of any hint of bizarre phenomena. Martin still maintained a fleeting curiosity about the esoteric world, but it was now assigned only a footnote in the book of life. He still entertained tender thoughts of Lily—a vision he could never quite forget—but decided romantic notions should be the exclusive province of poets. Almost in defiance of Aphrodite, he flirted with one of two of the female students in his tutorial group.

Term did not officially end until the middle of December, and for Martin the days became interminable. Short in hours they may have been, but his soul felt heavy, as if the world itself lay on his shoulders. The problem that occupied him most was his arrangements for Christmas. He simply could not resign himself to spending the day with his parents. After much soul-searching, he resolved to inform his mother that he was meeting a foreign student in a remote part of Europe, and celebrating the season with her parents. He told himself that the story could be true, as he had befriended a Japanese girl in his tutorial group, but his conscience inevitably still troubled him.

One Saturday morning he conceived the notion of surveying the city before it woke. From Pyms Hill—the highest point in Clinton—he looked down upon the tiled rooftops as they stretched into distance and fading into the dawn haze. When he ventured into the old Medieval centre of Barstowe, every kind of life filled the streets. Those who scurried to work, those who pretended that they were not engaged upon such a vulgar pursuit, all was an endless parade passing before him. Some were purposeful; others appeared to have lost their identity among the crowd.

Individuals obviously intent on marking a mark in the world passed others desirous of concealing their every thought. Men marched as if going to war, women sauntered as if leisure was their domain, and often the roles were reversed. Sadness, joy, despair—all was written in the faces that Martin observed. Occasionally he would catch the eye of someone then the moment would just as quickly pass.

He left the old city and ventured beyond the narrow, cobbled streets. Here lay towers of pressed concrete, at once proclaiming their own reality. Humanity seemed oppressed by the unrelenting greyness and gangs of narrow-eyed youths and dough faced girls glared at him as he passed. Martin kept to the way not daring to venture into the alleys that yawned on either side of him. Did he imagine the inviting glitter there?

Martin, realising his wanderings had lasted several hours, went into a cafe seeking sustenance. Blasted by the sound of a radio, the shouts of customers, and a curious wave of heat from behind the counter, he waited awkwardly in a queue. After ordering a pie that he saw in a Perspex case, he hurried outside, realising his mistake as he bit into something grey and suspiciously rubbery. Without thinking he hurled the pie into the gutter, narrowly missing a passer-by. Martin fled to the sanctuary of a patch of grass hosting a few broken benches and masquerading as a park. There he sat until dusk saw him returning to the more familiar surroundings of the streets of Clinton. The Moon rose early, and a ghostly disc high in the heavens stared down upon him. He thought of Anton and some of the things he had said. Martin was not to know that Anton was no longer upon the planet.

10

Quite why Mandy had been attracted to Florin Farish was a mystery to all, particularly among those in Rylock Wells. Love they say is blind, and that her suitor was so obviously a knave—and not even a plausible one—was apparent to everyone but the besotted barmaid. The gelled hair, leather jacket and shiny jogging trousers repelled many, and Florin always wore black, accentuating his secretive nature. Calculating, involved with his own nefarious business, and not particularly affectionate, he still possessed the qualities Mandy thought she needed. Not one to expect devotion, and she would probably have grown impatient with a swooning swain, the aloof Florin fitted the bill perfectly. With intemperate speed Mandy convinced herself she loved him deeply, this made her as helpless as a jelly fallen out of its mould

When she was alone Mandy saw nothing but visions of bridesmaids and bouquets, and heard no other sound except wedding bells. Other suitors had begged for her hand over the years and Mandy had ignored them, but when Florin had almost indifferently pledged his troth at closing time one night, she had eagerly accepted.

Women will put up with a great deal from their men folk in order to avoid being marooned upon the shifting sands of doubt. Commitment brings with it a sense of belonging. Mandy had always been content in the company of her friends, tolerating their vagaries and inconsistencies, but she knew it was never quite enough. From the moment she had acknowledged the existence of men she had sought a permanent union. Over the years the prospect had seemed as likely as two tides at opposite ends of the world rising at the same hour. Either her lovers did not notice her moods, or they ignored them, none ever anticipated her needs. Florin had appeared in her life at one of those moments when Mandy felt a desperate need to relate to another, and thus had chosen the rascally Florin Farish.

Thursday was her night off, and she and Florin had taken a cab into Barstowe. Mandy resigned herself to accepting that the entire evening would be at her expense, as her partner never seemed to have any ready funds. They went into Clinton and, discovering the *Pizza Internationale*, established themselves in one of the tiny booths near the window. Not that the view was particularly prepossessing—a Tosscos and a drab store selling carpets. Mandy was determined to enjoy herself and had gone to a lot of trouble with her accessories—the colour of her mobile matched her earrings. She was slightly resentful that Florin did not compliment her on her appearance, but she let this pass.

When the waiter appeared Florin ordered a Pepperoni and Mandy a Venus Special, attempting to be coy when she said it. Conversation flagged after that, even after more than a few sips of the Vino Licarta. Her companion seemed deliberately distant and Mandy finally broke into the silence.

"What's the matter with you tonight? Is something wrong?"

"Nothing. What d'you mean?"

His tone was almost belligerent.

"I just wondered if you were worried about anything that's all ..."

Florin was immediately defensive.

"No ..."

Mandy smiled.

"That's alright then."

He looked at her.

"There is something I want to know about though ..."

Thinking this was a prelude to a romantic moment, Mandy was enticing.

"What's that, sweetheart?"

Mandy went to take his hand, but he did not respond.

"What happened to that book?"

Mandy immediately blushed.

"What? What book?"

"The one Clifford found over by the stones and gave to you in the pub ..."

Florin was staring at her in a way Mandy didn't like. She tried to be casual.

"Oh ... that ..."

"So what did you do with it?"

His voice was harsh, and she was suddenly reminded of the tone Lord Folds had used.

"I ... I ... gave it to somebody."

Florin paused.

"Who?"

Mandy was now thoroughly confused.

"Does it matter? Why are you asking me about all this?"

The tone was unforgiving.

"Because I wanna know, Mandy."

He said her name in the way a policeman would, fear came rushing at her in waves.

"I … I … gave it to Lily."

Florin didn't say anything, just sat back, a strange expression on his face. At that moment the pizzas arrived, but when the wheel of dough was put in front of her, Mandy didn't seem to have any appetite.

Since the Eighties, Ollie had developed a pathological dislike of English pubs. Once they represented much that he found attractive about England. Charming, welcoming and unassuming like an old friend, that was how he remembered them. Since the majority had been refurbished into a caricature of themselves, Ollie had avoided them.

Perched on the brow of Spencer Hill, he just about tolerated *The Blue Badger*. Not that he had ever been a regular there. Ollie had a horror of personally engraved tankards and a barman who said 'The Usual?' To Ollie, that sort of carrying on was in the same league as washing the car at precisely eleven o'clock on Sunday morning, then mowing the lawn afterwards—just in time for lunch.

Intent on having a quiet drink before making his way the Department Christmas Party, Ollie wandered into *The Blue Badger* just before six o' clock. The usual crowd—a smattering of students who hadn't yet left for the Home Counties and a few locals—

occupied the benches round about. As he approached the bar Ollie was aware of a swaying figure in front of him. Suddenly thrown into profile, the features were eminently recognizable—Mick Benson—most definitely the worse for wear.

"Lo, Ollie …"

"Hi, Mick."

Ollie had not seen his friend since before his outing with Trencham. Recalling the details of that encounter, he wondered if Mick's catatonic state was not somehow connected. When he eventually spoke, however, it was the shortcomings of his colleagues in the English Department that appeared to warrant his displeasure.

"Post-ironic! *A greater ironic distance than irony* … What does it mean? Total crap! Charlatans! Clowns … with their power-point piffle! Foucault! Fuck off Foucault! Dumbo Derrida! Nabokov the Nob! Wankers, all of 'em …"

Temporarily running out of steam, Mick subsided. Ollie tried to ascertain just what had prompted Mick to castigate his colleagues so vehemently. Ollie somehow remembered that the English Department had held their end of session meeting earlier in the day. Had this become acrimonious, for some reason? He knew Mick saw those who supported the principles of critical theory, deconstruction and post-structuralism as orcs and the spawn of Mordor. Whatever it was it seemed that Mick had been driven to seek solace in the bottle, resulting in his present over-refreshed condition.

"It won't really matter what bollocks Derek Mint

and Bob Bride come out with in their *post-modernist* seminars soon will it? When the crunch comes they won't know what's hit 'em. Oh ... yes ... they're so smug now because they think they're going to get something out of it ... they won't I can tell you ... they been sold down the river ... all of 'em."

Ollie got straight to the nub, or at least where he thought that item might be located.

"So this is what's happening in the corridors of power then?"

Mick considered the question, as an astronaut might survey an alien landscape.

"Zandra Croop. Come across her?"

"Oh ... yes ... the 'Exterior Academic Advisor' ..."

Mick smiled, without mirth.

"She's gone up a rank or two ... 'Executive Coordination' is her title now ... authorized by Senate last week."

"But ... who is she? That's what keeps puzzling me ... I've never heard of her ..."

"You wouldn't. She's a nobody ..."

Ollie was incredulous.

"But ... she must have the same background as the rest of the staff ... or at least some University Management qualification. Where did she study?"

Mick was adamant.

"*Nowheresville* is the answer to that. The *University of Gresham* ... and it doesn't exist ... except on line. The actual place is simply a rather unprepossessing suburb of Portland, Oregon. No ... this is one of those web sites where if you a pay a thousand dollars ... then ... *Hey Presto* back comes a degree. You print off the smart looking attachment that comes with your email and that's it … you're qualified."

"I don't believe it …"

Mick merely grunted.

"Your Dick Trencham is in on this too … right up to his neck … and beyond …"

After all this speechifying, Mick decided he needed more refreshment. He made a valiant effort to remain upright as he tried to extract his wallet from an inside pocket. The exercise proved more difficult than he realised. Eventually he succeeded, but in the process scattered money, credit cards, and undoubtedly important papers, at his feet. Unbelieving, he stared at the carnage. One or two of the clientele, hearing the clatter, smiled ruefully, while the barman eyed Mick tolerantly—for the moment. Ollie hardly noticed. He had been deliberating while all this was going on.

"So what *is* Dick up to?"

Mick was recovering his possessions, stuffing them randomly in his pockets.

"He's Lord Folds' agent … gofer … whatever you want to call it."

Ollie wondered if anything he heard about Dick at the moment could be good.

"So … what I want to know is how Dick … once upon a time a perfectly decent bloke … and the V.C. it seems … are playing into the hands of this …"

"Toe rag? He might be a lord … but he's only one of Tony Blair's off-the-peg honours. No … what is comes down to is *dosh* … loads of it …"

"Has he got that much of a fortune?"

"Folds is pretty well-off … big place up in

Yorkshire and married into money ... but the real deal is his dodgy contacts ... and let me tell you ... he's mega-bent."

"Really?"

"Yanks mostly ... and Saudi oil money ..."

"I thought America was in big trouble with its economy right now ..."

"Doesn't affect you if you're money-laundering does it? Raking in tax-free income *and* counterfeiting your own currency as well. Folds has got an in with at least $15 trillion in funny-money ... plus the Saudi Oil ... and Chinese offshore investments. With that lot anyone could buy half the world."

Ollie agreed.

"No wonder Senate are eating out of his hand. But what I don't understand is this ... why the big interest in Barstowe? What's the big attraction? If he's that much of a crook there must be other things he could get involved in ... heroin ... porn ... I can't see how Higher Education is that lucrative as a racket."

Mick thought further about this—his heroic intake of alcohol causing him to take some time.

"That's what I don't know ... and I don't know any way I can find out either."

"No ... probably not."

With that Mick's thoughts drifted off into other areas. Surprisingly, or maybe not, these were on literary lines.

"Keep thinking about what Swift would have said ... but he was completely mad ... I'm sure. Then so many of them were ... weren't they? Virginia Woolf ... Poe ... the Brontes ..."

Encouraging this thesis in a half-hearted fashion, Ollie offered a few suggestions.

"Blake ... John Clare. Coleridge ... getting that way certainly."

Mick had reached that stage of drunkenness where he was intently staring at nothing in particular, but still capable of contributing to the conversation.

"Philip. K. Dick."

"Absolutely. Mustn't forget him."

"Maybe ... maybe ... lots of drugs ..."

"Quite possibly. Let's see ... Hunter Thompson."

"Oho ... ah, yes ... yes, indeed ... I should say."

Ollie, his drink finished, decided to act promptly.

"You off home now then, Mick?"

Several synapses, the ones that were still successfully connected, endeavoured to process the enquiry.

"Yeah."

Mick stared at his glass on the bar—a full pint, hardly touched. He shook his head laconically. They made their way to the door, amid a few farewells—some good-hearted, others expressing a profound relief at Mick's departure.

Once outside, the chill air seemed to revive Mick a little. Ollie was also aware that Mick's flat was only a short distance away. He was confident that, apart from any real act of malice by Dame Fortune, no harm would befall Mick on his return home. They stood together briefly on the pavement. A lone cyclist passed them, pedaling athletically up Spencer Hill.

"Cheerio, Ollie."

"Night, Mick. Happy Christmas. Take care of yourself."

Jollifications had been underway for around an hour or so when Ollie arrived at the Department Christmas Party. A muted hub-bub guided him in the direction of the orgy. In recent years, there had been often been doubt whether the Departmental junket would even be held at all. This year the custom of being greeted on arrival with a glass of champagne was notably absent. In former times, the catering staff had passed among the guests with trays of delicacies and constantly refilled one's glass. Now there was only an unseemly scrum to get at whatever booze and nosh were available. A plethora of soft drinks, outnumbering the cans of the cheapest lager, and wine-in-a-box, told the whole story. In these circumstances, unrestrained drinking was not only tacitly discouraged, but would have been logistically impossible.

Certainly a low-key affair, looking round, Ollie also detected a sourness in the atmosphere. Individuals were eying each other suspiciously and Trencham was definitely trying to hide in a corner, not venturing forth into the fray. The lack of any conversation was partially alleviated when some sort of music started up. Jack Filch, who happened to be standing next to Ollie, began pumping his elbows in an arrhythmic manner. Lucy regarded her colleague with a mixture of amusement and disbelief at this oasis of spontaneous jollity. Ollie distinctly had the feeling that battle lines were being laid in the Department, if not the whole university, and it would be a long and bloody conflict that was impending.

In the North of England, the weather was not the same as that bestowed upon the effete southerner. Beyond the window of Folds' office, snowflakes the size of fried eggs tumbled over each other in the sky. Score shivered involuntarily at intervals and prayed he would be able to return to Birmingham later that day.

"Florin called, my lord ... to say he was going to getting you another book ... better than the last one he said ..."

Folds seemed partly appeased.

"Yes ... alright. Good for him ... though I'm more interested in teaching this bloody little cow in Rylock Wells a lesson for pinching the other one. I was right that barmaid knew where the book was ... and Florin told you she gave it some other little hippie whore ... did he? That place is getting on my nerves ... I'd shoot every bloody one of them if I had my way. What they did to my car ..."

There was a knock at the door. Not waiting for a response, a figure glided into the room. Score, who had not encountered Stibs Gulley until this moment, could only stare in amazement. Folds, not so easily fazed, was still taken aback. In a black robe and, despite the cold, open-toed sandals, the priest looked around briefly before finally acknowledging the company.

"Lord Folds ... and ..."

"Royston Score ... my assistant ... he's just about to leave ..."

Score, relieved to be dismissed began to mutter.

"Yes ... must make my way back to the Midlands ... before this weather really sets in ... I hope everything will be alright on the M6 ... that's the worst bit ..."

A silence even colder than the air outside greeted his words and, grabbing his briefcase and coat from a hook, Score hurried out. This left Folds with his extraordinary visitor. Unbidden, Gulley settled himself in a chair and unflinchingly regarded his host. Folds returned his gaze.

"Lemme ask you somethin', Lord Folds ... how far are you prepared to go in order to gain ultimate power?"

Folds responded bluntly.

"I already have a great deal of power ... more than most people ..."

Gulley made a dismissive gesture.

"That's earthly dominion yer talkin' about ... baubles and bubbles. I'm talkin' here about the ultimate authority in the universe ..."

Folds was logical.

"I thought only God had that?"

Gulley smiled secretly.

"Oh ... there is one greater than Him ..."

"Tell me more ..."

"The guy who defied Him ..."

"Satan?"

Gulley put his finger to his lips.

"Speak his holy name with reverence, My Lord ... please!"

Folds regarded his visitor, not without a modicum of suspicion.

"So ... what are we talking about here? Devil

worship? Black magic?"

Gulley laughed, not a pleasant sound.

"Those are just the words of fools ... *I* am speaking of The Dark One in all his great majesty."

Despite his inner scepticism, Folds was keen to hear more. Any road that might lead to success he took, no matter where it came from.

"This sounds like the same sort of thing that our Cattermog comes up with ..."

Gulley interrupted, his sneer making Elvis look like an amateur.

"Hicks! That jerk! He's an actor ... a goddam amateur. I've forgotten more about the ways of The King of Hell than he'll ever know in a dozen lifetimes."

Folds was inclined to provoke his guest a little.

"Really? I thought he was the great expert in these ... circles ..."

Gulley almost spat in his derision.

"He don't know nothin'!"

Folds eyed him.

"And you do ... apparently. So what can *you* do for me that any of the other characters I've met in all this business aren't capable of?"

Gulley paused and put his hands together in a gesture of perverted prayer.

"What is it you *desire* me to do, Lord Folds?"

A few moments passed before any reply was forthcoming.

"There are a few people I want dealt with ... out of the way ..."

Gulley eyes glistened with an infernal light.

"Yes?"

"... one or two of them attached to that bloody university ... but I have ways of handling that riff-raff. I just keep hearing about another interfering little nuisance ... someone called Tonks ... *he* obviously needs to be told where he gets off."

"A piece of work ... huh? An' you want him outa the game?"

Folds was strangely hesitant.

"Yes ... yes ... I do."

Gulley's tone was as rock falling to the depths of a chasm.

"Mandatory ... I'll arrange it ..."

Folds nodded absently, glancing at the whitening landscape as he did so.

"Good."

Gulley's voice was a whisper.

"But yer thinkin' around someone else though ain'tcha ..."

Folds almost jumped.

"Yes I am ... actually. This bloody girl ... who's got my book ..."

"What book's that?"

The enquiry was almost casual.

"*The Garden of Squagbo.*"

"Ah ..."

Gulley was not impressed with Folds' revelation, regarding the volume in question rather as if it was *The Ladybird Book of Sorcery*. He took care, however, not to show his contempt.

"She's part of all that business down there ..."

"That Rylock Wells hang-out?"

"Exactly."

"Aren't you planning on doing another ritual at the Circle there?"

"Yes … another trail run … before …"

Folds stopped himself, no point in revealing everything.

"Lemme put it this way … why not deal with her at the same time as yer doin' yer ceremony … that seems kinda neat."

"Maybe. How would you propose doing that?"

"I can make it so if she's around she won't be able to stop herself going right through that Portal …"

Folds looked at him sharply.

"That's what the last one did … you know about that?"

"Oh … sure. That kinda thing happens all the time. That Portal ain't the only one on this goddam Earth y'know. There's a whole bunch of 'em … all over the place."

Folds was quick to reply.

"Yes … I knew that."

Gulley was deliberating.

"I knew this dumb dame … Philomena … the same one went into that portal and didn't come out again … oh … no. Let's just say I had some dealings with her before you ever saw her. She's the kind of chick that's very easy to persuade … to do anything …"

Folds looked away in mild disgust. He didn't want to imagine what Gulley, with or without his smelly robe, got up to.

"So you sent her there?"

"Exactly … and I'll do the same with this other

one. What's her name?"

Folds looked bored, he didn't know why, but he was rapidly growing tired of all this.

"Lily … I think …"

"Okay … I'll do it. But there is one thing I gotta tell you …"

Folds was alert once more.

"What's that?"

"I'm gonna run the show at the Winter Solstice Ritual … not that creep Hicks. He can assist if he wants … but no way is gonna be the magus in this set-up."

Folds shrugged. He did not want to be involved in any occult power struggles. Dealing with any machinations among people was not for him, he was too much of a dictator.

"Suits me. You can take over what's happening if you want. I'll tell Cattermogg … I'm paying him … he'll do what I say. I suppose you'll want a fee too …"

"A little discretionary money would more than welcome right now … yeh."

To Folds' relief his visitor stood up, looking as if he was about to leave. Outside, the snow was falling more heavily by the minute. Gulley surveyed the scene.

"Looks I'll have some kinduvva walk goin' back to the Priory …"

"You will … I should get on with it if I were you."

Gulley surveyed the skies.

"Nothin' ever bothers me. Magic is trippin' yer own trigger, man."

Folds agreed absently.

"If you say so."

Without another word Gulley flung open the door of the reception and strode off. Folds watched his disappearing figure, black against a whiteness now almost blinding in its intensity. The symbolism of the spectacle did not register in his unconscious. Nor did it occur to Lord Folds that by aligning his dark side with one who was almost exclusively malevolent, the universe would not easily forgive him.

11

Mr. Tonks always felt at home in the surrounds of Barstowe Library. The Reference Section, its marble pillars bestriding the alcoves, the comfortable chairs, had been home to him for countless hours in the past. Now he was welcomed once again, like an old friend. Even the books on the shelves seemed to exude warmth toward him. Mr. Tonks always mouthed a silent prayer for the staff member who had enough foresight in the 1960s to realise that the library's *Paranormal* collection was probably unique. Ensuring that it was under lock and key had removed temptation from any light-fingered Satanist and their ilk. On this occasion, however, the library assistant looked perturbed when she returned to Mr. Tonks waiting patiently at the counter.

"I'm dreadfully sorry ... I can't quite understand it ... the book you've requested from stack is missing."

"Really?"

"Yes ... I've hunted high and low ... I would have expected to have found it easily. It's all very odd."

Mr. Tonks mused.

"Perhaps ... not as odd as one might think ..."

"I'm sorry?"

"Nothing ... nothing. If it's not there ... then so be it."

"I do apologise."

"Not your fault at all. Thank you anyway."

Mr. Tonks turned away from the counter and returned to the table where he had left his notes. As he did so he was aware of a figure looking distinctly out of place in the library. Even slacking sixth-form students had some air of purpose about them, this particular person had none. Florin! This was no coincidence—here was the thief and probably still in possession of the swag! Mr. Tonks slowly packed his bag, planning his next move as he did so. A moment later he signalled to a bored looking security guard, who almost gratefully left his post.

"Excuse me ... I don't like to make a fuss ... but that man over there ..."

Mr. Tonks indicated the figure of Florin shuffling between the shelves.

"Yes, sir?"

"He asked me for some money just now ... got quite aggressive when I refused ..."

The man in uniform looked more than interested.

"Begging is most definitely against Library Rules ... I'll go and have a word with him, sir. Thank you for informing me."

Florin quickly made for the exit, but the guard was now on a mission.

"Excuse me, sir. I'd like a word ..."

Florin panicked and ran hither and thither. Over went a chair with a crash that echoed through the whole library. Students looked up from their dissertations, researchers appeared peeved. Florin bumped into a large woman librarian, slipped on the polished floor and skidded into a heap next to the photocopier. Several folios fell from a shelf above, tumbled onto him—all was pandemonium. When he had fallen a small, dark volume shot from beneath his leather jacket and landed at the feet of Mr. Tonks. He stealthily picked it up. Florin was now engaged in a heated conversation with several security guards and Mr. Tonks went to the counter. He requested that the book be issued to him.

Minutes later he made his way down the library steps and into the street, mingling with the crowds that massed about the cathedral. When he returned on the bus to Conkerville an email was waiting from Martin hoping to arrange a meeting at The Robe. Mr. Tonks smiled to himself—Martin had rejoined the cast. Mr. Tonks made himself a pot of tea and cast his eye over the contents of *Thule, Tibet and the Temple of Solomon*, the prize he had captured from Florin. A rare treatise, written in 1940 by one who was later to perish in the Holocaust, all known copies had been burnt by the SS. Somehow a few had survived. Mr. Tonks could now clearly see the methods Folds' intended to apply in his schemes, all had now fallen into place.

The principle was almost too simple—find the intrinsic code possessed by every kind of natural object, construct a calculation to combine those elements and you have control of every aspect of the world. Those who served in King Solomon's Temple believed they had the keys to such a symbolic system, and so did the SS. An organization calling itself *Zwansig Zwansig*, active when Hitler came to power and heavily influenced by the Thule Society, had inherited this knowledge. This secret society, who combined Old Norse myths and a belief in the supremacy of the Aryan race, had also systematically seized the Qabalistic treasures of Jewish scholars.

Along with any other occult treatises they could lay their hands on, its members had set about conducting rituals solely in pursuit of world domination.

They were aided in their evil pursuit not only by the Gematria, but by the Swastika itself, a symbol of Thor, the Norse God of Thunder and its German equivalent –*Donner*. Hitler too made much of the notion of *Vril*, the power allegedly owned by earth spirits. A chapter on *Agharti*—a subterranean land beneath the Gobi Desert—took the attention of Mr. Tonks. It all fitted into place! This was why Lord Folds centered his activities around Rylock Wells— here must be an entrance to this world. When he read that the members of Zwansig Zwansig had been convinced that the Aryan race came from Asia, and they were in contact with an exiled group of Tibetan Necromancers calling themselves Lodge 99 all was revealed to Mr. Tonks.

The reputation as a portal into the Otherworld had been known to the initiated for some thousands of years, almost since the monoliths had been erected in Neolithic times. Tonks was also certain that Folds, being no occultist, had only a superficial understanding of the power of Rylock Wells. He was correct in thinking that its network of subterranean passages, existing both in the material and the ethereal planes, formed a network that extended to the furthest corner of the kingdom, but that was only part of the story. The knowledge had attracted Folds, and he had surmised that by somehow directing magical power into this endless labyrinth he could control the very substance of nature. That was all very well, but there was an aspect of the stone circle and its Portal of which he was ignorant, Mr. Tonks was certain.

Beyond the portal lay—not just one, but *three* separate worlds—all existing on separate planes. It was possible to pass between them, and if the traveller was resolute, and perhaps fortunate, he would be able to return to the ordinary world. But beyond the Portal, the gods and goddesses who have authority over mortals exercise their will, for this is part of their domain. Mr. Tonks recalled the words he had first read when he delved into the esoteric tradition of Rylock Wells. Telling they were:

"Once any enter into Twyfin ... the first world they encounter ... they manifest an entirely separate personality ... one reflecting the dark side of their nature. Those who have a pure heart may pass into the other lands—Golbellen -the Land of Light and Gwallyog—the Place of Unreason. Those who have the making of evil as their intention will never pass beyond the borders of this first gloomy kingdom."

The month of December brought frosts and, upon the highways, mirrors of ice. Only by showing valiant resolve did Martin journey to Rylock Wells. A few hardy souls among the locals had braved the weather, but patrons were few in the Robe. Even Old Ted was absent, preferring to doze at home. Mr. Tonks was in evidence—as always looking slightly disheveled. He was one of those men who, even if he was fitted out at great expense in Saville Row, would have still lacked any kind of 'dash'. His coat, of the kind referred to as a 'British Warm', hung on a peg, the rest of the Tonks outfit being a Norfolk jacket, and a pair of trousers not recognizable as being of any style, or from any period.

Martin felt slightly awkward on being reunited with Mr. Tonks. Although he had recovered his faith, as he liked to think of it, he still experienced a twinge of guilt. Mr. Tonks, however, was at once all joy and gaiety.

"My dear boy ... how splendid to see you once more. And what have you been up to?"

Martin was hesitant but honest.

"Actually ... I've been trying to work out how I felt about certain things ..."

"Ah ... the great mystery of mysteries ..."

Martin shrugged.

"I suppose so ... although that all sounds a bit far-fetched now."

Mr. Tonks smiled comfortably.

"Mmm ... better to be a romantic than a cynic ..."

Martin was inclined to be impatient.

"Shouldn't one just be sensible? Although I know that sounds awfully boring ...

"Pragmatic perhaps ... but never dismissive. Sneering at the wonder and miracles that are most definitely to be found in the world ... that would never do."

Martin suddenly thought of Lily, not with the usual wistful air but with a certain anxiety. He continued with his confessions to Mr. Tonks.

"Sometimes I don't know how I feel about anything ... that makes me feel pretty fed up."

"Ah ... the darkness of doubt. We must all experience that ... although one eventually concludes that such an exercise is all rather pointless. Ananke— the mother of the Fates—having her own agenda you know ..."

Martin deliberated; he had embraced reason to an inordinate degree in the last few weeks and was not going to give up without a struggle.

"But surely we ought to ask questions?"

"Indeed ... always best to do so ... as long as we accept there are no real answers."

"Not even what makes good and evil ... for instance?"

Even though as a Philosophy student he had studied the great ethical questions to an inordinate degree, the whole business still bothered him from time to time.

"It is not The Devil who perpetrates evil it is man. The universe does not comprehend duality, Martin ... only that all things exist."

"But surely we make choices ..."

"If we do not ... they are made for us ... and it is our destiny to know both light and dark. How can we know them ... or discriminate between them if they are unfamiliar to us?"

Martin recalled his recent observations in Windleroot.

"I wasn't sure which was which there ..."

Mr. Tonks' looked interested.

"Ah ... yes ... Windleroot ... the Isle of Teflon ... not somewhere I have been for ages. I was a regular pilgrim there in the 1960s ... quite a devotee. I'm sure it was very different then ... only a few *eccentrics* like myself. It is now a New Age Disneyland I'm told."

"Worse than that ..."

"Oh ... that's a shame ... though I suppose some things have remained the same. The Dallas Well ... Windleroot Nob ... Blearyballs Hill ..."

Martin shook his head.

"... and all swarming with Japanese tourists ... and would-be witches in velvet cloaks they've just gone and bought in Lowe Street."

Mr. Tonks sighed.

"Dear ... oh ... dear ... has it come to that?"

Martin returned to the here and now.

"And how are your researches on the stone circle here?"

Mr. Tonks looked conspiratorial.

"There is a phenomenal amount of activity in the solar system at the moment, Martin ... it's all quite extraordinary."

Martin was puzzled.

"And that's connected with the stones?"

"All things are *connected*, Martin ... the microcosm and the macrocosm ... 'as above so below' ... as the old magi never tired of telling their neophytes. I don't know if you are familiar with *quasars*?"

Martin went for looking intelligent, and was successful.

"Umm ..."

"A group of stars ... held together by the energy from a black hole ..."

Martin pounced.

"Oh ... yes ... I've heard of those ..."

"Well ... one has just been discovered that is many millions of light years wide ... some scientists say it has no business to exist ..."

Martin tried hard to grapple with the idea of the biggest thing in the universe not actually being there. Was it like Birmingham not actually being at the end of the M5?

"Really?"

"Yes ... it's always been assumed that existence is uniform ... relatively I mean ... so something that size ... we're told by the boffins ... couldn't exist."

"So ... what does this amount to ... for ... ?"

Mr. Tonks smiled.

"Everyone here on the planet? Not much ... except ... I'm certain the magnetic impulses it gives off are affecting the circle ..."

Martin tried not to stare, unsuccessfully.

"How?"

"By investing the stones with more power."

"How does that happen?"

Mr. Tonks took over as question master.

"Weren't you there at Samhain ... at the ritual?

"Yes ... but ..."

Mr. Tonks looked stern.

"I think you'd better tell me all you saw ..."

"Not a lot really because ... I ... left. I remember someone ... it might have been Philomena ..."

"It was."

"Okay ... well she was walking towards this sort of light ... as if she was hypnotised. There were a lot of people in weird clothes ... sort of encouraging her. I ran for it ... I got really spooked."

Martin looked round, hoping no one else had heard what he had been saying. He need not have been concerned, George the landlord was at the other end of the bar and the few regulars present had wisely congregated around the fire. Mr. Tonks stayed engrossed in his thoughts.

"According to Mandy ... people in the village swear they've seen Philomena but then she disappears and pops up somewhere else later on."

"That's weird ..."

Mr. Tonks looked arch.

"Martin, *most* of what I'm going to tell you will sound rather extraordinary ..."

"Okay"

"First of all ... I'll leave out the occult stuff that came out of Nazi Germany ..."

Martin was relieved, History lessons involving the Third Reich had been more tedious than the speeches of Der Fuehrer himself.

"... and concentrate on the link between the Indonesian Islands and Rylock Wells."

"Really? Is there one?"

"I believe so. Nearly two thousand years ago the country of Malayu was invaded by a King Jayanasa. He was after not only the gold that was there ... but ... *magic power*. I don't think he succeeded ... but it's interesting that the Indonesian version of a wizard is called a *dukun* ... that covers healers ... mediums ... and the rest. Initiates would take part in some ritual ... usually near water ... or on top of a mountain ... the purpose being to communicate with spirits. These are generally benign … but on occasions terrifyingly hostile. They are … as I see it … the guardians of these places. In the same way the stone circle here will have one of these ... maybe several.

Martin raised an inquisitive eyebrow.

"Is that really true?"

"I think it is more than likely. One disturbs these entities at one's peril … and I believe they instinctively know the motive of anyone who approaches the stones. They are particularly responsible for guarding the Portal."

"I remember you said about that … the gateway into another world."

"The Otherworld."

An eyebrow ascended even more.

"Tell me more … I mean … what sort of world is it?"

"Where there is anything and everything … and maybe nothing …"

"You mean …"

Martin began to look anxious, prompting Mr. Tonks to smile.

"I apologise, Martin … I'm being far too enigmatic … it's just rather difficult to speculate upon something that only exists in the universal imagination … if at all. But … it most certainly may be experienced by those who have the power to perceive it … and it is certainly not an empty space. Think of it as place where everything is constantly moving ... the shifting planes of reality …"

Martin was none the wiser.

"Philomena … she's there … permanently?"

"That may be her fate … but I think not. You will journey there Martin … that is destined to be also …"

Martin gazed at the benches, worn tables and the now-familiar prints on the walls—hunting scenes and the gentry in flamboyant dress. He looked for something to hold onto, that would reassure him—a world he knew would remain forever. He wanted a universe that was comfortable, easy, where people would not surprise him, like Mr. Tonks had just done. In his heart he knew it was not to be. All had changed. Was he the plaything of fortune? An actor without a role to play?

"The Winter Solstice is this very day … an opportune moment to consider your future quest."

Martin tried not to stare—unsuccessfully.

"My Quest?

"Beyond the portal … through the Walls of Time and into the three worlds …

Twyfin—the dark … *Golbellen*—The Land of Light … and *Gwallyog* the place of Unreason."

Martin put his face in his hands.

"What? What are you talking about?"

Mr. Tonks persisted.

"You will travel there … only when the time is right … perhaps it will be at *Imbolc* … the first day of February."

"That's more than a month away …"

"There is no sense of time in the Otherworld …"

Martin looked around, somehow expecting to see Lily coming through the door but saw only a half-empty bar looking back at him. He saw a garden with a tailored lawn and trimmed hedges, beds filled with summer flowers. These things he could not take with him if he went upon the Quest. He was aware of Mr. Tonks once more, his words seemeing to echo in his mind.

"There is only really one thing to remember when you are there ..."

"What's that?"

"Anything could happen ..."

Had Martin but known it, Lily was at that very moment leaving the woods and making her way towards the stone circle. She went in search of Philomena. Piles of leaves, broken branches and runnels of water were at her feet. Ropes of ivy hung from the trees tugging at her clothes. As she came into the open a cruel wind cut into her cheeks, and stung her eyes. She floated barefoot over the frozen field, and until she was but a few yards from the portal, she might have been invisible.

Stibbs Gulley sensed her presence, and very deliberately took her hand leading her towards the Portal. She did not protest, but stood motionless before the entrance to the Otherworld waiting. Gulley let go his grip and faded into the shadows with the rest of those who were gathered for the ritual. For a moment all was still, time had ceased to be, the universe motionless. It was at that moment Folds chose to act, seizing the chalice from Cattermogg Hicks he ran forward and threw its contents over Lily, muttering ugly words as he did so. She did not flinch, as the holy water ran over her.

Thus was Lord Folds' plan—to imprison Lily in a cage of crystal ice within the Otherworld. He had called upon the spirit of water to aid him, for it was that very element Folds wished ultimately to control. Every emotion—even life itself—resided within water. Once he could master the glistening liquid that lay within the earth he would have power over the land and nothing could prevent his conquest of the entire kingdom. This was his gesture of power and domination! The one who had defied him would now be captive for all eternity. In the eyes of Lord Folds, she deserved this punishment, and he would show her no mercy.

Stibbs Gulley was as amazed as the rest who had witnessed this tableau, but before they could react, more was to come. The Portal was now lit with silver light, so intense that none could look upon it, the silhouette of Lily was visible for an instant before it disappeared and the light slowly dimmed. At last Folds could open his eyes and when he did so could only stare at the circle of stones about him. They all seemed to grow in size and strength and he fell back before them. The spirits therein were angry! Gulley, who had witnessed all manner of demons and darkness at one time or another knew when he was defeated. He gathered up his robe and quickly strode away, the others in his wake, all stumbling and running across the grass. Folds was the last to leave, though his fear was as great, if not more so than the rest.

Lily although she was in utter darkness was still aware of an endless stream flowing over her, even within her. She became as one with this silver tide, until the rain became as ice and snow. Before terror could become part of her conscious self, she became frozen—part of an immobile glacier. Her eyes were open but unaware, her mind locked in a world without time or hope. To the universe she had embraced death in the icy wastes, although some part of her had not. Lily knew of her purpose, to search for her friend Philomena and to bring her back to her own world. She was also convinced that she still existed—that she was aware was enough to convince her of that. She nurtured hope in her heart and, even in the obsidian darkness, a speck of light was kindled. Lily offered a silent prayer of thanks as it continued to shine.

One of the many absurdities in our thinking is the notion of misplaced time. An event occurs that we wished had happened either before or later than it did. It is a meaningless to suppose that anything happens at the wrong moment, all comes into being when it is right to do so. Those swirling invisible currents that determine our lives are not random, they are determined by Creation. The infinite power of the universe decides what shall be, in all things.

12

A meeting between the Senior Management Operations Group and the University Senior Management
Committee was to take place at the end of January.
Usually a somnolent affair, the current air of unease
made the occasion seem more than significant for
those who would attend. In what had once been
a grand Victorian drawing room, Mick Benson
and Norton Bradley took their places. The latter—
Professor of English—had a robust look about him
and, encountered in some country lane, he would
more than likely to have been taken for a farmer. The
rubicund cheeks and a Busby of curls were simply
begging for a tweed hat to nestle among them. Fearnley
Wilmot, senior lecturer in Ollie's department, stared
ahead of him. A visible mass of lines on his forehead,
etched like Pick-A-Stix, told of endless wrestling with
abstruse concepts. His immense beard, reputed to be
modeled on that of Rasputin, stood out at angles in
front of him.

If Willie Slate and Fred Bingley-Brass had assumed
the assembled company would accept the agenda they
were about to present without a murmur, they were
grossly mistaken. Mick, Bradley, and Wilmot did not
intend to let Senate, or Council, ride roughshod over
them in the matter of decision making. All three had
independently sensed this was the first skirmish in
a hard campaign and, if they did not win the day, at
least they would go down fighting. Under the watchful
eye of Zandra Croop, Bingley Brass got proceedings
underway in his usual bluff manner.

"I've really called us together ... this community of scholars ... to clarify certain issues about future policy for our university ... particularly in the seminal areas of finance and academic disciplines. Put simply ... we're talking about ways to make Barstowe more viable ... not only as an educational concern ... but as an economic unit. Some of us might even think that the two issues are in no way connected ... but as our present situation proves ... they very much are."

Some predictable muttering greeted all this.

"Now ... we are all aware of the crisis in funding that Barstowe University is currently facing ... and it has been my ... rather onerous task ... along with Willie here ... to find an answer to this ever-increasing problem. The good news is ... that we have succeeded."

Bingley-Brass paused, perhaps anticipating cheers, or even jiving in the aisles. Instead, an awkward silence met his words. Wariness was apparent even among those who were known to invariably support the Vice-Chancellor. A similar response came from those who rarely saw eye-to-eye with his policies, this group manifesting an even more tangible suspicion. When Bingley-Brass continued, it was with markedly less confidence. Willie Slate, all too aware of what was coming next, was seen to shuffle uncomfortably.

"The proposals ... and I realise that some of you may find you may have a ... a ... strong reaction to all this ... are far-reaching. I would suggest that we all remain calm when confronting this ... rather radical scheme ..."

Fearnley-Wilmot coughed loudly and the sound —like a pistol shot—resonated through the lecture hall. In the up-to-date buildings on the campus any trace of an echo would have been muffled. In this high-ceilinged space, the ripples of sound continued for a considerable time before fading away. The effect was to heighten the tension in the room, so that every nuance in the Vice-Chancellors' voice was magnified tenfold.

"There are two main objectives to be achieved here ... and I would strongly advise all those on Council to accept them for reasons which should be all too obvious ... *and* I would also ask for the fullest support from non-committee members ... a total restructuring of funding ... and ... a complete overhaul of academic procedures."

This was greeted with, not only a volley of rhubarb from the Operations Group, but remarks from other quarters that were easily discernible as hostile. Bingley-Brass waited for some moments before resuming, his tone now bordering on the truculent.

"Because of the serious nature of our financial affairs ... on behalf of us all ... I had to make a decision ... it was inevitable that a drastic solution was required. Both Willie Slate and our pro-vice chancellors have ... and I can assure you of this ... looked at the problem from every angle. The only workable solution that presents itself is for the entire administration of Barstowe University both financial and academic to be put in the hands of an outside agency."

Bingley-Brass delivered the last words in a rush then sat back in his chair. He removed his glasses with a gesture reminiscent of man who has just surrendered his country to the enemy. Whether Mick

Benson had even registered that allusion was unlikely, his reaction was more volatile than considered. His voice was raised in uncontrollable anger.

"That's a bloody disgrace! You should be ashamed of yourself for even *thinking* of saying that to all of us here ... you *traitor!*"

Uproar did not greet this outburst, more a discordant jumble of voices. Some were obviously critical of Benson, while others made noises that could have been approval. This seemed to go on for some time while Bingley-Brass sat rigid, in silence. He seemed unwilling to move or even communicate with those on either side of him. The distinctive voice of Fearnley Wilmot was suddenly heard; it had a particular timbre, one not easily ignored.

"Vice-Chancellor ... I am assuming that any proposal you might present to us this afternoon is hardly *fait accompli*. But I think it would help if you could briefly outline the nature of these changes. That would seem to be the most helpful course ... and lessen any further confusion."

At first Bingley-Brass seemed to be shaking his head as if he were not prepared to do this, but a whispered conference between him and Slate prompted him to address the meeting once more. It was noticeable that his voice now sounded strained with emotion.

"I have been in conference recently with Lord Folds ..."

At this, Benson began to whistle and wheeze like a traction engine. Norton Bradley laid a restraining hand on his arm, and he gradually subsided.

"... and I must say his offer is more than generous ... better than I could ever have hoped for. With a guaranteed investment in the area of the figures we discussed ... Barstowe would be more than restored to the prominent position that it once enjoyed in the academic hierarchy of universities in this country."

A few 'hear hears' greeted this mainly from those sat nearest to Bingley-Brass. Naturally, the loudest came from Slate. Somewhat heartened by this, the Vice-Chancellor regained some of his previous aplomb.

"Naturally ... Lord Folds has ideas of his own as to how to maximise his investment. He is ... after all ... a business man and ... in the world of commerce efficiency and productivity reign supreme. It is only fair that we should make his task easier ... see his point of view. As an institution ... we should be prepared to make certain concessions to a style of management that is in keeping with the sound economic principles of the twenty-first century."

Benson muttered 'bollocks' under his breath.

"Lords Folds has presented me a very comprehensive ... and I must say ... very impressive and well thought-out document as to how he envisages Barstowe being run in the future. We've formed a Senate sub-committee to discuss this document in depth ... and that body will be issuing a report as soon as we've discussed the major issues involved."

Bingley-Brass paused, then adopted a statesman like pose.

"I have to say that I truly believe this is the way ahead for our university. I know there may be a few dissenting voices in our midst ... that's bound to happen in any true democracy ... but believe me ... we are most fortunate to have the support of so munificent a sponsor as Lord Folds. He is really our saviour ... and a man who genuinely has the interests of Barstowe University ... and everyone in it ... at heart."

When this produced a spontaneous round of applause, neither Bradley nor Wilmot joined in, and Benson sat shaking his head in total disbelief. Others in the Operations Group looked confused or slightly forlorn. It was plain what had happened, Bingley-Brass had speedily, and comprehensively, swayed the opinion of the meeting his way. He held the field, and he knew it. Pip Driver—a smallish, bald article in a shiny suit—had been sitting on the other side of the Vice-Chancellor from Slate. As if on cue, he began to speak.

"First of all ... I'd like to thank the Vice-Chancellor for so comprehensively and ... if I may so ... so *courageously* ... informing members of Council the new policies that we *may* adopt in the near future. I for one am in total support ... in principle ... of the changes ... and I would wholeheartedly endorse the Vice-Chancellor in his view that we should be eternally grateful that such a fortuitous opportunity has presented itself to us. Frankly ... we would be most foolish to ignore this most generous offer from Lord Folds. No matter what reorganization or changes may have to take place at Barstowe to incorporate these new ... and I'm certain ... excellent ideas will ultimately pay enormous dividends."

This was too much for Benson who, throwing back his chair with a clatter left the room. This did not cause quite the stir it might have done. Driver, his tie flapping like a wilting tulip simply nodded at the retreating figure. Anything else that might have occurred would simply have been an anti-climax, but Bingley–Brass had not finished yet. There was one more announcement left to make.

"In addition to open-handedly presenting us with his ideas ... Lord Folds has generously organized a presentation for us. I urge all of you who are in any doubt as to the details of his proposals attend this. The presenter will be our own Zandra Croop ..."

A measured smile came from this quarter.

"... and she will at this event enlighten you all as to every aspect of our project. This will take place in the morning of March the Third. I'd like you all to be there ... I know it will be beneficial."

The Vice-Chancellor briefly surveyed his audience, left the dais and exited through a door at the back of the room. Slate, awkwardly clutching a heap of files, and smoothing back his hair with the other hand, hurried along behind him. Gradually, the rest of the company filed out of the main door, all except Wilmot who continued to stare at an empty room, almost in disbelief. His immense intellect pondered on the realization that finally bad feeling, jealousy and superiority were the paramount emotions in an institution he had once regarded as an august seat of learning.

He was aware that academic success had long been measured only in the size of a research grant or the sales of a text book, but this coming move was more comprehensive in its implications. With the advent of those such as Lord Folds, no longer were those who supported higher education from a class of patricians, scholars or gentlemen. The minds that now ordered the academic world would from now on be unfailingly small and mean. With the demise of original thinking, what would inevitably follow would be the tearing and rending of the soft flesh of debate and democracy.

Although Ollie had not been present at the Senior Management meeting, both Mick and Wilmot offered him their own version of what had transpired. The former's account, delivered in the Blue Badger the following day, was redolent with passion; the latter's more incisive and measured. Both versions, however, illustrated dramatically the zeitgeist of the University. Ollie was most perturbed by the news, and the inevitable discord had a habit of causing tempers to ignite around the Department. He was not at his most accommodating when it came to dealing with either colleagues, or his tutorial group.

Ollie wondered if it was ever possible for any two people to completely understand each other, in any circumstances. Philosophy was often a study of truth and misrepresentation—just how a belief could be regarded as totally erroneous. The lengths to which people would go to prove the viability of some pet notion was staggering. Wasn't this too a microcosm of what happened every day when two people interacted? Parents and children, lovers, friends—all vying for the prize of knowing they were right. The amount of effort expended upon such a course was ridiculous. Powering windmills might well have been a more sensible idea. A demonstration of such a thesis was never far away, such as during one fractious nine o'clock tutorial.

"Really, Eleanor … that is totally unbelievable you could think that …"

"I shan't be asking your permission for what I think about, Toby …"

Ollie felt he had to curb these outspoken sentiments and did so with as much grace as he could muster, but it was a close-run thing. As he was collecting up books and papers he found Martin standing there, a bemused expression on his face.

"I thought they might have a scrap … didn't you?"

Ollie smiled, more with relief than anything else.

"Hormonal levels high this afternoon would you say? You're probably a better judge of these things than I am …"

Martin laughed.

"Through the roof … *Second Term Second Year Angst* … they tell me. Smack bang in the middle of one's course …"

Ollie closed his briefcase.

"You're probably right. Oh … something I meant to ask you, Martin."

"Mmm?"

"Did you ever get to do any more research with that very interesting Polish chap you met … ?"

Martin shook his head.

"Fraid not. Actually … he died. It wasn't very long ago I heard about it."

Ollie looked serious, any mention of Death notoriously having such an effect on the living.

"Oh … I'm sorry to hear that."

"Yes … makes me wish I'd spent more time with him when I had the chance."

Tutor and student then both went about their business. For Martin it was a time of decision. As he returned to the flat, the words of Anton came to him. *'You can run as far as you like but you can never run from yourself.* Martin was decided—his mission was to enter the Otherworld, particularly as he somehow sensed Lily had somehow been spirited there. He must find her and lead her out of Twyfin and into *Golbellen* —the Land of Light. Philomena also needed to be rescued and Martin was determined to lead both souls to a place of healing, to become whole once more. His Quest was clear, his purpose absolute.

As is the nature of the world, the actual embarking on his Quest was almost inevitably guaranteed to include the ridiculous. This manifested itself when Martin got into his car, glancing in the mirror as he did so. The sight captured there was, even in miniature, wholly alarming. Astride an ancient bicycle, wearing a voluminous smock from which purple bloomers protruded, Minnie Short approached along the pavement, pedalling furiously.

"Make way! Make way!"

Her outfit was crowned with either a colander or a small saucepan, affixed with a red ribbon tied beneath her chin. Martin, wondering if the postman would be the first victim in any collision, watched events unfold. Although laden with a large bag, he neatly sidestepped, and Minnie went sailing past.

Martin, intent on leaving the city behind, took the now familiar route to Rylock Wells. Once there, he left his car next to the Robe. Setting off along the path that led to the stone circle, he entered the field, and felt his whole body vibrate with a strange energy. Not only did he see each of the stones haloed with blue light, but he was also acutely aware of everything around him. Every blade of grass was a spear of emerald, the trees at the edge of the field ancient sentinels.

As Martin drew nearer to the circle he detected the faint turquoise glow of the Portal. He was also aware that his town shoes were letting in water. The fields, soggy from the January rains, now made his every step ponderous. Eventually he stood before the entrance to the Otherworld, slightly unsure of what to do next. The light within grew brighter and more intense, almost tangible. Martin braced himself.

'Passing Beyond The Veil', as the experience is reverently described by the great occultists is one deemed to be most individual. For Martin it was like jumping into the middle of a giant pizza—one as a big as a football goal. He flung himself boldly at the fabric. With a screeching sound, and a heat that seared his brow, the barrier to the next world melted and disappeared.

At first everything seemed distorted and out of proportion, as he imagined things might have appeared during some psychedelic romp of the Sixties. Swirling carnivals of colour, and forms that attempted to depict reality and meant nothing, were all around him. What physical objects there were had a habit of changing, almost at will. Spheres became flattened into pancake shapes, and anything that owned a simple linear pattern had a tendency to become high, wide, long or short if it was regarded for longer than a few moments. Anything like the idea of *dimensions* meant nothing at all. Martin also enjoyed the sensation of all sorts of experiences happening simultaneously, like watching three tellies at once.

The Universe is ordered, our experience tells us that it is not common sense to believe anything else, yet ultimately we are relying on our own belief that certain things happen and at a certain point. Our reality is only a tendency to believe something is true. We only believe what we are capable of believing and always the observer, although there is really no actual observer at all. Existence is an entertaining unfolding of events, reality a shakedown of shifting scenarios, and consciousness which could be just a collection of clownish conundrums. Truth might just be true after all. Who knows?

If Martin had been a shaman, he might have journeyed to the place where the departed ancestors, or even the demons and gods dwell. Not on this trip—all was just plain *random*. His actual location, the space he occupied, was ambivalent too. Seeing a star above him, he might be very near or far from it, all was utterly unreliable—so might-be-if-you're lucky. His mind could not map the territory; he could not rely upon his senses to inform him of anything. Every moment was connected to the next but in a way that each one appeared to be separate. Any sense of continuity did not exist, nothing moved from a present into the future. Martin decided he was lost, and he was right.

Twyfin—the Land of Darkness. And it certainly was just that. Actual darkness—absence of light—is one thing, but this was something else altogether, a dark that was on the inside as well. Martin could not see anything and he wondered if that state was permanent. He didn't think that his eyes would, after a time, get used to the dark, this kind of darkness felt *permanent*. It was also thick and woolly, stifling almost, and it made noises, something like the rumblings of the sea when it was heard in a fog. Martin could feel some indescribable thing all around him, and all the time moving. Because he couldn't see what it was, that was all the more disturbing. Although, if he *had* seen it then he might have been more alarmed—a toss-up between one horror and the next. What he did realise was that he was being pushed, none too gently, in some direction—one he knew he didn't want to go in.

If Martin had known it, he was heading for the Pit—the transcendental trash heap, where skips full of souls beyond repair are emptied. Here, only despair rules. Some also say this is the place where warty imps poke their victims all day and night with toasting forks. At the moment when Martin could feel the air becoming like lumps of sticky goop, he decided things had to change. By having this thought, he learned the first rule of the Otherworld—that things *could* be changed.

The method he discovered was simple—evoke a new moment and make it your own, then it becomes the next one. A kind of planning for the future—a notion of which his father would have approved. So Martin learned that the most important thing is *not in the knowing but the believing*. If he was convinced he could travel to this or that place ... then he had permission to do so. There are exceptions, of course, as there are to any rule.

It is all a matter of faith combined with conviction, a basic premise of magic, though Martin would not have been aware of that. The brain, being part of the universe, has the power to create other worlds within and beyond itself. Creation is infinite; it has no beginning or end, and thus has no limitations. Perhaps the universe the ancients knew was the same one as our own, perhaps it wasn't. Things change, and time is dwarfed by infinity. The singular moment may exist to Historians, and those who wish to define the nature of events, but to the cosmos it's only another one among the trillions of its neighbours.

Martin wanted to run, and he did. He kept running, because fear makes you do that, it stops you thinking too much about what might happen next. He wanted to be away from the darkness, as far away as possible, and eventually he arrived at the edge of the world. There was enough light here to see, but what he actually saw was the void. He stared deep into its vastness, an experience he would not be likely to forget for some time. His feelings were of awe combined with a sense of terror at the complete and utter *nothingness* of it all. An absolute empty space was all there was. Logically, the place where space ended ought to have been zero—that was measurable—what he was seeing wasn't. The experience was so overpowering Martin had to say the words he heard in his head. Probably the same ones anyone would have said in the circumstances, and he shouted them, ever so loud.

"What does it all mean?"

The Cosmos must have heard him. Every atom of creation began to quiver, do a back flip and go on a paint-balling weekend together. At the same moment a billion light years tried to squeeze into a space only big enough for a Thursday afternoon. Martin felt like he had been flung into the furthest corner of the universe and back again like an interstellar bungee jump. He expanded and contracted, existed and disappeared and generally got messed about. Martin reasoned that if his present existence was a hologram, which seemed likely, the quicker he found the off switch the better.

Little did he know that at exactly the same moment when he had zipped and zapped into the Otherworld a powerful resonance had been ignited in this one.

Hughie Smigg had just left his BMW in the Prockleby car park when the pride of Euro-engineering exploded. The resulting ball of flame, sent waves of heat in every direction, scorching Folds' Rollers and more than tousling Lady Folds' expensive hair-do as she was passing. Score, watching this mini-apocalypse from the window in Reception cried out that it was an omen. Lord Folds, normally less sensitive than a Gestapo officer on a mission, wondered for a moment whether to agree with him or not.

13

The potential of the human brain, this singular tool of consciousness, far exceeds what it actually achieves. If, as some mystical voyagers have insisted, that we are as the totality of the universe, it is perhaps easier for us to wholly accept our destiny and embrace the vagaries of existence. Even knowing this would not have prevented Martin from feeling as if his whole being had been shredded into its component parts. The total of these he estimated would have been several billion items. His brain was in overload—most of the time the visions he could see and the things he was experiencing he did not comprehend. Even if these same phenomena had been repeated slowly and endlessly for him, Martin was still convinced he would have been baffled by their nature.

He wondered for some time how to set about the task of putting himself back together again, a project that had to be begun without delay. Essential parts of his personality seemed to be missing. Those characteristics he had always considered quite capable of dealing with anything life presented him with had let him down badly. Sometime he would have to give them a good talking too. In the meantime he ran his fingers through his tangled locks in total bewilderment.

What did it mean to be in the unknown? It meant his surroundings were unfamiliar, but he reasoned that everything that was happening to him *belonged* to him in some way, and thus could be defined and understood. Such an ambition was understandable as a part of the human psyche. Taming and, at a later stage, conquering the world has always been the preoccupation of the pioneer. It was all a matter of putting things into perspective, or perhaps labelling them correctly. Twyfin might seem to be the domain of demons, phantoms, and creatures that leapt about among the crags, but in the end it did not matter a hoot.

The Moon rose, not a bright snowy globe but a cold harsh version. Like a cardboard cutout pinned to a black curtain, surrounded with pretend silver stars. This cartoon Isis still reflected enough pale light to illuminate the forbidding towers and limpid pools Martin saw about him. The gothic stage set now revealed was not an inspiring sight. Peering into the gloom he wondered if he would come upon Lily. He had kept an image of her in his mind most of the time, which had not been an easy task. Since he had entered the Otherworld, there had been more diversions than at a road works in Milton Keynes.

Without any warning, the depressing mists parted like stage curtains and there before him was a brilliant light. It appeared to originate from inside what looked like an immense crystal—transparent and resembling a block of ice. Within, assuming an inevitably frozen pose was the figure of a celestial dancer—Lily, her features lit with a ghostly light. Martin stared and stared again. He started shouting, dancing round in circles and cheering. Having done that he wondered how the heck he was going to get her out of there.

If he had referred to the previous intelligence test, he would have simply *thought* Lily out of her situation.

But, so excited was Martin that this simple approach did not occur to him, and he set about the task using a more direct method. He took up the nearest rock and started chipping away at a corner of the crystal. As might be supposed, this achieved absolutely nothing, except for sending a shower of glassy splinters into the air.

Martin, partly through frustration and an understandable weariness, lay down on the ground and after a few minutes went to sleep. As he was to discover, slumber in the Otherworld was not quite the same as that which he was used to. He simply entered yet another world, one of the numerous planes of existence in this place. Confronted with a feeling that he was somehow entering his own mind, he allowed this to happen. Fortunately for Martin, this was the most sensible course he could have followed.

Lily was before him! Smiling and looking at her most wondrous and entrancing she was free from her crystal prison. Martin, who ought to have responded to this with another show time extravaganza suddenly, experienced, in contrast, a tremendous sense of fear. What he was he so frightened about? Mainly of who he was—his whole personality was a false premise, his entire notion of himself based on a myriad of illusions. The idea terrified him; he could find nothing that could in any way contribute to an identity. His self had disappeared, and he was no more than a speck of anti-matter in a black hole, or even less. If he was totally and completely without a personality, how could he actually be?

He concluded that if he did not exist, he meant

nothing to anybody, particularly Lily who still stood before him, still smiling. Perhaps she did not know of his dilemma or, much worse, she did. His realized that his greatest fear had been that of realising his utter unsuitability as a hero. Martin would freely admit that his knowledge of the female psyche was minimal, so he really had no idea of what she might think. It did not occur to him that Lily knew exactly what Martin was like in the first few seconds she had laid eyes on him but, as is the way of feminine wisdom, she did not let on.

The other possibility was that he was still dreaming. Was he? Somehow he thought not, although the crystal was nowhere to be seen, as if it had miraculously disappeared.

"Oh … thank you … thank you."

It was real! For a glorious moment Martin thought Lily would fling her arms around his neck and kiss him endlessly. Instead she smoothed herself down and stretched her limbs, as if she was glad to know she still could still do these simple things. She then looked around her, uncomprehending.

"What is this place? Where am I?"

"Twyfin."

"Yeh?"

"That's what Mr. Tonks told me …"

Lily tried to make sense of what Martin was saying but for the moment abandoned the idea.

"I felt like I would never be able to talk to anyone again …"

"Not so good …"

Martin recalled his first encounter with the

dark World, when the very weight of existence itself crushed even his will to live. For Lily, being trapped inside the crystal must have been like that.

"I came here to find Philomena."

"I know …"

"How do you know?"

Martin hesitated.

"Well … actually I saw her disappear …"

"I don't believe it! Why didn't you tell me?"

Not for the first time in his life did Martin question the dictum that 'honesty was the best policy'.

"I didn't know you …"

Lily considered this.

"I remembered who you were … in the pub."

"Mmm."

"Do you think I'll find Philomena? Will you help me look for her?"

"Sure …"

He was aware that Lily was looking at him curiously, assessing what part he played in the game of life.

"Are you a student?"

"Right …"

"What … um … course are you doing?"

From her hesitation Martin realised Lily was not *au fait* with the academic life.

"Philosophy."

Lily considered.

"That sounds awfully clever."

Martin looked around at the unforgiving rocks and the mountains of midnight blue in the distance.

"Not as clever as figuring out what's going on

here."

Lily looked at the landscape with him.

"You're right ... you wouldn't believe what happened to me ..."

Martin looked at her ...

"No ... I don't think I would ... I'm not sure what I believe any more. There's one thing I do know though ..."

"What's that?"

"We ought to get going somewhere else. C'mon."

Without thinking Lily followed him. The sombre landscape seemed to stretch into infinity. Together they made their way among broken stones, some with edges sharp enough to slice salami. After some time these were less menacing, their shapes becoming round and flat. In the middle of this new terrain they came upon a pool of clear water. Lily knelt down and stared into its depths.

"Do you think it's okay to drink?"

Martin scooped some of the liquid into his palm and sniffed it.

"I think it's alright."

Feeling less thirsty, and the draught apparently having no adverse effects, they continued on their way. Ahead was a chasm, its sides stretching up towards the black of the sky. The entranceway was narrow, and it was impossible to see the way ahead. Lily stayed close to Martin, and suddenly she felt afraid.

"Don't leave me will you ..."

"No ... of course ... I won't."

"I just thought what it would be like if I was here on my own."

"Lonely."

Lily thought for a moment.

"Really I suppose I was ... until you came ..."

"To rescue you ..."

Martin's voice might have been muffled in the world of stone but the meaning of the words went straight to her heart.

"You did ... didn't you? Thank you."

Lily touched his shoulder in gratitude, but also to reassure herself Martin was still there. The chasm became even narrower and they were forced to crawl along the sandy floor. Finally they came out into an open space, odd tufts of vegetation and shapeless bushes surrounding them.

"Now where we are we?"

"I've no idea ..."

Martin wondered momentarily how he could possibly have known, but considered it more important to decide what they should do next. As soon as this thought came to him, it grew dark again. He decided to try an experiment. When all doubt disappeared, the dark went with it. Martin wondered if he thought about making something—being creative, as it were—everything would grow more light. His first attempts looked like the fourth prize in a pottery competition, but when he really focussed on what he was doing something solid soon appeared. Tall, imposing, and made from bright red brick, it featured an entrance arch that invitingly presented itself. So pleased was Martin with his efforts that he didn't notice Lily crying quietly to herself.

"What is it? Don't you like what I've ... um ... built

..."
...

Lily smiled on him, in the way that he had come to know.

"No ... it's lovely ... I was just thinking about Philomena ... all alone ..."

Martin was consoling, in his own fashion.

"Right ... right ... well ... maybe we can find her in here ..."

"You think so?"

"It's worth a try ..."

Such unbounded optimism usually wins the day, and with a nimble step they passed through the entrance and into the brick house. There seemed to be a lot of passages opening out in front of them. Some turned to the left and others, as would be expected, to the right. They followed these in turn until

Martin, by scratching a cross on one of the walls, proved that they always returned to where they had started from.

"We're in a maze ..."

"Yes ..."

"In fact it's more likely to be a labyrinth."

"Is there a difference?"

"Yes ... a labyrinth is usually some kind of ritual path. A maze is just a kind of game really ... constructed to amuse ... there's no real purpose in it."

"I didn't know that ..."

Martin paused. He had never before realised how much knowledge he possessed. Whether any of it would be the slightest use in the present circumstances was another matter altogether.

The days now felt distinctly different. A warmth in the air, a dash of yellow forsythia and a benign sky— all hinted at Spring. Ollie was making his way to the outskirts of the campus. As he did so, he remembered that two fine Georgian houses had been demolished in order to construct the Mulberry Conference Centre where the presentation was to be held. This grey edifice, with all the charm of an inner-city job-centre, seemed an oddly appropriate venue for Zandra Croop. Having only encountered her personality through ubiquitous emails, Ollie was curious to see if his image of her matched up to the actuality.

Inside the centre, muscled roadies were man-euvering massive steel boxes, obviously containing technological hardware, onto the stage. The panoply of audio equipment and visual aids already set up was overwhelming; the speaker cabinets alone would have not looked out of place at a rock festival. A sound-engineer, bulky headphones perched on the side of his head, sat at a large consul facing the stage. All around, teams of technicians and gofers in a *de rigueur* outfit of a fluorescent jacket and joggers scurried about. So mesmerized was he by the sight that Ollie did not notice Lucy approaching. She waved her hands in the air, apparently in supplication.

"Ee … by 'eck … wot's all this?"

Ollie was cool.

"Zandra's big day I think …"

"I should bloody say so … looks like when they have the Presidential Elections in America …"

"I rather think the new regime takes its cue from the American model of Higher Education too … they've got very different ideas about how things should be presented over there."

"They've got different ideas about everything. Don't you remember Zandra was singing the praises of *The Land of The Free* in the last email?"

"Uh … remind me …"

"About society would only survive if the universal consciousness changed."

"Oh … recycling your baked bean tins that sort of thing …"

Lucy pretended to look dismayed.

"No, Ollie … she meant a bit more than that. Obviously you *don't* read her mails. This is 'a common awareness of the world' …

"Corporate thinking?"

Lucy did not reply as she was staring open-mouthed as the gigantic screens at each side of the stage sprang into life. One showed what was obviously a government-issue puff intended to promote the attractions of student life—scenes of young people, dancing frantically and then engaged in communal fraternization. Another ostentatiously displayed the heraldic logo of *The Pride of Prockleby*. Lucy noticed that the places in the theatre were rapidly being filled and she nudged Ollie.

"C'mon … or we won't get anywhere to sit."

They found seats near the front of the stage, as it happened, next to Fearnley Wilmot. No sooner had they sat down than a voice assailed them from the banks of speakers, although its owner was not apparent. Lucy half-expected the form of Zandra to appear above their heads—floating down from the heavens. More prosaically, she appeared from behind some logo-embossed screens, the source of the ethereal voice being a radio-mike in her lapel. Her appearance was striking, blonde hair glistening as it fell onto the shoulders of her smart, charcoal suit. Despite the no-nonsense cut, the décolletage was most evident, the skirt short and tight across the hips. After glancing at her audience, Zandra launched into her spiel with all the power of an Exocet missile.

"In my role as Exterior Academic Advisor at Barstowe University I'm here to make you aware of many proposed changes … involving of course brand new opportunities for students and staff alike."

Ollie was aware of ambient music being faded in behind Zandra's voice. As she got into her stride this subtly altered, to the kind of rousing stuff played by some airlines on take-off.

"Our remit is … primarily … to provide a more than first class student experience … it will be one sustained by the community. Participation is the way ahead … and it is most assuredly our way ahead also. We are totally committed to being progressive and realise that we must compete … and succeed … to the highest level in the global knowledge stakes. World-class research and vocational training must be at the highest level. If an individual wants training in managing a golf-course … then we should be providing that service on the same level as any subject in the academic field. Above all *The Pride of Prockleby* lives in the real world."

Lucy's eyes traveled skyward. Ollie and Wilmot exchanged glances.

"The key issues are in the ballpark stage right now and they need to be implemented ... attitudes have to change ... and rapidly ... or we shall be left standing ... still at the starting gate. We recognise that all our top universities have always desired autonomy ... now we know we can provide it ... beginning at Barstowe. No longer will we have to be reliant on government hand outs ... a system that is demeaning ... and one that is ultimately damaging to any community of scholars."

Wilmot's whispered remark was almost audible.

"And what on earth does she know about being a scholar?"

"The time has come to banish inward-thinking and move on ... into a better ... more fulfilled and rosy future ... one full of exciting ... dynamic ... new prospects ..."

Wilmot's response was somewhat louder this time.

"Sounds about as exciting as a soggy sandwich ..."

"... and ultimately ... there can be no genuine or meaningful opposition to our plans for the future of Barstowe ... or indeed any other educational institution in Great Britain ... because we aim to achieve the best for all concerned ... and ultimately for all future generations."

So bland were these sentiments that the effect might ultimately have been soporific had not a sudden glitch occurred. The music suddenly got louder, drowning out Zandra, then fading to be replaced by howling feedback.

"… our *whang* mission … *kerrraaang* … is to bring back *squeearrrk* … a sense of … .*whhheeeoowww* … egali … *waaarrkk* … itarianism …"

The man at the consul looked like he had been struck by a high-calibre bullet. He began to move faders wildly up and down as if he were doing an impression of The Phantom of the Opera. Many of the senior members of the audience could be seen covering their ears. Some of the younger set openly smirked. Zandra alternately drew in her cheeks, glared at the sound man, and struggled to keep her cool. A long minute elapsed before things finally settled down.

"Many an established approach thought suitable by previous administrations will be swept away … to be replaced by new methods with guidelines and parameters that are appropriate to our times."

A lot more in this vein followed. As if to underline the significance of her words Zandra chose to balance a pair of reading glasses on the bridge of her nose and adopt a quasi-gothic tone.

"Only *The Pride of Prockleby* is prepared to address the real academic issues of the moment … what is currently in place … the traditional … closed methods … is now redundant … tired … and in the way. Now is the time for real … genuine *change* … *and we shall bring it.*"

A beatific smile of somewhat longer duration than the introductory version followed. On cue, loud clapping and some orchestrated cheering came from the serried ranks of the university hierarchy. Ollie was certain he detected a canned version coming from the speakers to enhance the effect. The ubiquitous music started up again, the screens then becoming so animated as to resemble the disco cult in its heyday. Zandra appeared to be surrounded by fans and admirers and she had some difficulty leaving the stage. Ollie glanced at his colleagues. Lucy was looking round quizzically, while Wilmot held his head to one side, stork-like.

"Very interesting this kind of corporate thinking that she's proposing ... in some ways I'd have to agree that controlling our thoughts ... following some kind of template ... might stop the mind controlling us. On the other hand experience shows ideas have a habit of flocking on the perimeters of our consciousness ... like starlings ... and going in all directions. A lot of the time they simply contradict themselves ..."

Ollie was less abstract.

"She's a control-freak ..."

"Undoubtedly. After I'd mildly commented on one of her multifarious proposals she sent me a pithy little email. It was saying that I couldn't expect the university to invent a special sub-category for someone who has such an idiosyncratic attitude as my own."

Lucy was desolate.

"What I can't understand is ... how can anyone believe that what she's saying is right ..."

Wilmot was judicial.

"I'm afraid that for the most part people *are* dull and stupid ... it's something one doesn't want to accept ... in fact one feels guilty in doing so ..."

At that moment Trencham shuffled past them, head down as if looking for some sand to bury it in.

Ollie stood around with his colleagues a little longer then joined the tail of the crowd making their way to the exit. When he came out of the Centre, the sun had inconsiderately decided to disappear. He drew his coat around him, lost in thought. At that moment he remembered the mysterious envelope Martin had given him months before, and his insistence that it was somewhat significant. He promised himself that he would investigate it when he returned to his room.

Martin, by refusing to believe that they were lost, led them out from the interminable labyrinth. This done, The Land of Twyfin still continued to drain their energies. The landscape stubbornly refused to alter its tedious and predictable character. It was rather like realising that an old friend has, for whatever reason, become a total bore. Temporarily abandoning their trek, Martin and Lily decided to perch on a convenient log. This example did not possess the lethal spines most of the trees roundabout owned.

"I remember reading about this German guy called Edmund Husserl ..."

Lily spotted what was coming.

"A philosopher?"

"Yeh ... he said the world exists without us considering it. I mean when I'm concentrating on something, *that* becomes my concern ... my reality if you like. But then there are ... of course ... all these other worlds existing along side of it."

Martin could see that Lily was not impressed.

"Well ... that's all very interesting ... but how does it help us get out of here?"

Martin thought for a moment.

"What it means is ... I don't think we're supposed to get back to the *real* world yet ..."

Lily almost stamped her foot.

"I don't want to be here for the rest of my life."

Martin hastened to be reassuring.

"I'm sure we're supposed to experience a few things before that happens ..."

"Like what?"

Martin did his best, which might have not sounded like much.

"I'm not sure ... I can't tell ... but I do know what we ought to do next ..."

"Yes?"

"Think about where we want to go."

Lily did this for about half-a-minute.

"I keep thinking about my cats ... all I want to do is go home."

Martin was patient.

"I'm sure they're fine ... and you'll see them eventually ..."

"I hope so. So what are you thinking about?"

"I don't know yet ... I'm still thinking about it ..."

They both burst out laughing and then looked at each other. One of those unexpected moments came, and they were holding hands.

"Golbellen!"

"What?"

"The Land of Light ... that's where we're going ..."

"Lovely ... it sounds like a fairy story."

Martin was adamant.

"Suspending belief sounds like a good approach right now."

Almost immediately they found themselves descending down a way lined with tall trees, except that weren't actually trees. They were just huge plants that had grown to an extraordinary size, as if they wanted to prove they could do it. It started to rain, but the sensation was nothing like getting wet, more like being stroked with an oily cloth. Eventually that stopped, and at the same time the ground before them flattened out.

"Look ... over there ..."

Lily looked in the direction Martin was pointing. A light like polished gold appeared on the horizon. They had arrived in Golbellen- the Land of Light.

14

Ollie's early arrival in the Department that morning was prompted by a stultifying guilt. The perpetual demand for journal articles, a continuing obsession in academia, had of late taken its toll on his patience. He realized all too acutely that if he did not submit his current piece by the end of the week he would miss the deadline. This, and the prospect of the Departmental Meeting due to be held that day, did not prompt him to launch into any abandoned yodeling.

After an hour or so he left his room to fetch a cup of sub-standard coffee from the vending machine. In the corridor, Lucy hailed him. Pleasantries were speedily exchanged prior to her lobbing a hand-grenade into the conversation.

"Have you noticed that nobody speaks to anybody else anymore?"

Ollie detected the innate sadness in Lucy's voice, but tried to make light of it.

"Nobody ever talked to me anyway."

Lucy wasn't laughing.

"Since *all this* started … everyone's frightened to say anything to anyone else. Head down and rush back into yer room … that's the way it is now. This used to be a nice place to be. I don't look forward to coming here anymore."

"I know what you mean. It's not a lot of fun."

Lucy stared at the floor.

"What's Dick going to say at this meeting?"

Ollie shrugged, wondering whether he wanted to add to the gossip that at present ran like a renegade mob through every department in the University.

"Search me. The top dogs are keeping very close about it all. Obviously things are going to change ... but it's almost impossible to know how they will. Dick might announce redundancies ... chucking out the junior lecturers and putting post-grads in ..."

"But that's so unfair ... they work so hard ..."

"I know ... but it's all about saving money here there and everywhere ..."

Lucy was almost pleading.

"But you've talked to Dick haven't you? I mean what does he say ... off the record I mean ..."

Ollie was evasive, though he hated himself for doing it.

"Basically ... he won't let on ... he certainly won't confide in me anyway. I will tell you this though ..."

"What?"

"He's drinking a helluva lot ... must feel he's under some kind of *big* pressure ... I've never known him fire down the beer like he did when I last saw him."

Lucy caught her breath.

"Oh ... no ... and he's got a heart condition ... blood pressure too ... silly booger."

For an awkward moment Ollie thought she was going to start crying.

"Never mind. It'll all come out in the wash."

Lucy sighed deeply.

"I've arranged to see Dick after the meeting. It's ages since I had a real heart-to-heart with him. We used to do that all the time."

Ollie couldn't think of what to say. He contented himself with patting her on the shoulder in a way that he hoped was comforting then disappeared into his room. Around noon, he picked up his briefcase, turned out the light, and let restful shadows invade the room.

The meeting was held in Seminar Room 'B'—a particularly dreary venue. The modern features inside the university buildings were uniformly grotesque, designed by someone with a permanent grudge against humanity. One wall was made entirely of unpolished wooden slats set opposite a line of windows, all resembling a tumbledown greenhouse. Trencham had placed himself so that he faced squarely into the room. Behind him the power-point screen on the wall glowed faintly.

Some of his colleagues were already settled in the front row and Ollie put himself between Lucy and Wilmot. As he sat down, Lucy winked at him, and Fearnley offered a half-smile. Jack Fitch waved from the other side of the room. The visiting lecturers, all hailing from various parts of America, were lined up in the second row. A common nationality did not bond them, and they sat stiffly apart. Ollie idly reminded himself of their antecedents. Mimi Schwartz—Yale, Romita Simek—Stanford, Jello Parkes—UCLA, Tomita Schneider ... somewhere in the Mid-West.

Ollie glanced over at Trencham in a subtle bid to gauge his mood. The clue was always to be found in his facial colour—right now it was Beaujolais and suggesting mild hysteria. Ollie thought he was looking a little flabby round the jowls too, and deep shadows below the eyes told of sleepless nights. Conversation—not very animated anyway—ebbed to a murmur and the meeting began.

"Morning, everybody. Now ... even though I've convened this as an *informal* Departmental Meeting ... we'll still be minuting apologies. Prof. North and Dr. Burnside won't be joining us I understand ... Paul's got car trouble ... and Richard's not very well apparently."

Ollie sat back, waiting for whatever would transpire. Business would be conducted with that academic formality known since Medieval times, not like the free-for-all manner that passes for discussion in lesser grades of society. There, balls are thrown in the air with little concern where they might land, if at all. Today might be different, Trencham certainly did not look at ease, and when he spoke it was with a thin rasping tone.

"Now ... as I'm sure you're aware ... certain changes have been mooted in the ... uh ... corridors of power ... Zandra gave you all an idea of how these will pan out at her presentation."

Wilmot shook his head pointedly.

"And although these are in the main confidential issues ... I've called this meeting as a means of reassuring everyone in our department that ... contrary to what the rumour mill might have been saying ... there is absolutely no cause for alarm ... .uh ... none at all."

Trencham's features were strained, like a ghastly mask. He looked round, as if fearful that any of the assembled company might actually contradict him. After a moment or two Jack Fitch spoke up.

"Dick, can I ask ... quite simply ... how *Lord Folds*

fits into these plans for the future of the Department and perhaps the entire university?"

Wilmot shook his head again, as if to say no one knew, but Trencham took the enquiry badly. His hue switched rapidly to burgundy. For one alarming moment Ollie thought he might start shouting. The atmosphere in the room had, in a few seconds, become uncomfortably tense. The Americans began to exchange puzzled looks.

"I totally refuse to discuss what goes on in senior-management meetings. That's no business of anyone else … no business of yours."

This was going too far, and everyone knew it. An astonished silence followed, one that seemed to continue … endlessly. Then Lucy's voice was heard—a plausible imitation of a junior school teacher admonishing her charges about rough play.

"Dick, I'm sure you're doing your best to deal with what might turn out to be massive changes in the university … who knows … and I'm also certain that must bring an enormous pressure with it. Jack's had his say … which I'm sure Emily has minuted … so p'raps the best thing would be just to move on. Don't you think?"

Lucy beamed about her. The next few moments were still awkward. Everyone waited to see what Trencham would do next. To the relief of all in the room he apologized, although with the minimum of grace.

"Sorry, Jack. Not a very good way for us to start is it?"

Filch said nothing—which meant everything. A

slightly longer pause then ensued, as if no one was willing to speak. Eventually Wilmot began his slow drawl.

"Something that rather puzzles me at the moment … more than anything to do with *Lord Folds* … is the *degree of authority* that our erstwhile Zandra Croop actually now commands. I personally have the impression that … since her presentation … the directives one now receives … and they have been increasing since then at an extraordinary rate … are actually *orders from above* that cannot be rescinded."

Ollie waited in suspense for the possibility of another explosion, but this time it did not come. Instead Trencham's features returned to something like rosé, and a smile appeared on his face.

"Now … I'm sure you're all familiar with one of Kant's maxims, 'All human knowledge begins with intuition … proceeds from there to concepts … and ends with ideas."

Trencham looked round, still grinning. One or two nods of recognition greeted this gobbet of scholarship, but its relevance to the business in hand seemed remote.

"Senior Management … along with myself and those in Senate are confident Zandra Croop will fulfill all of Kant's maxims."

His audience waited awkwardly, noting Trencham's desperate embarrassment. His performance had become bottom-of-the-bill, stuff, and realising that more was somehow expected from him, he almost yelled the next bit.

"All I can say at this point is that Zandra will quite

probably be the person responsible for inaugurating the new policies ... after first detailing them through the usual channels of communication ... thus bringing them to ... er ... the attention of all of us."

The smile assumed the look of a cut melon—the features the colour of old port. From his manner, it was obvious Trencham considered the matter closed. To the astonishment of all present he simply got up and shuffled out of the door. It was not his, or the Department's, finest hour. Lucy was seen to follow him.

When she discovered him in his office her first thought was how old and fragile Trencham looked. The lines that now scored his features were the same as those she had seen during the months after his divorce. Lucy had spent many an hour consoling him then. It was some time before Trencham could even look up at her. Finally he did, with eyes that told of confusion and anxiety. His words when they came were in a voice that was worn, defeated.

"I don't understand what's going on in the Department, Lucy ... in the whole damn university. Things are changing much too quickly for me ... I can't keep up."

Lucy's words were measured.

"Bit too fast for all of us, Dick ... that's the problem."

Dick didn't respond to this, he was determined to continue with his own lament.

"I'm too old for all this kind of ruckus. Why is everybody in the Department against me?"

Lucy noticed how defensive he was. Trencham,

always sensitive to criticism, was more touchy than a hedgehog with a skin complaint.

"Dick, nobody's against you."

He rounded on her.

"They're against Zandra then."

"That's hardly the same thing."

"Yes … it is. She's been brought in to make the Department … the University be run better. How can anybody object to that?"

Lucy was at a loss as to where to begin.

"None of these *improvements* have ever actually been discussed out in the open, Dick! That's why everybody's on edge … hostile you could say. It's all cloak and dagger stuff with Senate and Council. All we get are these new directives *hinting* at what's going to happen … most of them are just gobbledygook … and nobody actually consults the staff to see if they agree with them."

"Zandra always runs everything past me."

"And you always rubber-stamp it."

"Well … of course … if I think it's sound policy … it always seems to be. Zandra's a very competent woman. You can't argue with that."

Lucy knew she could, and quite convincingly, but she was also aware it would achieve little.

"But, Dick … this autocratic style of running things is bound to cause resentment sooner or later. People don't like being told what to do all the time. These *timesheets* for instance … they're on the lines of what it must be like to be working in bloody Toscos. There's no dialogue any more. I mean you once got us together and asked us all quite seriously if it was okay to move the furniture round in the Common Room."

Dick smiled at this, if only briefly.

"God … the *Common Room*. Times are very different now … aren't they? That must have been more than thirty years ago."

"It was."

"Well … we can't live in the past. I'm sure it's all for the best. Zandra's the new blood the University needs …"

An image of Zandra as a vampire came unbidden into Lucy's mind.

"… Bingley-Brass is certain of that. If the VC and Willie Slate are supporting her we can't argue with them can we?"

"But I'm sure there's another way to go about things, Dick … more involvement with everyone …"

Dick wasn't listening anymore.

"And why's Ollie being so difficult? I just can't understand his attitude."

Straightaway Lucy protested.

"C'mon, Dick … you can't suddenly single out *Ollie* as a trouble maker."

Trencham scowled, as petulant as a hurt child.

"Fearnley's another one … he's in on it too … and Jack …"

Lucy was aghast.

"In on what?"

"This campaign they've got going … accusing the Committee and the Senate of being underhand. It's them that are the ones who are trying to discredit Barstowe."

Lucy could only stare in disbelief.

"You mean if anyone questions these changes they're seen as *the enemy* ... by Senate and Council?"

Trencham was almost triumphant.

"They want to be careful ... they go too far ... they'll be kicked out ..."

"What!"

Trencham deliberately turned away.

"I'll tell you this ... Fearnley Wilmot's definitely on thin ice ... he's a senior man ... he ought not to behave like he does ... it's not professional ..."

Lucy could not believe what she was hearing. She looked at her head of department, seeing a man bewildered, controlled by forces he did not recognize, let alone understand. Lucy said nothing more, just quietly left the room leaving Trencham to the hell of his isolation.

What was that sound that could be heard? The soul of Barstowe University in her torment mingling with the cries of men yearning for true scholars and poets. Whither are they now, O Phoebus? Let us pray they are merely hidden, remaining eternally, waiting only for the call so they may shine once more upon a kingdom now lost and abandoned.

The perpetual gloom the travellers had known for so long began to disappear, as the streak of light over the horizon grew wider. Now they could see more clearly, the colours of their surroundings also changed, from the previous dull greys and murky blue. In the lush foliage luminous yellows tinged with emerald began to appear. A tall specimen with a mass of red, bulbous fruit came into view, as did other tree-like apparitions. Some had crinkled fronds, others tapered leaves, but none of it was soft or welcoming like the green of Olde England.

The circle of the horizon deepened until it was a shimmering halo about them. The air was warm and the distant landscape grew more inviting. Some of the tree-things they came across were so huge they would have been impossible to embrace even if they had felt so inclined. Tree hugging was not predominantly on their mind—food was. They had considered sampling the crimson globes, but on inspection they appeared singularly unappetising.

"I wish we could find something to eat ... anything ..."

They continued to forage, eventually finding something that looked like grapes. Martin picked one from the tangled vine above him and tentatively sampled it.

"Mmm ... that's okay."

He and Lily feasted on these until they could take no more. Somewhat sated they, carried on walking. They could feel nut-brown sand beneath their feet and next, a sea of opal was before them, its surface gleaming radiantly. The waves rolled in, one after the other, as if they had done so forever. The sun made the surf gleam brighter and each splash of water was hurled skyward in celebration.

"That's incredible ..."

"We can go swimming."

Amazed, Martin watched Lily throw off all her

clothes and run naked towards the edge of the tide.

"Wait!"

The voice sounded so alarmed that Lily paused at the water's edge.

"What's the matter? Are you shy?"

She laughed uproariously.

"No ... it's not that ... it just that might not be our kind of water ... I mean ..."

Lily stared at him for a moment, then at the sea.

"Well ... it certainly looks like *my* kind ..."

With that she plunged into the surf and was soon turning over and over like some beautiful fish.

"Does it feel okay?"

"It's lovely ... really warm ..."

Without any more hesitation Martin stripped and ran into the waves. Soon he too was held in the arms of Poseidon's nymphs, though he might have wished it was Lily doing the holding. After they knew not how long, they left the water and lay on the sand. Lily drew her clothes about her, Martin being a gentleman, did the same. They stayed gazing at the sparkling water until it made them blink.

"Doesn't it make you want to paint or write?"

Martin agreed.

"I do ... um ... write ... poetry ... and stuff ... sometimes."

"Yes I know."

Martin looked surprised.

"How did you know that?"

Lily put her head on her knees and looked sideways at him.

"Oh ... I just did ... you can read some to me some

time."

"I'd love to."

"Okay ... that is if we ever get back from here ..."

"Oh ... we will ..."

Martin surprised himself at how determined he was when he said that. Lily looked wistful.

"Wouldn't it be great to hear some music ... ?"

"Yeh ... that'd be cool ..."

"I really miss not having my favourite tracks to listen to ..."

Martin thought about this.

"I'm sure we could hear music if we wanted to."

Lily looked interested.

"You mean imagine it ... like ... in our heads?"

"Yes. Don't think about it and it'll just happen I'm sure."

Lily shut her eyes.

"Here it comes ..."

Martin heard music like he had never heard before, an aural version of all that was around him. He could vary the tone the tempo or the mood too, as it suited him. Feeling became colours, thoughts shapes, and all transmuted into the most wondrous melodies. Cadences and counterpoint he had never dreamed of was determined by a flick of a neuron, the dance of a synapse. He was so involved with all this that he almost forgot Lily was there.

"Wow ... I'm sorry I was somewhere else ..."

Lily drew her knees up to her chin and smiled.

"That's okay ... I was too."

"Oh ... that's okay then ..."

"Perhaps we were in the same place ..."

Martin looked like he hadn't thought of that possibility.

"Yeh ... yeh ..."

She touched his hand for a moment.

"I think we were ..."

"Maybe ..."

"You don't think so?"

Martin detected the slight hurt.

"No ... I mean ... yes ..."

Lily laughed.

"What *do* you mean?"

Lily smiled at him in a way that Martin knew they were about to kiss. When he opened his eyes, Lily's smile seemed to be the whole world.

"Oh ... I ..."

She put a finger to his lips.

"Don't say anything ..."

"Right."

He was suddenly aware of her whole body and wanted to take her in his arms and possess her, but somehow he knew that wasn't to be. Martin closed his eyes again, and then suddenly felt her lips on his again for a moment and her whispering.

"Not yet ... we must wait. Like you said ... this place is like that ... everything happens when it's supposed to."

More than reluctantly, Martin drew away from her. The eternal Sun beamed upon them.

To the ears of Score the usual arrogance that

accompanied the roar of the BMW bearing down on Prockleby was absent. He sensed Julian Flora would have a difficult time of it in his meeting with Lord Folds that morning and he was right. Folds' bellicose shout from his office set the tone for the encounter, even before Flora had come into reception.

"So that prat has shown up has he? Don't show him in right away ... he can cool his heels out here till I'm ready."

"Yes, my lord."

Score resigned himself to knowing that another difficult day lay ahead, sometimes he wondered how much longer he could endure the endless regime. Flora duly appeared and carped at being kept waiting in reception. Score did not offer him any refreshment, believing that if he bore this yoke others must suffer under it also. Finally Flora was thrown to the lions.

"What's all this about the Unions kicking up at Barstowe?"

Flora parried this opening thrust as best he could.

"I hear there was some difficulty when we presented the new wage structure."

Folds took a glossy leaflet from a drawer, and slapped it on his desk.

"I'm not surprised if you gave them this load of bollocks to look at."

Flora was inclined to protest.

"That document was commissioned from one of our top contacts in London."

"I don't give a toss. Listen to this ... *emerging paradigm to drive productivity ... liquid labor specific skill sets ... project-based personnel rationalising payroll expenditure ... monetizing skills ... across the board."*

Flora looked hurt.

"That's standard terminology in a situation like this ..."

"As they say ... 'Bullshit baffles brains' ... but not in this case apparently ..."

"One or two of their representatives questioned what we were proposing ..."

Folds leant across the desk.

"Look ... we're about to clinch this deal with those Senate wallahs ... and I don't want any trouble from *anybody* at this stage of the game. Understand?"

"Yes ... but ... if ..."

Folds made a dismissive gesture.

"I don't care how you do it ... tell 'em it was a mistake ... wrong info. included ... just get these people in line ... promise 'em anything. We can always change it all back later ..."

Flora looked dubious.

"I don't know whether ..."

Folds glared.

"Just sort it! Couple of faxes ought to do it ... they always impress people. Go down there if you have to ... ask to speak to these union reps of theirs ... be nice to 'em. Know what I mean?"

Flora did.

"Alright. I'll get on to it."

Folds did not let up.

"Do that ... and pronto. Right?"

"Okay."

Folds rallied his forces.

"Now then ... little Zandra ... your pet Rottweiler

..."

Flora winced.

"Yes ..."

"I want her to sort out this Vice-Chancellor dude."

"How d'you mean?"

"Simple. Tell him she's in the driving seat now and *she gives him* the orders."

"Will that work?"

Folds almost leered.

"I'd be very surprised if it didn't. I've never met the woman ... I wouldn't want to ... I've got a first-class bitch for a wife myself thank you. But the way I see it when she says 'jump' down there ... they all do."

"Zandra certainly has got one hundred-per-cent results in the Barstowe campaign ..."

"Yeh ... and I want it to keep being like that too ... especially now."

"Okay ... I'll tell her to ..."

Folds finished the sentence for him.

"... inform Bingley-bloody-Brass that she's in charge of Barstowe University now."

Zandra had been working hard at breaking down the existing channels of communication at Barstowe and replacing them with a system that referred back only to her. Operating in a vacuum did not feel alien to Zandra; she lacked anything approaching human qualities. When informed she was given *carte blanche* to put the Vice Chancellor firmly in his place, Zandra set about the task with relish. She immediately made an appointment with his secretary, and when she entered his office the next morning regarded Bingley-Brass in such a contemptuous manner that he quivered from head to toe.

"Lord Folds is extremely disappointed with the speed of our changeover ... he would like the situation rectified immediately."

"Oh ... right ho ... yes ..."

Zandra regarded him in a way that renewed the tremors.

"All arrangements must be finalised ..."

Bingley-Brass was bluff.

"Aye ... aye ... I'll do what ah can ... this very day in fact ... make sure everything starts to move faster ... that's the ticket ain't it?"

Zandra's eyes were as points of light, blinding him, searching his very soul.

"By the end of the week ... any later date will be unacceptable to Lord Folds."

"Oh ..."

Zandra showed her teeth, in parody of a smile.

"Lord Folds insists this is all made very clear to you ..."

Bingley-Brass made the mistake of returning to his casual manner.

"Oh ... aye ... well tell 'im I've got matter in hand ... won't yer ..."

Zandra was not going to let her prey escape that easily.

"I think you should insist that Senate ratify your decision ..."

Bingley-Brass waved his hands about in a pantomime of protest.

"Oh ... can't do that wi'out convening special meeting of executive committee ..."

The teeth were now slightly more evident.

"You and Mr. Slate have sufficient authority I believe ..."

"Well ... ah suppose so ... boot it would be highly unofficial ..."

Defeat was giving him a baleful eye.

"I'm sure it can be done. I shall be contacting Lord Folds shortly ... and I'll inform him that you've issued the Senate's authority ... University Council approval as well of course ..."

"Okay ... then ... you do that ..."

Zandra stood up.

"I'll be checking up on that ... of course ... shall we say on Thursday lunchtime?"

"Right ho."

"Just as a formality."

Zandra held out her hand. The Vice-Chancellor took it, very gingerly.

"Raht then ..."

"Thank you, Vice-Chancellor ... I'm sure Lord Folds will be glad to hear my report now."

Bingley-Brass could think of nothing to say. As soon as Zandra had left, he collapsed in his chair. When Slate came into the room some time later, the Vice-Chancellor had no more life in him than a punctured Lilo.

15

When the Sun went down in the Land of Light it started to get cold. Having earlier been glad to throw off their clothes, now Martin and Lily wished they owned more. Sleep eventually came to them, and with it dreams. As Martin had discovered before, the act of dreaming was not the same in the Otherworld. Not only were he and Lily transported to a fantastic realm, those they knew from the past, the present and figures unknown—all became players in a strange drama. Martin and Lily flitted in and out of each other's dreams too, sometimes lovingly embracing, but often passing in silence as if they were strangers. When Lily woke, it was to find Martin already alert and immersed in thought.

"Good morning."

Martin returned her greeting but still carried on contemplating.

"You know ... I was wondering if it isn't ..."

Lily leaned her head on his shoulder.

"Tell me."

"... all too much of a good thing here."

Lily stretched out her arms towards the rising sun.

"I don't mind if it is. It seems pretty nice to me ... wherever we are ... maybe we should just enjoy it."

"Yeh ... but ..."

Lily was distracted by the sun appearing over the horizon, looking like a great big jar of mustard pickle. The sight oozed warmth and merriment Martin would have had to agree.

"Anything would have been better than that other place."

"Yes ... but that's the point ..."

Lily looked puzzled.

"What point?"

"We didn't want to be there ... so now we're here. We made it happen ... like the music."

Lily lay back on the sand.

"Oh ... just relax ... it's fine."

Martin didn't say anything for a moment, just concentrated on putting into words what he was thinking.

"You know if you have a really posh chocolate ..."

"Oh ... yes?"

"And then you have another one ... it's not as nice is it ..."

"I know what you mean ... even if it's a different flavour ... it's not so ... so ..."

"Amazing?"

"Yeh ... total ..."

Martin tried not to look smug.

"I think I know why that is."

"You do?"

"I believe the brain invents a totally new pattern of sensations the first time ... then the next time it doesn't bother ... just gives you the same again."

"Yeh maybe. So ..."

"I think here ... it's different. Every moment *really is new* and every time we experience something it's like it was the first time ever ..."

"Yeh ... I feel that ... like I've never seen anything like this before. Which I haven't I suppose ... but ..."

Martin was insistent, working it all out as he went along.

"No ... hold that thought ..."

Lily felt like saying 'Which one?' but didn't.

"... about feeling every moment is new ... and knowing we can choose where to go next. We've got the power to do that ..."

Lily felt the sun warming her, it was difficult not to forget everything else but such delight.

"But not right now, Martin ... it's so lovely ..."

"We've got to ... got to move ..."

"Why?"

"Because now it's all changed ... it's not like it was before ... and if we don't go soon we'll be stuck here ... maybe forever. I'm sure the longer we delay ... it'll be harder all the time when we do want to go."

Lily sat up, reluctantly.

"Okay ... I'm sure you're right. You seem to know all about these things."

Martin was determined to keep on track.

"Will you do what I say?"

Lily's smile was wide, and slightly provocative.

"Of course ..."

"Right ... now just empty your mind ... don't think about anything."

"I'll try. That's not easy for me you know ..."

Martin frowned.

"I'm not sure it is for anyone ... but we have to try."

They sat on the shore a little distance apart, each endeavouring to stop the mind from working—a thankless task. If they had been Zen Buddhists they would have got there straight away. After she didn't know how long, Lily opened her eyes. She faced Martin.

"We're still here. Why isn't it working? We haven't gone anywhere."

"We haven't moved ... if that's what you mean."

"Isn't that the same?"

Martin thought about that.

"No ... it isn't really. We're not connecting with the idea that nothing stays the same ... we're still believing that it does. We're still stuck in the old world because of that."

"But we were able to come here ... to Gol ... Goll ... whatever it's called."

"Golbellen ... I know ... but that was somehow easier because the Dark World was so heavy and inert ... this is different. The problem is that ..."

Lily stopped him.

"... because it's so nice here ... or ... *I* think it is ... were being held back ... and can't leave."

"Exactly ... we don't know what's coming next ... so we keep returning to the same place ..."

Lily didn't follow that, but thought it best to agree.

"So what do we do instead?"

"I think we have to totally become what's around us first ... and then change that ..."

"Okay ... but what do we change it into? I mean ... what's the best thing to imagine?"

"Anything or nothing."

Lily screwed up her face in mock horror.

"Martin! You'll have to do better than that."

"What I mean is that by thinking of nothing ... that helps to make the connection ... then it's as if what's supposed to happen takes over. Then we get ... sort of sent ... to wherever we're going."

Lily took this in.

"Well I hope it's going to be as nice as this ..."

Martin was inclined to be impatient.

"Thinking like that is just hopeless ..."

Lily sighed.

"I'm sorry ... I'm not helping much am I?"

Martin looked at her, with love.

"You're fine ..."

"And you're so sweet ..."

She went to kiss him.

"C'mon."

"Aye ... aye, Captain. I'm ready ..."

They closed their eyes. Nothing happened that was different until Martin was aware of there being a split in the space he was seeing. He focussed on this, all the time working on making it wider until there was a gap in the fabric of reality. Martin reached for Lily's hand, calling out as soon as he felt her grasp his fingers.

"Jump! Now!"

They were moving faster than anything else in their universe so, inevitably they squeezed into a time tunnel, one that linked the worlds. They bounced against the walls of space, speeding towards infinity. When they came to the very rim of existence, it was neither here nor there. This was perhaps inevitable as their destination, though they did not know it, was Gwallyog—The Place of Unreason.

In a bid to topple the tyrant, Mr. Tonks had set himself the task of finding out as much as he could about Lord Folds' empire. The more he delved, the greater the amount of base metal that he discovered. In an obscure financial journal was a brief exposé of one of the many questionable methods that Lord Folds had once employed in his business dealings. He had been party to a scheme for providing advice to investors in hedge funds. The fees subsequently charged by the consultants far exceeded the value of any dividend, and eventually swallowed up any investment as well. Simple—a swindle always is.

For decades, Folds had been a prominent member of companies that subsequently collapsed, ruining shareholders in the process. That his lordship's shares in these companies were always sold prior to the inevitable demise was almost guaranteed. Mr. Tonks had seen enough, the man was a crook through and through and justice would soon exact her price. His ancestors also had much to answer for, particularly a judge who presided at several witch trials. On this occasion the daughter of Old Meg Hampton had not only been burnt, but savagely tortured. Old Meg had cursed the family, not only for seven generations but seven times seven. Retribution was at hand, and coming from all quarters.

The night promised a glimpse of the fate waiting for Lord Folds. In the world of dreams the dreamer has no sense of responsibility, abdicating any control of what happens to him or anyone else. Nor does he expect there to be any rhyme or reason for anything experienced. A dream it was that felled the pride of Lord Folds.

In his dream Lord Folds did not know where he was, which was not surprising as he had entered another's dream, that of Mr. Tonks. To that gentleman, Penelope's Patisserie in the High Street of Conkerville assumed a significance that a visit to the Valley of The Kings, or The Hanging Gardens of Babylon, would to others. Mr. Tonks owned such an idiosyncratic blueprint of reality that no other version could possibly exist alongside it. All other spheres of reality were simply swallowed up to become a footnote in his personal consciousness.

Thus did Lord Folds begin at a disadvantage. When the surroundings in his dream took shape they had more than an air of the grotesque, much more so than he had ever experienced. He appeared to be in some bakers' shop, every detail of the establishment engraved upon the parchment that recorded the ethereal tale. All was very busy, among other tasks the staff seemed to be engaged with a mountain of Danish pastries which at intervals collapsed and restored itself of its own volition. Folds attempted to gather the cloak of his conscious personality about him and failed, such is the way in dreams.

A figure appeared to him, kitted out in a bottle green corduroy suit, a livid tie and what looked like brogues of an extreme vintage. They seemed to shine so much that they winked at Lord Folds in a way that he regarded as the height of insolence.

"Good morning. Archibald Tonks ... at your

service ..."

The smile seemed to expand and grow larger until it filled the whole world. It was a look that spelt power ineffable, the very seed of creation, the stuff that made up the most ancient of gods. Lord Folds could only see that the deference he always expected from others was at this moment most definitely absent. This Mr. Tonks, whoever he was, was actually regarding him as an equal! Even in his dream, this realisation made Folds angry, but the emotion manifested itself in a strange and unpredictable manner. He began to leap from one foot to the other, as if executing some obscure and long-forgotten folk dance. Up and down, and round and round he went, sometimes falling, and then recovering at the last moment and on again in an endless whirl. When eventually he stopped the mad dance and tried to speak, to give vent to his emotions, nothing he said made any sense.

"Follicle ... barnacle ... icicle ... meadowsweet ... Marylebone ... cheese ... bicycles ..."

And this Mr. Tonks was laughing at his efforts! So loudly and uproariously did he laugh that he took to rolling on the ground and kicking his feet in the air! Lord Folds grew more and more angry so that eventually the heat in his cheeks made his face melt and his features to disappear. Where was his nose? His chin? It was all too much and becoming more so. To top it all, this Mr. Tonks was taunting him with an impertinence he had never ever experienced.

"What a funny fat man you are! Silly old Folds! In disgrace ... hasn't got a face!"

Lord Folds stared and stared, and Mr. Tonks carried on completely regardless. Then Folds discovered he could speak again. He bellowed so loudly that cars in the street turned over, and all the chimneys flew from the roofs of houses.

"How dare you speak to me like that!"

Mr. Tonks did not seem in the least bit interested in how his lordship felt. He continued to caper around, at one point removing his shiny shoes and throwing them at Lord Folds. One hit him on the ear making him yell in pain.

> "*Because I dare*
> *I do not care ...*"

For the first time in his life Lord Folds feared, a feeling he could not ignore. He thought he might die—perhaps he was dead already. The thought made him shiver and he woke in his bed, bathed in sweat, shaking and in the grips of cold terror.

Around six o'clock, the Department 'Rebels'—a title they would have vehemently denied—convened in the relative privacy of the back bar of the Blue Badger. A more morose gathering it would have been hard to imagine. Light conversation between Lucy, Jack Fitch and Ollie did not flourish, and the late arrival of Fearnley Wilmot caused some alarm. Known always to be obsessively punctual, this seemed an ill omen. When Wilmot did finally appear, one glance at his ashen pallor confirmed that all was not well. Whether his demeanour resulted from extreme trauma or plain rage was initially impossible to discern. With only the briefest of nods Wilmot went to the bar, returning with a pint of Guinness—itself an uncharacteristic gesture.

"Bastard! Patronizing little sod."

Shocked silence greeted this outburst as Wilmot was always a most quiescent character. That he considered he had been wronged in some way was blatantly obvious. Lucy asked the pertinent question.

"Who is?"

"The Registrar … Willie Slate. I couldn't believe it. Did he thank me for forty odd years service to the university? Did he … buggery. Just seemed incredibly pleased I had agreed to take the blasted redundancy … which was forced on me. It was either that or nowt. I wouldn't stay here now if I was offered a million quid a week. The bloody toe-rags that run this dump … *and* he had the cheek to make me sign something to say I'd complete my tenure.'

Lucy wanted to disappear through the floor; she could not believe that Senior Management could be so vindictive. She was certain Trencham must have supported, or even pressed for, Wilmot's dismissal. His mentioning of 'disciplinary measures' to Lucy when they met after the departmental meeting confirmed this. For Slate to treat the most senior member of the Department as if he was a bumptious post-grad, and summarily terminate his contract was not only grossly unfair, it was inexcusable.

The aggrieved party took a goodly swig of his

pint and simmered down a little. After a few muttered condolences they could hardly bear to look at each other. Jack Fitch appeared particularly glum.

"Looks like we're beaten before we've started doesn't it? Tow the line or you're given your marching orders. If they've done that to you, Fearnley ... our senior man ... what hope is there for any of the rest of us."

Wilmot took a second pull at his drink and sat back in his seat.

"They'll put somebody in my place y'know ..."

"Really?"

"... at half the salary. Somehow they've got to fund the new management structures they're putting in ... and that's probably how they've decided to do it. And we can guess what sort of candidates they'll be looking for can't we?"

Fitch groaned.

"I knew it ... so we'll now have a university run by people who don't know anything about universities ..."

Fearnley continued for him.

"Every department will have an executive team appointed to it ... two senior management and a chief information officer. That number will be increased within two years of course ... doubled. I got all this out of Dick when Slate gave me the glad news I'd been sacked. He didn't see any reason to keep it a secret anymore. Kept telling me how clever Lord Folds' people were to think out all this. Good God!"

Lucy shook her head.

"And everybody's agreed to this happening?"

"In A & H they have ... definitely. English ... History and Classics were given an ultimatum. Falling in with the new regime ... or mega-redundancies right and left ..."

Ollie didn't want to believe what he was hearing.

"And no one said anything?"

"They all gave in without firing a shot—all of 'em. Barker Compton ... Head of History ... was particularly craven apparently. Congratulated Zelda on being 'tough with the terrorists' and hugged her in front of everybody. A particularly nauseous spectacle I'm told."

Ollie was not surprised by the behaviour of Compton, who he had always suspected of being a weasel and a turncoat. The English Department was no better. Since Maggie Brougham had lost the ear of the Vice-Chancellor she had no citadel to defend. Mint, Usher, Bride, and the rest of the charlatans would have whooped for joy. Mick Benson had either committed murder or left the country, probably done both. It was the mention of Classics that stabbed at his heart. Had Professor Harptree and the others really thrown in the towel that easily?

"Bob Harptree put up a bit of a fight ... but it didn't do much good ... it's *fait accompli* now ... *Folds rules OK*. Of course ... this all ties in nicely with the government move to introduce the 'National General Award' scheme—N.G.A."

Lucy could not stop herself.

"Sorry? What's that?

Wilmot smiled, but without a trace of humour.

"It's a pop version of joint honours. You take five

subjects and you're awarded a qualification at the end of two years. I've only seen some rough layouts of the idea but it seems you can actually fail three of them and still get a pass."

There was a collective gasp. Wilmot regarded them all placidly.

"I know. Insidious isn't it? It's all to do with government targets of getting eighty-five per-cent of school students in higher education by 2015. Lord Folds' regime may even fit in with the official plan to keep school leavers off benefits for two years … make them pay for their education with increased fees … of course … tripled by 2016 … everyone's happy."

"But why do they think this is a good idea in the long run? Or am I being incredibly naïve about it all?"

"No … I don't think you're being naïve, Ollie … you're just looking at it from the point of view of an academic. What we're seeing is the diluting of the process of learning … abandoning any real debate … what we call 'scholarship'. The sort of management who will take over wouldn't know a footnote if it came up behind them and bit them on the bum. Government departments responsible for Education don't include academics in their advisory committees. Maybe one token member, so they can use him as a spokesperson on T.V. to justify what they're doing."

Fitch carried on being gloomy.

"It all started with that 'Widening Participation' scheme. What our far-thinking government didn't like was that some places … Barstowe for instance … maintained a high standard. Students wanted to come here, not just for the social side of it, but because the departments had a good reputation. So they started to make universities accountable. 'Why aren't you letting this student in?' 'Because he's no bloody good'. End of story. Not now. Unis were going to be fined if they didn't allow entrants with lower qualifications in."

Lucy fizzled.

"Or build new ones like C.W.B. ... and those places are such a joke. Less than a 25% pass rate? That's a youth club not a uni."

Ollie was genuinely puzzled.

"But what about research?"

"What about it? This new lot will control all the funding. The old established bursaries that keep on going year after year will be milked until they don't exist. Funds for A & H research are already so low now ... they might as well not exist. Any funding that's coming in is from the U.S ... .and that's right across the board. Even Cambridge ... your old *alma mater*, Ollie ... now relies on Macrotuff for money. I actually thought the proliferation of our American cousins in the department this year was because they were all reps. from Dapple or somewhere ..."

Fitch pondered.

"So Folds could see the opening ..."

"Precisely. It's this sort of political climate that is perfect for someone like Folds to prosper in and my thinking is that won't be satisfied with taking over Barstowe. If he succeeds here then it's a case of *encourager les autres*. The others might give in without a fight ... but here's the billion dollar question ..."

"What?"

"Why did they choose to target our department?"

Lucy looked puzzled.

"Did they?

"I think so … and that's what intrigues me …"

"Dick! It must be some deal he's got going with …"

Wilmot shrugged.

"… somebody or other. Obvious when you think about it."

Lucy whistled audibly.

"So really we should have assassinated him and the V.C. on the first day of this academic year."

Wilmot looked grim.

"You know what Slate said to me? 'You just don't seem to realise that things have changed in universities in the twenty-first century.' Now I bloody *do* … thanks to riff-raff like him."

He downed the rest of his pint, pausing before he returned to the bar.

"The other thing you've got to remember is that Zandra now handles all the university funds. She is in effect the new Director of Finances as well as Exterior Academic Advisor."

"Oh … no …"

Wilmot took out his wallet.

"The cheque the Registrar gave me this morning is bloody well signed by her. Now … can I get anybody a drink?"

Lucy spoke up straightaway.

"I don't do this sort of thing usually but … as you're offering and I feel it's called for … I'm going to have a very large brandy."

16

Dimensional quirks have a habit of assuming characteristics all of their own. They are inclined to allow other realities to intrude only if the original sphere desires to include some variation in its agenda. No one could possibly hope to provide an ordered description of *Gwallyog* because it was *The Place of Unreason*. Any attempt was bound to be considered unreasonable. All of Gwallyog, from beginning to its impossible end, was illogical. Hadn't this world been created from the unpredictable, and good old-fashioned chaos? It stayed like that too. When there was the slightest hint of one thing actually leading to another, anarchy took over. Nothing was ever as it seemed, even less so, if that made sense—and nothing ever did. The way this world worked was so much of a caricature that Gwallyog must have been ruled with an ironic fist. Our intrepid travellers didn't know what to make of it, right from the moment they arrived.

With colours, of such exotic and tempestuous hues, almost blinding them, they wandered around in a dormant daze. Above them were purple skies lit with lemon yellow orbs, and a thick, grey and green dust scrunched beneath their feet. Creatures of great size, some with more than one head, stared at them and wandered off. Swarms of something resembling insects made a hideous noise over their heads. Had they known it, the rejected versions of numerous forms of life resided in Gwallyog. Aberrations, and just plain ridiculous notions by Creation, were ferried here and unceremoniously left to fend for themselves.

By far the most numerous of these were the green-toed Querbs that slithered along the branches of the more robust plants in a vain attempt to escape being hunted down and killed by flying Lymatts. The latter were a combination of bat and squirrel, equipped with night vision and predatory teeth. The constant screams of the dying Querbs caused Lily to feel most unsafe, as if she might be their next victim.

Intellectually, Martin was most disturbed by not being able to reconcile Gwallyog with his acquired philosophy of the structure of the Otherworld. If, as he firmly believed, all was part of a holistic universe—such as that described by the more scholarly of New Age pundits—there were certain questions to be answered. Gwallyog could only be considered in the context of being some arcane appendices to the published plan. It was as well that Martin did not know that the world they now found themselves in was so tightly surrounded by fractal geometries it was impossible to enter. That he had worked out a way of achieving this was greatly to his credit. Even more impressive would be getting back out. Martin would certainly have preferred a respite from all this weirdness. Instinctively he knew that he and Lily were going to get a double dollop more before it was all over. And what did the idea of anything being 'all over' mean anyway?

There was one enormous compensation for all this continuing turmoil however—they had found Philomena! Lily saw her in the middle distance, sitting beneath a vermillion shrub with bell-like leaves looking a touch forlorn. She hailed her, and the grateful girl came running towards them almost crying with joy.

"Oh ... this is amazing! How did you find me? How fantastic to see you!"

Naturally Philomena had many questions, all of which Lily did her best to answer, with an occasional contribution from Martin. As might be expected, the foremost of these concerned the prospect of returning to Rylock Wells. Lily was most optimistic, almost casually so. She proceeded to take Martin's arm proprietarily.

"Martin will get us home. I know he will ... he's so clever and wonderful ... and I think I love him to pieces."

The object of all this praise and affection smiled modestly. Philomena looked immensely relieved, confident that Lily was not simply weaving a fantasy about a new boyfriend. So joyous were they that both Lily and Philomena spontaneously began to dance. Martin preferred to sit this one out, quite content to watch them, as their eyes closed and they moved to an unseen rhythm. Lily mingled so totally with the air around her, it was as if she were invisible. So entranced was Martin by the sight that he temporarily set aside planning their return. He consoled himself with the thought that it was better to live in the moment, as that was where ultimate happiness resides. At least, he had heard the spiritually enlightened advocate such an approach to life. He had often enough advocated the use of the moment to travel through the dimensions, so it was only right for him to embrace such a belief.

The evening of the first day of May brought a rich pink tinged with grey to the sky over Rylock Wells. The trees that overlooked the car park of The Robe were painted with a fine brush. In the bar Mandy and Mr. Tonks exchanged confidences. It seemed inevitable they would, the cast of this particular play having dwindled somewhat.

"There ain't nobody left now … Lily and Philomena are gone somewhere an' I don't know where …"

Mr. Tonks was at his persuasive best.

"You really have no idea at all …"

Mandy's features darkened.

"Well … it's strange see … but folks have seen both of 'em walkin' around in the village but when they talks to 'em they don't answer … as if they was ghosts …"

Mr. Tonks was all wonder.

"I see …"

Mandy's eyes filled with tears.

"What's happened to them? They're my best friends … will I ever see 'em again?"

Mr. Tonks deliberated; he was not one for bestowing empty assurances.

"I think so, Mandy … but I cannot say for sure."

Mandy almost wailed.

"Where are they then?"

Mr. Tonks braced himself.

"You remember the book …"

"The one I give to you …"

261

"Exactly. If you had looked at it you would have known that it consisted of writings on magic. Therein lies more than a clue to the disappearance of your friends."

Mandy was stupefied.

"What! They been magicked away?"

"I rather think so … and through the stone circle …"

Mr. Tonks waved in the direction of that Neolithic monument.

"That ain't right? Now that's funny …"

Mr. Tonks was alert.

"Really?"

"Yeh … that *bloke* I was seein' …"

"Florin?"

"That's 'ee. He were askin' me about that book …"

"Oh?"

Mandy was overcome with shame.

"I told 'im Lily 'ad it. He was 'orrible to me bullyin' an' goin on … ."

Mr. Tonks made no judgment.

"I see. You've no idea why this Florin should want to know about the book?"

Mandy looked thoughtful.

"You know … when I think about it … I reckon he was workin' for that 'orrible bloke what come in 'ere. I fink Florin was nickin' stuff for 'im …"

Mr. Tonks pounced.

"Was this *Lord Folds* … by any chance?"

Mr. Tonks was prepared to wait.

"You're right … Florin talked about him once … when he'd had a few … then he shut up quick … like he'd been caught sayin' what he oughtn't to 'ave like."

"Did he say what this Folds was up to?"

Mandy thought harder, Mr. Tonks waited once more.

"Not really except that book was something to do with it … and he was getting him another one like it. He was really mad about losing the first one … kept goin' on about where it was … and did I know …"

Mr. Tonks spoke gently.

"But you didn't tell him it came to me in the end?"

Mandy looked defiant.

"No way was I gonna do that. It was about then when I went off him like. I knows about blokes an' what they're up to … an' he weren't up to no good."

Mr. Tonks ordered another half of Guinness and silently reflected upon the wisdom of woman.

Score was at this moment in the all too familiar position of listening to his employer blowing his top. When he did this, he often resembled a constipated parrot.

"Can't I trust *anyone* to do a simple job? It's completely beyond me the way people carry on. This little twerp … first he says he'll get the first book back … then he says he'll get one that's better … *and he ends up not doing either*. He's completely bloody useless."

"It seems that way, my lord. Not the best choice of …"

Score, noticing the deathly glare, obliterated any hint of criticism just in time.

"And he's got something else ... the document to do with the origins of Barstowe that's mega-important to all this ... or at least he told me he had. I don't believe a bloody word he says these days ..."

"No, my lord."

Folds snarled.

"... and now you tell me this idiot's gone and disappeared off the face of the Earth!"

"It looks that way, my lord ... nobody seems to know where he is."

"Hiding somewhere like the little rat he is."

Score wondered if he was ever referred to in those terms by his employer. Depressingly, he reasoned that it was likely.

"I've almost finished compiling all the material you've asked for ... on the members of Senate ..."

Score had been set to seek out any skeletons hiding in the cupboards of the members of the Senate—tax fiddles, affairs with students and the like.

"Right ... I'll decide what I want done with all that. See what you can find on Lord Lupin as well ..."

Score looked mildly questioning.

"He's this character who's been asked to form an investigative committee about higher education funding ... definitely trying to get us in his sights I'm sure. I want to make it hot for him too if I can. The government and these university types don't like any scandal hanging about round them."

"Yes, my lord."

"And send a message to Flora ... tell Zandra to put the squeeze on anyone else in that bloody university who she suspects of giving us the slightest bit of trouble ... there's still one or two loafing about spreading loose talk."

Score scurried away, discovering, when he returned to reception, that the less than attractive figure of Stibs Gulley had taken up residence. Folds had mentioned his forthcoming arrival, but confronting him, particularly in a relatively small space was less than pleasant. He ignored Score and marched into Folds' office.

"Ah ... there you are ..."

Folds noted that Gulley reeked even more than usual. His robe seemed to have acquired an extra layer of dirt and filth turning it an even darker shade. He did not offer Gulley a chair, and to his relief he seemed to prefer to stand some distance away. The latter regarded Folds with a patronising air. After the way his lordship had behaved at the Winter Solstice ritual, Gulley concluded he was a candidate for the funny farm.

"You wanted something ..."

Folds, remembering his dream, shivered involuntarily.

"Have you done anything about that Tonks character yet?"

Gulley's expression did not change.

"Next item on my list ..."

Not for the first time did Folds consider that Americans were only able to do things by numbers.

"I always thought he was just some bloody Professor Brainstawm ... but he's dangerous. These educated types think too much ... then they start shouting off to rest of those idiots and they listen."

Gulley's face hardened dramatically.

"Terminally subjective jerk that guy is ... gettin' too close to the wire too ... that's fer sure ... he's gotta be put back in line ..."

Almost casually, Folds slid a bulky envelope across his desk towards Gulley.

"What's this?"

"Ten thousand pounds ... in cash."

"Yeh?"

Folds adopted a faraway look.

"I thought that might be a little incentive ... for doing the job *properly* ..."

Gulley paused. He thought for a moment, at the same time picking up the envelope and secreting it in some inside pouch of the smelly robe.

"I see what yer sayin' ..."

"So I can leave it up to you to deal with him then ..."

"Right ... right. I'll fix that ..."

Folds nodded. Inwardly he congratulated himself. No professional hit man would have come so cheap.

"Good. Sooner the better. Oh ... and there is one other thing I want you to do ..."

"Huh? Whut's that?"

"I need some sort of ritual ... incantations ... or whatever you call it ..."

Gulley looked curious.

"Yeh? What you tryin' to get goin' now?"

"I've decided to abandon doing any Summer Solstice Ritual ... too much going on at the moment ... but I want to seal off that Portal so that no one gets back out of it ... I have my reasons ..."

Gulley regarded him wryly.

"Makin' yer revenge permanent … huh? Boy, you sure crossed some boundaries when you grabbed that cup and threw the holy water around …"

Folds glowered.

"I'll do what I want … I've every right to … if people give me trouble and interfere in my affairs."

Gulley shrugged nonchalantly.

"Yer karma, my friend. You gotta live with it."

Folds deliberated.

"That bloody Rylock Wells place gives me the creeps … but I'll go down there … tonight maybe … sooner the better. I'll put half-a-dozen curses on it if I have to …"

Gulley did not react to all this, only thinking that the men in white coats were well overdue.

"Right."

Folds looked up.

"I don't suppose you want to be there … give me a hand …"

Gulley could think of nothing less he would rather do.

"Nope … not if you want me to settle that other business. That'll take a little plannin' …"

Folds was bland.

"I thought you might throw in a quick spell …"

Gulley appeared to make a decision.

"Okay. I'll give you what you want …"

Pulling a notebook from somewhere inside the reeking robe Gulley tore out a sheet and scrawled a few words in a florid hand. This he gave to Folds who received it as if he had been handed a dead fish.

"And that'll do the trick will it?"

Gulley was laconic.

"Oh … yeh. Stand in front of the Portal and say all that a coupla times … then get the hell outa there."

Folds eyed him, not with a little respect.

"How do you mean?"

"Just you be careful, mister … that's all I'm sayin'. You've already upset the spirits round that place … they don't dig to be messed with too much y'know …"

Folds looked defiant.

"I can take care of myself … thank you"

"Sure … sure …"

Gulley drew his robe around him, sending a waft of something rank in Folds' direction. Didn't the man know anything about personal hygiene? Folds couldn't help noticing Gulley was in a hurry to leave, and this prompted him to depart for Rylock Wells immediately. The power of the spell might wear off if he didn't get casting as soon as possible. He called for Score and together they stuffed the Rolls with the artefacts Folds considered necessary for his magical excursion.

The prize item was a ceremonial hat, a ravishing titfer which, owing to its vintage, periodically needed maintenance—a plume replaced here, a clasp tightened there, its sheen painstakingly restored. A crimson cummerbund, made from enough material for a sizeable pair of curtains, a waistcoat with a glistening jewel resting in folds of white satin, robes inlaid with gold and tangerine filigree thread—all were carefully loaded into the boot. The staff of Thule and a pair of antelope leather sandals adorned with brass studs were laid on the back seat, along with a casket of rings of astonishing gaudiness.

Folds, by driving like a lunatic, arrived at Rylock Wells just before dusk. An air of foreboding hung over the field and the stones in the circle appeared to glower at Lord Folds as he approached them. Bedecked in his wizard's clobber and clutching Gulley's grubby note, Folds made ready for his ritual. What he had conveniently ignored was the invisible presence of the Guardian, an entity of fearsome power and awesome appearance. This elemental being was inclined to ignore the spectacle of pagans dancing naked in the firelight, but this was somewhat different. The sanctity of his domain had been violated by this insolent mortal. Such impertinence could not be ignored, retribution would have to be meted out in due time.

Oblivious to all this, Folds waved his staff and did his best to recite the words Gulley had written. Most of it was half-remembered gibberish from some séance conducted while he was stoned teenager. Incredibly, a vision did manifest itself in Folds' mind, but not one he particularly wished to behold. As if posing for some holiday snapshot Martin, Lily and Philomena stood grinning at him. Folds realised that yet again he had been mocked by the universe. He tore off his magical hat and threw it onto the ground in his rage. Unluckily for him it landed in a cowpat.

17

Ollie was woken in the early hours. He thought he heard someone scampering along the street outside. Just a plastic cup caught by the wind—rattling, hollowly along the street. He did not go back to sleep, and it was with a slow tread that he arrived at the Department in the morning. Waiting for him was an email requesting that he see Bingley-Brass. Ollie knew the axe was about to fall.

The Vice-Chancellor—following Lord Folds' diktat to the letter—was now setting about removing both Ollie and Mick Benson from the fold. Rather deviously, he decided to open his interview with Ollie by listing Mick's sins, calculating this would soften the blow when his own dismissal was announced. Bingley-Brass started on this tack straightaway.

"Trouble wi' Mick is he's thirsty lad … don't yew agree, Ollie?"

"He likes a drink certainly … so do a lot of people in this university."

An image of Trencham quaffing in The Willows came unbidden into his mind.

"Health and Safety … that's what's doon it. Not sayin' they're insistin' … boot my understandin' of regulations is that it's been decided he's a danger to oother staff and the student body in general."

Ollie was almost speechless, but not quite.

"You're telling me that's the reason for his dismissal? I'm presuming you've decided to sack him … and the reason being that he likes a drink occasionally. How can you possibly justify that? Has been seen ... or reported ... drunk in the English Department?"

Bradford-Bingley knew that if he embarked on debating the issue he would lose ground. He wanted to be the one holding the power when the moment came to inform Ollie of his own removal.

"That's not point is it? Decision's been made ... and that's final. All out of my 'ands now."

Ollie was acid.

"Of course."

Bingley-Brass nervously adjusted a few bits and pieces on his desk.

"Now comin' to consider yer own case ... which we have to do ... it's a bit different."

Ollie could feel the anger surging in him.

"My case? Am I on trial or something?

The Vice-Chancellor was blunt.

"Well ... I suppose in a manner of speaking you are ... yes ..."

"Really?"

Bingley-Brass ploughed on.

"As I say ... different ... more a disciplinary aspect ... Senate hasn't taken kindly to your obstructive attitude ..."

"I see ..."

"You know what I'm sayin' don't you?"

"No ... I don't really ... but it doesn't really matter does it ..."

Ollie saw red and it was the colour of blood, he wondered if he would get away with whacking the Vice-Chancellor across the chops. What would Health and Safety make of that?

"We'll be raht sorry to see y'go ... o'course, Olluh. You've been mainstay of Philosophy Department for well, ah don't know how many years ..."

The platitudes continued to ooze from the flaccid lips. In the end Ollie got up and left, in the same way he had walked out on Dick Trencham some months before. When he returned to his room he met Lucy who, in the manner of the female sex, divined immediately what had happened. On this being confirmed by Ollie she burst into tears.

"It's all over now in't it ..."

Ollie sighed.

"Doesn't look too good I must admit."

In all their years as colleagues, Ollie had never seen Lucy look so distressed. He attempted to comfort her, with a modicum of success.

"If Dick can do that to Fearnley ... and the V.C. treat you like that ..."

"And Mick Benson ... he's been booted out too."

Lucy wailed the more.

"And at one time Dick and Fearnley had a lot of regard ... and I think affection ... for each other. They've lost all sense of perspective ... turn on anyone ..."

Ollie put his hands in his pockets dejectedly.

"They get their orders from the court and hang the offenders ... and none of them seems to be particularly bothered who gets the rope put round their neck ..."

Ollie found a box of tissues on a shelf, and Lucy went off to see about repairing her appearance. Ollie was left to contemplate his fate, and more so that of

Barstowe. Was this how the saga was supposed to end, with everything honourable or noble abandoned—a world where truth had no place? Had the antics of Zandra Croop along with the ruthless ambition of Lord Folds finally conquered? The cowardly surrender of those who should have resisted and defended their principles was incredible to behold. Now he knew how Mick had felt when he got wind of the whole sordid plot in the beginning.

The next blow fell swiftly. Ollie heard that Seymour Widgeon had suffered a heart attack in Beechdale Road. It would have been ironic, bordering on the macabre, if his end had come outside the Department, but that was not to be. The Reaper had made a final appointment with him outside The Willows.

Seymour Widgeon could have been regarded as an icon of the Fifties, but he belonged to a much earlier era—some corner of England forever Edwardian. His was a world of silver threepenny bits and hansom cabs. Ollie remembered how Widgeon had looked on the last occasion he had seen him. A linen jacket and fawn corduroys, a tie—with an insignia of some personal significance—flapping across his chest. Like one of those old gentlemen that are seen every year at Henley, only the straw boater was missing. Ollie also recalled what they had been talking about.

"You know I can't help thinking about Himmler …"

Ollie had, understandably, been puzzled at this.

"Really … why?"

"In Germany in the Thirties the only people who wouldn't swallow the Nazi line were the universities.

They even tried to discredit Einstein without any success. Makes you wonder what would happen now doesn't it. I think they'd welcome the bloody SS in here ... even if they haven't already."

Then, Ollie was still hopeful that sense would prevail.

"I hope not ..."

Widgeon had adopted a distant air.

"All that we've known will be soon be gone. Take my advice ... don't take it all too seriously. It's not our problem ... as scholars ... to be teaching people anything anymore."

Ollie had offered his own, as he thought now, rather wistful contribution.

"I used to think I was following in your footsteps ... you know ... the old school way of doing things."

Widgeon had chuckled.

"I didn't think there were any schools *apart* from the old ones."

Ollie forgot about Widgeon for the moment and thought about Tonks. The name suddenly came to him ... and at the same time Martin ... and the document he had been given. All of this suddenly seemed significant. Ollie went to his desk and rummaged about until he found it. Reading the document, he was even more convinced he should find Mr. Tonks. The future of Barstowe—his future—might depend upon it. But he wasn't quite sure where to begin any search for him. At that moment the gods decided to make their play. As if guided by an unseen hand, Ollie went into Beechdale Road. There, not a few paces ahead of him was the man he sought.

"Excuse me ... is your name Tonks?"

He who was addressed made a mock bow.

"Archibald Tonks ... in person."

"How amazing!"

"Is it?"

Ollie was all confusion.

"Well ... yes ... it is actually ... I sort of wanted to see you ... and there you are."

Mr. Tonks smiled enigmatically.

"Often the way things work out isn't it ... that is ... when you really want them to. So you're here at Barstowe?"

"Yes ... Philosophy ..."

Mr. Tonks eyes lit like small lanterns.

"Seymour Widgeon ..."

"He's gone ..."

"Really?"

"Yes ... the other day apparently ... eighty-five ..."

Tonks shook his head in wonder.

"And were you fortunate enough to know him?"

Ollie nodded

"He was my tutor ... in the early Seventies ..."

Mr. Tonks considered this.

"Ah ... you must have been here a few years after I left ..."

"Yes ... I must admit I knew about you only vaguely ..."

Mr. Tonks smiled in the grand manner, as only he could—without the slightest hint of pomposity.

"The world of Academia ... where memories are short ..."

"I don't think many people knew about Widgeon

either ..."

Mr. Tonks allowed himself a reflection or two.

"He was very much the essence of real study. Philosophia—a love of wisdom—that was him personified. Wise ... conscientious and always kindly. Plato was his great inspiration ... you know. Like him ... he always encouraged others to develop their own view and to be ready to defend it. 'Tell us what you mean ... we are all ready to listen to your wise words.' That's how he put it to his students ... some of them almost worshipped him you know ... but that was in a different time ..."

"Yes ... I'm not quite sure what they worship now ... their I-Pad ... I expect."

Mr. Tonks assumed his thoughtful air.

"And do you have a student called Martin?"

"Martin Callow? Yes ... I do ... he's probably the best I've come across for some time."

A twinkle came in Mr. Tonks' eye.

"Have you seen Martin in your tutorials recently?"

"Yes ... but come to think of it he's been a bit quiet ..."

There came a sound of small muffled explosions— the sound of Mr. Tonks laughing.

"That's only one part of him ... his doppelganger ... the rest of him is ... shall we say ... taking care of business on another plane."

For a moment Ollie wondered if he was being mocked, he was not really in the mood for that sort of thing.

"What d'you mean? I don't follow ..."

Mr., Tonks laid a reassuring arm on his sleeve.

"You must forgive me ... forget what I just said. We must have humour to allay the pathos of life ... it is a principle of mine."

"But ..."

"It doesn't matter ... I assure you all will be revealed at some point ..."

Ollie was in utter confusion, but somehow he remembered he still clasped the document he had retrieved from his desk.

"This is supposedly a 'Charter of Entitlement' giving the family of Folds ... and their antecedents ... some sort of say in the original foundation of Barstowe University. It's dated 1883 when the land in Clinton and roundabout was originally acquired. I have the feeling you might be able to tell me something about it."

Mr. Tonks had been listening carefully to all this without reacting in any way. A bench in the garden of The Willows presented itself, and he sat down on this, Ollie beside him. He took the document and began to examine it, his eyes darting over the text, assessing and evaluating. He took an eyeglass from the top pocket of his jacket, and with this fixed firmly to his eye continued to scrutinize the text before him. It took but a few moments more before he delivered his verdict.

"A forgery. Not a particularly good one either. Those who wish to deceive are convinced these days that technology will unfailingly serve their purposes. This is not the case. When something is not convincing ... it does not become more so ... no matter how much it may have been digitally enhanced ... or what's it called … photo-shopped."

He handed the document back to Ollie.

"I would have thought you had a valuable piece of evidence in your possession there … and in your favour."

Ollie was more than thoughtful.

"Yes … I think so too. Your verdict on that might even restore our university to its previous … not glorious but at least honest state."

Mr. Tonks studied the sunlight playing on the roofs of the departmental buildings for a moment.

"I'm very glad to hear you say that."

"Are you?"

"Yes … because it a noble sentiment and I will also add that the greatest weapon you have at your disposal is to be subversive. The English are good at that. They're good at being defiant too, mocking their enemies, not taking them seriously even though they threaten and swagger. Our spirit is unquenchable."

"Lord Folds and his ilk shouldn't really frighten us … should they … ?"

Mr. Tonks was adamant.

"Certainly not … the man is an ass … he has a brain the size of a pickled walnut."

Ollie certainly laughed at that, and he also realised that Mr. Tonks possessed no fear. He was as an elusive spirit that flitted to and fro in the sunlight. The eternal liberty that he represented would prove to be decisive in the ultimate downfall of Lord Folds.

Lady Folds put down her cutlery with a more than audible clang. A footman, new to his post, winced. She fixed a look upon Lord Folds that would have done more than adequate service as a laser-beam.

"I have been hearing things, Douglas."

Folds crumbled his bread roll and pretended he was not listening.

"Really?"

"Really. About you being mixed up in some mega-fraud ... and that all manner of unsavoury characters are coming out of the woodwork to denounce you. I feel I have every right to be concerned. And I have noticed that our little army of thugs here ... I do apologise ... security personnel ... have suspiciously bulging pockets."

"Yes ..."

"I have always been particularly nervous of firearms since one of my uncles discharged a punt gun in the smoking room when he was drunk. I do not like the thought of armed men roaming about willy-nilly in my garden. But more important are these rumours ..."

Crumble. Crumble.

"People say all sorts of things ... there's no reason to believe any of them."

"Unfortunately, Douglas ... a lot of people do believe them. Friends of mine for instance ... and also people I do not know ... but whose opinion I value."

The bread was now almost the consistency of powder. Folds signaled for a replacement.

"What does anyone else know about my business affairs ... ?"

"I know enough to realize there's something about all of this which is most definitely fishy, Douglas. At first I thought you were just pulling off some deal and raking in as much gelt as you could ... now I'm not so sure. All I *am certain of* is that it's going to end in tears."

Folds took to scowling at anything and everything around him.

"I stand to be mega-rich if all this comes off ... *and it will* ..."

Lady Folds was almost casual in her tone.

"But how can you be so sure?"

Folds had abandoned the bread and was now applying himself to screwing his napkin into smaller and smaller knots.

"I've got everything sorted out ... right down to the last detail. It won't go wrong ... it can't ..."

His wife shook her head.

"It *will*, Douglas ... and I don't want to be around when it does."

Folds regarded his wife with indifference.

"Don't be then."

Very deliberately Folds took out the four mobile phones that he now took with him everywhere and laid them in a line on the tablecloth. Even he was surprised when they all rang at once. Lady Folds, still fuming, went into the attack once more.

"Have you gone completely mad, Douglas? First I find out that you're messing about with black magic ... now somebody sends me the front page of *The Guardian* where it's shouting about your ridiculous plans to take over Barstowe University and all the rest of them. They described you as the 'biggest threat to higher education since Thatcher'."

Folds was unrepentant.

"Business ... it's all business ... doesn't matter what it is ... or how you go about it ... as long as it makes money."

Lady Folds glared.

"You make it all sound so convincing ... and I'm damn sure you've got yourself mixed up in something that is way beyond you this time. You're completely out of your depth."

"I know exactly what I'm doing ... I've had top advisors from London ..."

"Exactly those spivs in their BMWs I've seen sneaking about ... ... and another thing ..."

Folds grimaced.

"What?"

"... and this is really too much. Your name's to do with some girl who's disappeared in some rural village in god knows where ... Mumbleshire. That's all over the papers too ... I suppose that's part of your Satanic Rites ..."

Folds could not disguise his alarm.

"What! Who said that? What's her name?"

His wife fixed him with a venomous look.

"So you do know something about it!"

"Of course ... I don't. What a ridiculous thing to say. You're mad ..."

Lady Folds lowered her voice, almost to a whisper.

"When you start blustering like that, Douglas ... I know you're lying. I've lived with you long enough. You're in big trouble ... and don't expect me to support you when the poopie really hits the fan ... because I won't."

Folds stared.

"I don't need your support ... or anybody else's. All of this will make me a pioneer of education in this country ... you just wait and see ..."

A peal of laughter, louder than Bow Bells hit the air.

"A pioneer of education! And why are you so keen to have that title? Because you couldn't get into university yourself ... and we all know why that is don't we? You're so bloody thick!"

As a parting shot it served. Folds stared as his wife rose from the table and left the room. They would never look upon each other again.

If this was to be Lord Folds' finest hour—the inauguration of the new order at Barstowe University—it did not begin well. The organizers of the *The Pride of Prockleby* launch knew it would be incumbent upon them to invite Lord Lupin to the event. Folds had vehemently resisted this believing, correctly as it turned out, that the rival lord intended somehow to disrupt proceedings. The invitation was, however, still proffered. The arrival of Lord Lupin at the entrance to the marquee in the University Gardens caused as much stir as that of the honoured guests if not more. This his lordship regarded with wry amusement, he had no illusions about Folds and the toadies who surrounded him.

Having studied some of the initial reports that had been offered to the investigative committee he chaired, Lupin considered Folds' triumphal air to be premature. His own view, which he kept strictly to himself, was that Folds and his cronies would inevitably be the victims of hubris. He had also been informed of the campaign by Score to dig up scandal for the purpose of discrediting the senior members of Barstowe University. That the Vice-Chancellor had not always conducted himself blamelessly during the negotiations was unfortunate. Lupin reasoned, however, that ultimately it would be a better outcome if Bingley-Brass should save face and Folds be exposed than any other course. He cupped a canapé in a manicured hand and languidly surveyed proceedings.

Although there were over two hundred guests invited barely half that number had bothered to attend. Those were most obviously divided into two distinct camps. The Folds entourage seemed to regard safety in numbers as their paramount priority. They were disinclined to mingle, conversing among themselves in low voices. Equally, the university contingent kept to their own end of the marquee, away from the low stage that had been erected. The delicacies on the buffet tables remained untouched; the drink did not flow too freely. The atmosphere was distinctly low key.

Zandra it appeared was not on this occasion to address the company, that honour being left to Julian Flora. When the time came, he stood behind the microphone nervously fingering his tie in a state of abject anxiety. His address, although peppered with catch-phrases and rabble-rousing sentiments received only scant attention. The affair might well have turned into a damp squib had not Norton Bradley, with some alacrity, marched on stage to replace the previous speaker. A ripple of expectation went through the crowd as a figure in a velvet jacket joined him. To the horror of Lord Folds and the rest of his contingent, Lord Lupin was being warmly introduced, proceeding to then fill the air with his rich tones.

"Now … some of you may be wondering exactly why I'm addressing you on this occasion … when perhaps by right that should be Dougie's job. But he … for whatever reason has declined the honour … so you've got me representing the nobs this afternoon."

A wave of laughter followed Lupin's sally while Folds began bristling with annoyance. The speaker knew he had the attention of the crowd and he intended to milk the moment for all it was worth.

"In my role as chair of the committee I'm currently involved with … various things have emerged about the state of higher education and perhaps what needs to be done to make some changes. I thought you ought to hear about that. My good friend Douglas …"

Here Lord Lupin made a grand gesture in Folds' direction, the other's obvious discomfort prompting more laughter.

"… has offered us his own ways of going about this … I'm inclined to differ from his views."

Bingley-Brass was agog, Slate also. Several members of the Senate stood open-mouthed.

"Students these days are sometimes quite shocked to discover that they are expected … not only to actually read books but take in what they say … and then later discuss them. Not only that ... but a certain amount of graceful handling of language is expected. It always helps when a tutor reads an essay if he knows exactly what it is the student is trying to say."

A few mutterings of assent could be heard from the academic corner. Lupin beamed in their direction—encouraging and nurturing their responses.

"Too often schools are guilty of not encouraging genuine debate in the classroom. This leads to students being unable to formulate ideas or any argument in their writing. A page of unrelated ideas is considered to be a 'creditable piece of work'. This is why our universities have had to introduce ... to my mind ... the rather ridiculous notion of a student having to spend their first year bringing their work up to an acceptable standard."

This time the sounds of agreement were most audible.

"Learning *per se* has enough to do with acquiring virtues as to be the most valuable exercise for the human mind. Thus ... education should be inviolable ... not subject to the dictates of ambition or the whims of the market place. The motives of Lord Folds and his advisors are questionable to say the least. They seek to reduce the great opportunity and privilege for a young person of entering one of our universities. They advocate an approach where knowledge will be reduced to triviality ... understanding reduced to a formula. This is not what we want ... and I'm sure you would agree ..."

Some time later, it was unanimously agreed this was the turning point in Lord Lupin's speech. The majority of his audience wholeheartedly agreed with his views and started to voice their support.

"In the last months I've been looking closely at what *The Pride of Prockleby* ..."

Here Lord Lupin paused as if waiting for a response; it came in the form of a few giggles that quickly became open laughter. After this, a palpable sense of relief was felt in the room. *The new regime could be mocked!*

"... has undertaken to achieve. I have to tell you that I was not impressed ... and I regret to say these were empty promises that I saw."

The speaker paused once more and there was a distinct rumble of voices, all undoubtedly with him.

"One is forced to conclude that with the proposed *Prockleby* system the acquiring of a degree would be merely a business arrangement between a student and his alma mater. This is a travesty of what the acquiring of knowledge should be. To reduce several thousand years of intellectual toil ... debate and sheer delight in the exchange of ideas ... to something that has no more significance than filling up with petrol in a garage is wrong ... very wrong. We do not want a situation where gobbets of information are force-fed to students who rapidly cease to have any interest in what they are being taught."

A lot of involuntary shuffling started up. Folds was furious at this turn of events. Lord Lupin had been given the opportunity to encourage open rebellion against him!

"In the media ... opinions are served in bite-size chunks all ready to be absorbed by the mind and with no thought involved. If we neglect to study ideas comprehensively then we are left with a series of slogans and catch words. Language is devalued and undermined … turned into brand names."

Cheering started up and continued until tLord Lupin closed his speech. This was a call to arms!

"Knowledge and wisdom are two distinctly different things. One cannot exist without the other … though we might be better vowing always to pursue wisdom. We cannot always rely on reason and niggardly analysis to show us the way ahead. Is there any wonder we have a plague of plagiarism in our universities? *Plagiarius* literally means kidnapper … let us not encourage a situation where the very minds of our young people are usurped. The role of higher education is to teach people how to think … not what to think."

What followed could be fairly described as a standing ovation. The floodgates had burst, bringing a wave of liberty and freedom of thought back to Barstowe. In less than an hour the popularity of Lord Folds had sunk to a low ebb. He was physically shunned, only his hard cores supporters now clustered about him. His lordship was aghast, shaking his head in disbelief and few attempted to console him.

18

At any moment the cosmos is capable of splitting into a zillion universes. Within a few nano-seconds, a brand new version could appear in the middle of our own. The interloper might even engulf the whole of our solar system and, if this happened our notion of time would also disappear. With the birth of any new universe, time begins again. If it were suddenly to contract until the point where it vanished, time would simply disappear with it. This change might take thousands or millions of years to complete and, if there was still life on the planet, it would experience extreme weightlessness. Gravity, which is simply time slowing down, would cease to exist.

Ideas similar to all this kept intruding into Martin's mind, along with new ones about how 'moments' actually worked. This wasn't just him wondering about odd things he wanted his speculations to lead somewhere—mainly home. It was useful to have worked out how he and Lily could shift to another world, but the next stage—returning to their own might need a different approach.

It was possible that any particular moment could lag behind, or get ahead of its neighbours, in the same way that some people thought quicker than others. Any 'now' did not have to be located in any fixed 'present,' it could reside in the future or the past. The challenge was to control time, and one way to do this was to stop the universe. In theory, that could be achieved if every action was immediately superseded by its opposite. The result of this stultifying equilibrium would be to cause the universe to come to a halt and, to an observer; all would appear to be frozen.

Right now he, Lily and Philomena were looking out through an enormous window at their own world, and wishing they could be part of it. Martin had begun working on another theory that any experience could be transformed into molecules and these could interact along neuron paths. Events not being composed of solid matter, merely traces of energy, perhaps they could be turned into flashes of light or snatches of melody. If he could somehow reproduce the reality they were seeing, and combine it with a powerful enough thought form they would be at the winning post. Fortunately, Mr. Tonks was at that same instant thinking along the same lines. Would these two trains of thought meet? It seemed they would, the terminus was already in sight.

In his researches, Mr. Tonks was working on some way of retrieving the travellers' collective memory of Rylock Wells and relocating it in the present. The idea of 'memory' simply meaning the act—in the present—of retrieving some incident from the past, then that should be possible. He hoped the resonance would be strong enough to manifest an actual shift in time and space. Gwallyog must give up the three travelers and return them to where they belonged! Intent on securing this end, Mr. Tonks now stood in the stone circle, his sleeves rolled and ready.

His determination blazing like ten thousand beacons, Mr. Tonks approached the portal, not just as himself, but as a myriad of minds each with its own perception. In that way he met the Otherworld on its own terms—having access to as many variations as that sphere.

There was only one winged insect in the unguent—Stibs Gulley. Mr. Tonks had already observed him entering the field, his filthy robe flapping about his ankles. His pace quickened as soon as he espied Mr. Tonks, until he was almost flying across the grass. Unmoved, the figure among the stones continued to concentrate on enunciating his words slowly and carefully, until he had concluded the ritual. The next moment he heard Gulley's agitated shouting.

"Jesus H. Christ ... what's going on here?"

Mr. Tonks waited, calm and still.

"Good morning. Splendid day ..."

Panting for breath, Gulley was now only a few yards away.

"What the hell are you doin, mister?"

Mr. Tonks turned a smiling face upon the newcomer.

"How are you? Well ... I trust?"

Gulley snarled in reply.

"Don't gimme no oyster crackers, bub. Time I squared up this whole deal with you ..."

Mr. Tonks feigned surprise, he was playing for time—literally.

"I'm not sure I follow ..."

Gulley faced him.

"Listen, wise ass ... don't act up with me okay? You may think yer some fun guy in the mix but you ain't. I knew you wuz up to sumpin' all along ... I aim to fix yer little wagon but good."

Mr. Tonks could not help but chuckle, not at what

was said, but the Bronx- style delivery. Combined with the Father Brown outfit it made for an incongruous combination. Gulley stared at him, his eyes bulging in fury.

"Quit the laughin' will yuh? Yer in big trouble ... whichever you want it. A slug fest prolly ain't yer style I'm thinkin' ... huh?"

Mr. Tonks was even.

"I warn you ... you are completely out of your depth ..."

"I yam am I? Right you axed for it ... interfering allatime in what's going on around here! I aim to make sure you ain't gonna be givin' nobody no trouble tuh anybody ... ever agin."

Gulley was now stood in front of the portal, one arm raised. If his intention was to unleash a volley of diabolic oaths or something worse, he never got the chance. At that moment a blinding silver and blue light flashed from beneath the stone nearest to him. Gulley, taken totally by surprise, made to shield his eyes. He was now tottering from side to side as a billion shards of space dust enveloped him. Waves from the cosmic seas struck time and time again and more was to follow. Emerging from the depths of the portal, in a cascade of starry incandescence came three figures one after the other. Martin led them, followed by Lily and Philomena. Like champagne corks at a wedding, they popped out and flew through threw the air pinning Gulley to the ground.

As the three stood about getting their bearings, the portal renewed its dazzling glow. Mr. Tonks watched it change to a vermillion and tangerine hue.

The fiery light seemed to reach out and engulf Gulley, who began to scream in terror. Unable to resist, he was slowly sucked head first into the now reversed vortex that lay beyond the portal. His robe billowed about him revealing undergarments that in any other circumstances would have provoked endless merriment.

Prockleby had the air of being abandoned to some inevitable fate. Although the guards still patrolled the grounds and the staff went about their chores in the main building, there was little sign of life anywhere else. Folds remained permanently in his office, having his meals sent over from the kitchens. He had grown stout in recent months, and had taken to sporting mutton-chop whiskers making him resemble a pantomime villain.

Lady Folds, tired of her husband's antics, was staying with friends in the West Country. While there she visited Windleroot, surprised to see that this inconspicuous town, as she remembered it, had become a haunt of soothsayers and peddlers of trinkets. In Lowe Street, her curiosity was aroused by a sign proclaiming *Annie Fannie the Fortune Fairy*. On being informed that the services of this exotic personage were available, Lady Folds immediately booked an appointment. This corpulent clairvoyant appeared from behind a velvet curtain and led her into a small chamber festooned with plaster statues, wolves' heads and angels appearing from clouds, looking aloof.

Pungent incense made curlicues in the air, patchouli oil added a sickly undertone to the atmosphere and Lady Folds wondered if this had been a good idea. Her companion, festooned in beads of every hue, took down a distressed tome from a shelf and asked about her birthday. Lady Folds gave her the information and, after consulting its pages with many a portentous sigh, Annie Fannie set the book down reverently. A fleshy hand then shuffled a pack of cards and several colourful images were laid out on the brocaded cloth of the table in front of her ladyship. In a sonorous growl the clairvoyant began to intone the messages being relayed to her from the aether.

"I see dark energies ... a dangerous man ... this card here. He is powerful and thinks he may command others ... but he is doomed to fail and will suffer the worst fate. You will only be available to escape from this yourself if you act immediately ... within the next nine days ... yes ... nine. I see the number in the air above you. The great house and possessions you now have will be taken from you and you will wander ... visiting places ... for the next year ... perhaps longer."

Lady Folds was astonished; she could feel herself gripping the handle of her handbag tighter and tighter. She listened in a trance to a lot more of this, all in the same vein. At last the woman's voice stopped. She gazed at her with an expression that Lady Folds considered was both knowing and imbecile.

"That's all there is ... but it's probably quite enough isn't it, dear?"

Lady Folds recovered, partly.

"I … I … rather think it is …"

Annie Fannie regarded her in rather a bored manner.

"Do you desire to know about future love?"

Lady Folds was decisive.

"No … I don't think I do … thank you. That was quite enough … what you've already told me."

"Alright, my dear."

Lady Folds unclasped her handbag.

"Now … what do I owe you?

Lady Folds paid the woman, took in the hippie nick-nacks and exotic wall-hangings one last time, and took her leave. She found herself in Lowe Street not knowing in which direction to go. Feeling unnerved and confused she went off in search of a cup of tea. The emporia that served refreshment were equally as odd as the rest of the premises in Lowe Street, but she located one that did not cause her too much offence. Phrases that the fortune teller had said kept coming back to her as she sipped her lapsang suchong.

Later she drove back to Pokey Fiddleton where she was staying. It was the next village from Rylock Wells though Lady Folds would have no notion of the significance of that place in the life of her husband. Fate it seemed was having many a jest at the expense of both of them.

Lily's garden was the sort of place where anyone might find fairies. Enchantment had hovered in so many odd corners here, and for so long, that it was bound to breed elves and princesses. There was a pond with dragonflies kissing the surface of the water, and other delights of Wonderland. Lily and Philomena, in all their make-believe finery, fitted the scene perfectly. Martin in his jeans and t-shirt, thought he ought to be wearing tights and a velvet jerkin. The endless happiness that the two girls displayed on returning home was infectious too and Martin opened his heart to both of them. His reward was to be feted and fussed over until the evening, when Philomena decided she must adjourn to the Robe and renew other friendships there.

"They'll all be so pleased to see you …"

"It will be lovely to see them all too …"

She skipped away, and Lily and Martin were left alone together. Love has the power to preserve a moment for all time. With its universal touch, beauty is unfettered and undiminished as poets and minstrels have always known. Martin had all sorts of fine speeches prepared but none of them he could remember, so he made do with improvising.

"I want you so much, Lily …"

Lily took both his hands in hers and looked into his eyes, searching.

"I will be yours forever if you wish it … that I promise … but first you must know what I am really like …"

Martin didn't think that was on the agenda.

"I'll always love you whatever you're like …"

Lily looked even deeper into him.

"So you say … but … loving someone doesn't necessarily mean you should be with them forever."

Martin considered this.

"Well … no reason why we shouldn't try."

The thought of being robbed of Lily's presence was not comforting. Men wish to possess, and with desire inevitably comes pain—as Buddha said. No one may own anything in this world, it is all out on loan—I said that.

"You're very smart, Martin … but I don't think you know how strange the world may really be …"

Martin was inclined to disagree.

"What? After all that stuff we went through …"

Lily smiled once more and held his hands even tighter.

"That was nothing …"

Martin looked out over the garden and the dragonfly that he had seen earlier seemed to fill his mind, until there was nothing else he could see. The creature stayed there, hovering ecstatically. Martin's entire world was a vision in shimmering gold, emerald, saffron and vermillion. The colours that made up its form were of pure light. Wings, like veined glass, disappeared into infinity amid rippling flashes of silver. This vibrating kaleidoscope of atoms was suspended in the air, part of the space that surrounded it. Somehow, Martin remembered that dragonflies had been on the planet for a hundred-and-eighty million years—that rather put humans in their place. When the dragonfly flew off, it was as if the sun had gone out. Martin had just about got things back in focus when he realised Lily was talking to him.

"You know … I read this book that Mandy gave me … and I was supposed to because it showed me all the darkness in the world and beyond the world. I read it over and over again … that's why I could go through that Doorway of Darkness and become part of that world. I thought I could just go there and bring Philomena back though … I believed I had the power to do that … then I found out I didn't. I'm too much part of the light … just like you are."

Martin agreed.

"Golbellen … The Land of Light."

Lily nodded.

"That's right … and I knew someone would help me to get there but I didn't know who it was going to be. I was amazed when I found out it was you and then I remembered when we met the first time … .but I didn't *know* you then … afterwards I realized that you really were a part of me … but I still wasn't sure. Then when you looked after me … protected me … sometimes from myself … I trusted you then … completely. You were holding my soul in your hands … though you probably didn't know that."

"Probably not … I don't know everything."

Lily laughed, and took his hand, leading him.

"Come with me I shall show you beauty of the Goddess … the beauty of woman … you will be completely in my world …"

Martin took in all the extraordinary beauty that was in Lily's world—the room where she slept—the universe that surrounded her. They sat on the end of the bed looking at each other.

"This is amazing …"

She took his hand once more.

"I've never made love to any man before."

Martin tried to appear terribly worldly for about ten seconds, then gave up.

"Well that's okay ..."

"I went to bed with someone once but I knew it wasn't right ... so before anything happened I got up and ran away. I only just managed to grab my clothes ..."

She laughed again, and the next moment they lay together naked, holding each other like children do. Martin was laughing too and thinking how delicious it all was and how much he loved life—and Lily. She was his life—all the world, all creation. Lily looked up at him and her eyes answered his request. Lily wanted his caress and it was duly given, for Martin loved her. Suddenly, that wondrous and eternal love showed how profound it could be and they began to make love—as if they were the world itself being created from nothing.

When they woke the next morning, their souls were entwined. All else had been left behind. They had created this paradise themselves, one far greater than Golbellen or any other world. The design followed the one traced by an unseen hand—the Divine Will. When Martin looked out at the land, and the stone circle in the distance he believed he had never seen anything look so beautiful before. Apart from the goddess beside him.

19

The cad's moustache Score owned had become so pencil thin with constant trimming it had become almost microscopic. Perhaps unconsciously he wished he could deny owning it. Unfamiliar with Biblical texts, Score would not have considered his situation to resemble the Damascus Road. His epiphany might not be of a celestial nature, but it certainly came as dramatically as the drama heaped upon Paul of Tarsus. The moment when he decided to abandon Lord Folds employ came when, arriving at Prockleby on this particular morning he saw the security guards were openly carrying guns. Not a discreet holstered pistol, as one sees at continental airports, each man was furnished with an AK47. As soon as he came into the reception room, he could hear Folds in his office, screaming into the telephone.

"Foreign investments? What about them? Inconsistencies in our records ... what is all this? Impossible to continue on that basis? I can easily get another firm to do all this y'know ... you're the one who's missing out. If you take that attitude ... you won't get a penny out of me until you've returned every scrap of all the documentation. You must think you're dealing with someone who's bloody wet behind the ears ..."

Score waited until the phone was slapped onto the desk. Perhaps strengthened by his sudden resolve to quit, he marched into Folds' office.

"Morning, my lord."

Ignoring the greeting, his lordship continued to rage, not only against fate, but all creation.

"I knew I should never have put any faith in that Flora ... that hoity-toity bitch Zandra has jumped ship too ..."

"Really, my lord?"

Folds turned on him.

"Where's Gulley?"

"He has not been in touch lately, my lord."

"Another one who's run out on me ... *and* without doing what I asked him to do either. I'll bet that bloody Tonks is still strutting around making trouble ... no one around stopping him that's for sure ..."

Before Folds could become more enraged he picked up one of his many phones.

"Yes ... get me the Vice-Chancellor. I don't care if he's in a meeting ... twenty meetings ... get him out of there and talking to me."

Score could feel his heart racing; this is what it must be like to have a panic attack he thought. The sound of Folds' voice was a cacophony, worthy of bedlam. If he did not silence it, he would guarantee being on a fast train to madness himself.

"Excuse me, my lord ... I must just ..."

Folds did not even hear, and Score stole away, never to return to the sinking ship that was Prockleby. He left behind a despotic Folds issuing orders that any dissidents at the university must be liquidated. The whole scene was beginning to resemble Hitler in his bunker. Later, real bullets would feature when the next night three armed groups independently laid siege to Prockleby. The security guards were hard pressed to defend themselves against concerted attacks from Breguna's hit squad, Israeli Freedom Fighters, and a random Mafia contingent from Reno. The local Police Inspector decided not to bring in the Swat Teams to aggravate the debacle but, more pragmatically, to announced annual leave would be granted early that year instead.

Bingley-Brass regarded the framed photograph of his wife, a permanent fixture on his desk. Today was their wedding anniversary, and he reminded himself yet again that he must buy a suitable bouquet of flowers. Away from this domestic bagatelle, the Vice-Chancellor was not at ease and could not understand the reason. He soon found out. Slate burst into the room looking more than haggard, he could have auditioned for a part in Macbeth.

"Summat's wrong ..."

"How d'you mean, Willie?"

"She's gone' ..."

"Who has?"

"Zandra ..."

"Zandra! Wha'? ... Why?"

Slate waved a sheet of paper frantically.

"Resignation ..."

Bingley-Brass could only manage a feeble echo.

"Resignation?"

Slate muttered darkly.

"Aye ... an' that's not all ..."

"Oh?"

"She's demanded big payoff ... an' I mean big ... an' she's told me ... joost now ... to me face ... if she don't get it she's blowin' whole gaff about Folds and oos."

The Vice-Chancellor adopted a haunted look.

"She can't do that … she doesn't have …"

Slate returned his look with another, more placid.

"Oh … yes she does. She's got a transcript of every phone call we've ever made to him … all the emails … faxes … she's not missed a trick I can tell yew."

Bingley-Brass leapt out from his desk, as if it was on fire.

"She had no business havin' access to any of that lot."

Slate spoke deliberately.

"I think we agreed that she was the only one to have the master password to all the university electronic files didn't we?"

"Did we? I don't remember any of that."

Slate looked arch.

"Well … whichever … she's certainly got me and thee over a barrel now."

The Vice-Chancellor stared, as if desperately trying to think of some corner of the universe where he could find some solace. At the same time there was much discussion about Lord Folds in the Department. Although both Ollie and Wilmot had been officially relieved of their duties, they continued to meet in each other's rooms whenever they felt like it. Without the slightest emotion, Wilmot was detailing some of Lord Folds' previous financial dealings.

"It's all coming out now he's in disgrace with the city. Apparently he ran Staple Investments in the Nineties … they offered ridiculously high returns on investment ... saying they had offshore accounts so it was all untouchable. Their folio was put about as a hedge fund naturally ... but one where future returns were absolutely guaranteed. Told investors they were onto something hush-hush ... opportunity not to be missed ... all that sort of thing ...

"And people fell for this ..."

Wilmot looked bland.

"The capacity for self-delusion is extraordinary."

"Indeed."

"Usually stimulated by lust for power ... or greed which I suppose is the same thing really."

"But they must have paid out something ..."

"They did ... oh, yes ... and went on doing so ... for a bit ..."

"And then ..."

"The city got on to Staple Investments ... and that was that. Just as they've got onto Folds again."

"Right."

"It was the six month audit that did it. They had put in false returns ... the audits themselves were complete fairyland too. Then the boss man Waitley-Priest was his name I think ... couldn't be contacted anywhere. Hey Presto! Then everyone wants their money back ..."

"That must have been a bit embarrassing for ..."

"One of our major high street banks got hit very hard I can tell you."

"I'm not surprised ..."

"No ... someone working for them was in on it ... of course ..."

"Then there was the gold scam ..."

Ollie frowned.

"Spare me that … one scam at a time is enough."

Wilmot even managed a grin.

"It wasn't for Folds obviously … no sooner had one fallen apart than he was onto the next …"

Changing tack, Ollie told Wilmot about the forged charter. Ollie had never seen him so animated, particularly while he was relating what Mr. Tonks had told him.

"But that changes *everything* …"

Ollie looked blank.

"Does it?"

"Don't you see? Most certainly it does … come on we've got every right to go and see Bingley-Brass about this … and stinker Slate …"

Wilmot was almost rubbing his hands together in glee."

"Come on!"

Ollie dutifully followed Wilmot out of the Department and into Beechdale Road.

After his own country had turned against him, America then rejected Lord Folds and all his works. In the inimitable manner of justice in The Land of The Free he was denounced and condemned in one move. In the American Way, there were either sinners or saints, nothing in between. You were either with them or against them, and Folds had definitely become the enemy. He was pilloried in the Press as a maverick and a fraudster, and there were even snide references to him as 'that now redundant institution—the European nobility'.

Folds had never felt less noble than he would in the coming weeks when he would become a fugitive from justice—a man on the run.

Discreetly made aware of all this, and a few other revelations, Lord Lupin considered he might best serve the cause by attempting to save Barstowe University from disaster. With this in mind he immediately drove to Clinton, his first port of call being The Willows, the venue for a discreet meeting with certain parties. At the appointed hour, Wilmot, Ollie and Mick took tea with Lord Lupin.

"Thank you for agreeing to meet me, gentlemen … I'm much obliged. I mainly wanted to see you three in particular as it seems to me you have been very unfairly treated. I first of all want to inform you that you will all be instated by the university that I shall insist on … though I would be obliged if you would not mention that to anyone at the moment. Rome has not quite fallen yet … so to speak."

Lord Lupin beamed on the company, and they beamed back. Wilmot was the first to speak.

"Much obliged, Lord Lupin … though I must admit I vowed not to ever work here again … but one can always change one's mind. What really bothers me is the way our masters … if you know who I mean … have behaved in all this."

Benson could not contain himself.

"Appalling is the word …"

Ollie merely nodded, he was undoubtedly relieved to have his job back, but he wondered if matters were as simple as all that. Lupin surveyed them all in kindly fashion.

"I think the key word here is caution. One doesn't want to cause a stink if it doesn't achieve anything. I must say though that when the papers get hold of all this ... and they will ... then things are bound to come out that The Vice Chancellor and others would rather didn't. It may be that he and Mr. Slate might be wiser to resign ... or at least announce their retirement. That's between ourselves ... of course."

Benson, as always, was inclined to speak his mind.

"I rather think 'stink' is the word here. What worries me is if it could happen again. It rather does show that the university is not run as a democracy when it comes down to it ... and worse still ... when a fat enough carrot is being dangled in front of some people they can't resist taking it."

Wilmot put in his bit.

"Also what scandalized so many people was that everything was done in such an underhand fashion. It's only really the luck of the draw that Lord Folds has shot himself in the foot ... if he'd been kosher the whole thing might have worked and I wouldn't be sitting here talking to you."

Lord Lupin acknowledged all this.

"Yes ... it has been to our advantage in some ways that we are dealing with a total crook. He got in right out of his depth with the people he'd been dealing with too ... all far worse than him apparently. Anyway ... I'm informed that as of yesterday a warrant was issued for his arrest ..."

Ollie who had said nothing so far felt it was

relevant to mention the forged document. At this, Lupin looked immensely interested.

"What an extraordinary stroke of luck! So we presume Folds commissioned a spurious document that would enable him to have some hereditary authority in how the university could be conducted. Plausible of course ... in theory ... equally odd covenants do exist but ... in this case highly fraudulent. You say you told the Vice-Chancellor all about it ..."

Wilmot was blunt.

"When Ollie and I presented it all to him ... *fait accompli* ... he behaved very oddly. Basically, he didn't want to know ... denied that he had ever seen it and that Folds had never mentioned it to him. It didn't make sense to me ... if he didn't know about it in the first place ... why did he take such so much trouble to deny he did?"

Lord Lupin steepled his fingers in judicial fashion.

"I think, gentlemen ... my next call will be upon Messrs. Bingley-Brass and Slate ..."

Mick was succinct.

"They've certainly dug themselves into a hole ... it'll be interesting to see if they can get out of it."

Lord Lupin concluded proceedings in his usual adept manner, but not before making a final comment.

"The lesson I have learned is that in all sorts of place s you would least expect it there is still a far-too-cozy relationship between government ... business ... and ... how shall we say ... *funny money*."

20

As the month of August drew to a close there was already more than a hint of Autumn. This was not evident in the warm days, those deceiving everyone it was still High Summer. The cool evenings held a distinct undertone of the stillness of September. Martin had asked Lily out to dinner in Clinton. Although it was in some ways a formal affair, they both had a touchingly casual attitude to the evening. All promised well as they approached the restaurant. Above them was a sky that resembled a detail in some renaissance painting, one where clouds are sure to reveal angels if you looked hard enough.

Le Chat sur les Tuiles hovered just this side of being pretentious, but its prices were not too extra-terrestrial. By the time they arrived, the place had filled up enough as to be cozy, and their candlelit table was endearingly corny. When the uniformed waiter handed him a menu the size of the Dead-Sea Scrolls, Martin could hardly stop himself from giggling. Lily decided that was just one more thing she loved about him, the way he laughed whenever he felt like it.

"Shall we have some wine?"

Martin asked the question as an amateur not a connoisseur.

"Of course! We should have champagne …"

Martin hesitated

"Why not?"

"Don't worry I'll pay for it …"

A bottle arrived with another liveried type, and glasses were filled. Bubbles do make a difference, everything becomes so light, and soon the lovers floated away into sweet nothings. They returned to eart when all sorts of dishes full of fancy stuff arrived on their table.

"Oh … lovely! What's this … so exciting …"

Sweet talk was temporarily suspended during the handling of cutlery, topping up of glasses, and the actual business of eating. After all that, they returned to romance. Martin produced a tiny box, one exquisitely wrapped.

"I want you have this … it's …"

"A way of saying you love me …"

"… and you love me … I hope …"

Lily seized his hand.

"Of course I do …

"Then …"

The silver ring, engraved with hearts, slipped onto Lily's finger as if it had always been there.

"Now we shall be together forever and ever."

Their lips met over the table and, in another dimension, crowds of people clapped their hands and sang out loud. This world had been left behind, and all that remained was the aura of love. They drove back to the flat on Cloud Nine, and others equally significant. At the door, Martin paused.

"I did tidy up a bit …"

Lily put her arm about his shoulders.

"It doesn't matter. Soon you can come and live with me in my house. Would you like that?"

Martin encircled her.

"I think I would."

The next day when they left to return to Rylock

Wells, Martin waved to Minnie. She seemed to have abandoned the bicycle for a skateboard, and was now zealously practicing wheelies on her front door step.

Score had been arrested that morning; he had almost been waiting for the inevitable knock on the door and feeling of the collar. The neighbours watched with interest as he was led away by the Birmingham C.I.D. Boxes of papers, taken from the attic of his house, filled most of another vehicle brought specifically for the purpose. His initial statement, declaring that he did not know Lord Folds and had never seen any of the confiscated documents, was given short shrift. Score, who had always worked on the theory that people did not find the truth palatable, quickly surmised that the law took a different view

In the early hours all the groups who had been laying siege to Prockleby, as well as a few opportunists, attacked the buildings with ground missiles and firebombs. The security force, knowing the next assault would mean the end of them, moved out—the staff in their wake. Just as the most junior of the under-gardeners scampered past the lodge, the holocaust began. By dawn the mansion was a flaming pyre, hours later a mere skeleton in a pile of ash. The county fire brigade, as had the police earlier, decided to absent themselves.

Folds had quit the place hours before, grabbing cash from the safe and any other valuables and throwing it into the boot of the Rolls. As he drove across the Yorkshire moors he was aware of his destination only too well. He would be returning to the stone circle, almost against his will. Driving maniacally through the night, like a man possessed he finally reached Rylock Wells. He flung open the car door, almost falling to the ground, and then loped along the path towards the stones like some monstrous creature of the wilds. The moment he entered the field, he sensed something was following him—but he knew not what. Wheezing and grunting his way towards the stones, he felt the power of the spirits weighing upon him.

Pausing before the circle, he saw a vision of Mr. Tonks, much as it had been in his dream. The words he spoke now were not tomfoolery but seared into his soul.

"'I do not judge, Lord Folds ... all may do as they so wish ... it is not for me to decide what occurs in this world or any other. But you have dishonoured your knightly vows and cast aside the code of chivalry ... and the spirits are aware you have profaned this sacred place with your evil ...'"

The words echoed in his mind, gradually seeping into nothingness. Lord Folds knew instinctively that his doom was approaching. He was aware of the presence of a colossus, intent on destroying him and, within moments this lumbering stack of tawny red rock charged upon him. The Guardian was intent on crushing the interloper in his kingdom. Only one place remained for its victim to flee, and that was through the Portal into the Otherworld. In Twyfin the darkness would receive Lord Folds as one of its own.

There he would exist as less than a wraith, until such time as all traces of him would cease to exist.

Lady Folds, now permanently in exile in the shires, found herself falling upon the mercies of those obscure relations she knew who had a home there. In the coming years she would live as a hermit in a tiny cottage in Pokey Fiddleton, her pride somewhat dented but not entirely vanquished. Right now her ladyship was forced to endure the attentions of the Red Tops, for the Press did not take long in locating her whereabouts. A barrage of questions from insistent young men of the media was her lot.

"Lady Folds do you know where your husband is at present?"

"Do you have any comment to make about his disappearance?"

"Has he been in contact with you?"

"Lady Folds ... do you think you will ever see your husband gain?"

She rather hoped not, but was not prepared to admit that and present *The Sun* with a juicy headline.

The last fixture of the season had been played on the village green at Rylock Wells. A rather melancholy atmosphere accompanied the last few overs of the match, and stumps were drawn with a solemn finality. The English take sport and the state of the weather very seriously indeed, and always with a sense of fatalism. As much a supporter of village cricket as everything else English, Lord Lupin had organized an informal party at the Robe. As well as the triumphant return of Barstowe University to its scholarly traditions, the victory of common sense was also to be celebrated.

The cricket team, along with everyone else in the village, had been cordially invited to the event. On hearing that she would be in the company of at least twenty-two athletic young men, Mandy chose to wear her most daring outfit, one that plunged and swooped like a bevy of swans. The landlord was just as enthusiastic about the coming junket. Lawrence Groves, who played an electronic keyboard fitted with more effects than the Millennium Falcon, got the gig in preference to H.P. Umber. George had also tapped a new barrel of *Hefty XX* and set it up on the bar next to a vast jar of pickled onions. Nobbs Dyer, the local odd-job man, was prompted to spend some time staring at this and peering intently into its vinegary depths.

"What I wants ter know is why some on 'em floats and the uvvers stays down the bottom …"

Such a profound observation could not go unheeded. Clifford spoke knowledgeably about dirigibles, while Old Ted insisted it was something to do with the weather. Throughout the evening countless theories concerning onions and their physical properties were proposed and confounded. Even Mr. Tonks when he arrived was drawn briefly into the discussion, though that gentleman was soon to be monopolized by Lord Lupin.

"I have no wish that the tenor of the evening be one of gloating over the demise of Lord Folds … that I would consider most unseemly …"

"Quite … quite … the sort of glee that sometimes accompanies the passing of an unpopular politician …"

"We have achieved what we wanted at Barstowe and that is enough. Don't you agree?"

Mr. Tonks acquiesced.

"I do … most certainly. One can only reflect upon the power of the universe to always retain the balance. The wild card is always there to be played … a chance happening is our greatest asset when there is the threat of any sterile regime."

Lord Lupin smiled in an accomplished manner.

"I so agree … and that Folds type … they get so easily drunk with power …"

Mr. Tonks delivered his verdict.

"Ah … yes … *power* … one of the great illusions of man … and possible the most debilitating. Yet another anthem of artifice … sung at the top of their voices by the deluded … and *so* grossly deluded are they. It would be better if they put their considerable energies … not into strutting about in tight boots and uncomfortable uniforms … but in a moment's reflection … which might just possibly become *realisation*. One may always hope …"

"Indeed. Lovely to talk to you … I feel I must mingle …"

Lord Lupin glided away as if he was on well-oiled wheels. The party was livening up, more guests arriving by the minute, so that bar was soon stuffed with every class and disposition of folks. Fuelled with Hefty, Todge and Old Wicksniffer, Ollie, Jack Firth and Mick Benson were hooting with laughter.

Sensing there were larks afoot with these newcomers, the locals gathered about them, beaming and bucolic. Mick Benson amused the company by performing an impromptu dance, a combination of flamenco and Fred Flintstone. His efforts brought the house down, every man cheering for an encore.

From the wicket-keeper to the opening bat, the cricketers all flirted with Mandy, and her eyes twinkled like clusters of diamonds. Wilmot was gossiping with those of the Americans from Barstowe who had come to imbibe a little of the English atmosphere and more of the ale. Jello Parkes was volunteering the latest instalment in the saga.

"I hear yer Dick Fearnley won't be back next year ... he sure looked like he needed a li'l R and R last time I set eyes on him."

"I think you may be right ..."

"Yer Vice-Chancellor and his buddy are high-tailin' it too ... I'm thinkin."

"I believe so ..."

Mimi Schwartz was also keen to get in her two-cents-worth.

"They sure screwed things up gettin' all hoochie koo with that Folds guy."

Romita Simek added in her small change.

"Yer Lord Lupin sure whumped his ass ... if you don' mind me sayin so ... he's a real English lord ... a adorable gentleman. Not like that other phoney."

Wilmot chuckled.

"We say ... 'Breeding always tells' ..."

Clifford who was passing spoke up.

"Ar ... now ... Mister Tonks ... he's got breedin'.

Like ... a prize bull 'e is ..."

Mr. Tonks, next to him, spluttered into his Guinness.

"A wonderful compliment, Clifford ... you're a gentleman."

"Ar ... maybe but I ain't no *scholar* like thee ..."

When Mr. Tonks offered his credentials as an alumnus of Barstowe, Jello Parkes became quite animated.

"You know ... if you ever wanted to go teach again you could always hit America y'know. They'd love you there."

"A man of my vintage? Surely not ..."

"I dunno one of those small colleges would have yuh ... Tulane ... Oxford ..."

Ollie, who had wandered into the conversation, looked surprised.

"Oxford?"

"I'm sorry. Oxford, Ohio that is."

Romita Simek offered her views.

"Things are changing so big time in education ... not just here but in the U.S. too. It just seems more kinda dramatic here. You have all these old places that look like they haven't changed since forever. We're only just finding out about what education is really about back home ... we could do with a few Brits to teach us a coupla things. Like you Mr. Tonks sir."

That gentleman continued to demur, leaving Jello to shrug.

"Just an idea ... make you feel like yer wanted somewhere."

He waved in supplication and wandered through

the crowd to where he came across Martin and Lily, tucked in a corner. He sat with them being introduced to Lily, and heard all their tales. When these were told, Mr. Tonks began, for no obvious reason, to discuss his cat Guadalupe. Lily, who adored all felines, was delighted.

"How old is he?"

"Do you know ... I've no idea. He arrived one day and simply moved in ..."

"He likes you ... that's enough ..."

Mr. Tonks looked wistful, and continued to do so for some moments.

"Without understanding between two people ... or better still ... love ... life has no meaning."

Lily warmed to him. These were the men she admired—the thinker and the poet. They could not see her looking upon them, for she had the power to be invisible, leaving only a shimmer of beauty. And Mr. Tonks sat and wondered whether to journey to Golbellen to find love himself, or to take the next flight to San Francisco.

About the Author

Gordon Strong is an author, teacher, musician, and Tarot reader. He has written numerous books on the Arthurian legends, Neolithic sites, the Tarot and Magic. Five of his novels have also been published.

He makes regular public appearances in the UK and the USA and is known to be a knowledgeable and amusing speaker.

Gordon has made appearances on the National Geographic Channel and featured extensively in *Travels in Deep England* a documentary about druidry. He also described the Stanton Drew stone circles in *Symbols of Transformation*, one of a series of documentaries by explorer and researcher Herma Koornwinder.

Of his work, he says, "I observe, reflect, experiment and, from all this awareness, my writing appears."

Gordon Strong lives in Somerset, a part of England renowned for its spiritual connections with the land.